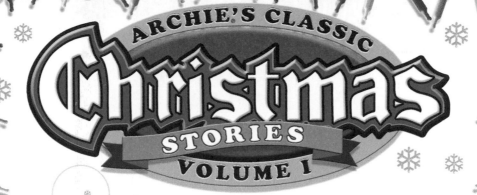

ARCHIE'S CLASSIC Christmas STORIES VOLUME I

MICHAEL I. SILBERKLEIT
CHAIRMAN AND CO-PUBLISHER

RICHARD H. GOLDWATER
PRESIDENT AND CO-PUBLISHER

VICTOR GORELICK
VICE PRESIDENT / MANAGING EDITOR

FRED MAUSSER
VICE PRESIDENT / DIRECTOR OF CIRCULATION

COMPILATION EDITOR:
PAUL CASTIGLIA

ART DIRECTOR:
JOE PEP

FRONT COVER ILLUSTRATION:
REX W. LINDSEY

COVER COLORING / PRODUCTION MANAGER:
ROBBIE O'QUINN

PRODUCTION:
NELSON RIBEIRO, CARLOS ANTUNES, PAUL D'ONOFRIO, MIKE PELLERITO

Archie characters created by JOHN L. GOLDWATER
The likenesses of the original Archie characters were created by BOB MONTANA

Visit Archie and his pals at www.archiecomics.com

ARCHIE'S CLASSIC CHRISTMAS STORIES, Volume 1, 2002. Printed in CANADA. Published by Archie Comic Publications, Inc., 325 Fayette Avenue, Mamaroneck, New York 10543.

ISBN 1-879794-10-1

4 FOREWORD
by Santa Claus

5 CHRISTMAS SOCKING
Mistletoe, a Christmas tradition! Just don't stand under it with Midge, or Moose will make you see lights... and we don't mean the lights on the tree!
Originally presented in ARCHIE'S CHRISTMAS STOCKING #3, 1956.

11 I PINE FIR YOU AND BALSAM
Even though Mr. Lodge can afford to buy a whole forest, Archie volunteers to cut one down for him... in the woods near Mr. Lodge's mountain cabin!
Originally presented in ARCHIE'S CHRISTMAS STOCKING #4, 1957.

17 DIS-MISSILE
Betty and Veronica offer to help the post office by reading letters to Santa and even making some wishes come true, especially when they get wish lists from Archie, Jughead and Reggie!
Originally presented in ARCHIE'S CHRISTMAS STOCKING #4, 1957.

23 IDIOT'S DELIGHT
All Betty wants for Christmas is to spend more time with Archie, even if she has to play "dumb" to do it!
Originally presented in ARCHIE'S CHRISTMAS STOCKING #4, 1957.

29 DRESSED TO KILL
Will Archie be able to make it to Betty's Christmas party? Find out in this poignant, illustrated text story.
Originally presented in ARCHIE'S CHRISTMAS STOCKING #4, 1957.

32 SLAY RIDE
It's lovely weather for a sleigh ride, but with Archie at the reins it's a sleigh slide!
Originally presented in ARCHIE'S CHRISTMAS STOCKING #5, 1958.

42 RING THAT BELLE
A classic Archie concept: Betty mistakenly thinks Archie is going to give Veronica an engagement ring for Christmas!
Originally presented in ARCHIE'S CHRISTMAS STOCKING #5, 1958.

48 VERONICA'S PIN-UP
Veronica makes trimming the tree glamorous!
Originally presented in ARCHIE'S CHRISTMAS STOCKING #15, 1962.

49 SEASONAL SMOOCH

Reggie convinces Moose that Santa won't bring him any presents
if he doesn't let Reggie kiss Midge beneath the mistletoe!
Originally presented in ARCHIE'S CHRISTMAS STOCKING #5, 1958.

55 FEATHER MERCHANT

Archie decides to get Mr. Lodge a rare bird for his collection,
but he wouldn't know rare from well done!
Originally presented in ARCHIE'S CHRISTMAS STOCKING 6, 1959.

61 THOSE CHRISTMAS BLUES!

This heartwarming tale finds Archie's parents reminiscing about yuletides
past, complete with Little Archie flashback sequences!
Originally presented in ARCHIE'S CHRISTMAS STOCKING #10, 1961.

67 NOT EVEN A MOOSE

Archie loves to play Santa, especially when the girls sit on his lap!
But if Moose catches Midge there, Archie may have to trade his Santa suit for boxing gloves!
Originally presented in ARCHIE'S CHRISTMAS STOCKING #10, 1961.

75 A JOB FOR JINGLES

A milestone in Archie Comics history: the first appearance of Jingles the elf!
Originally presented in ARCHIE'S CHRISTMAS STOCKING #10, 1961.

85 ESCAPE

Mr. Lodge tries to avoid the catastrophes of Christmas's past by getting
away from Archie. A great plan, until Archie makes the (re)arrangements!
Originally presented in ARCHIE'S CHRISTMAS STOCKING #20, 1963.

91 THE RETURN OF JINGLES

Jingles proved so popular, he became a Christmas tradition himself,
returning year after year to bewilder and delight Archie and his friends!
Originally presented in ARCHIE'S CHRISTMAS STOCKING #20, 1963.

A note about ARCHIE'S CHRISTMAS STOCKING. You may notice some disparity of dates between issues, such as #10 being released in 1961, #15 in 1962 and #20 in 1963. This is because ARCHIE'S CHRISTMAS STOCKING became part of the ARCHIE GIANT SERIES which included other titles like THE WORLD OF ARCHIE and ARCHIE'S JOKEBOOK. ARCHIE'S CHRISTMAS STOCKING alternated with these titles. Therefore, if THE WORLD OF ARCHIE #14 was the ARCHIE GIANT SERIES preceding ARCHIE'S CHRISTMAS STOCKING, the CHRISTMAS issue was #15. Each year, there was one ARCHIE'S CHRISTMAS STOCKING in the ARCHIE GIANT SERIES.

FOREWORD

Hi! Kris Kringle here to share with you some of my Yuletide experiences with Archie and his friends. You're probably wondering how I can possibly focus on just a few teenagers in Riverdale when I have to deliver gifts to millions, maybe even billions, of kids in one hectic evening. Actually, some obscure law of physics enables me to slow down real time for as long as it takes me to make my deliveries. I'm sure Einstein and his cohorts can give you a much better, if not simpler, explanation.

Be that as it may, some moments really stand out. Like the Christmas Eve that Archie and his pals, armed with a camcorder, all gathered together up on Veronica's roof in order to capture me in the act of sliding down the chimney. Fortunately, I was able to outwit them by sending my smallest elf through the pet door and having him open up the main door to Veronica's place for me and my sack of presents. As I rode away, I couldn't help but feel sorry for the Archie Crew as they froze their buns off trying to trick ol' Santa. On my Christmas visits many kids like to leave me cookies, but leave it to Jughead to do them one better. He goes out of his way by ordering a giant pizza with all the toppings in my honor. Wow! What a magnificent gesture! And by the time I arrive there's usually at least one whole slice left over for me, bless his heart! I've been asked if I experience any difficulty deciding what to give Archie and his pals. Veronica is the biggest problem because she already has everything. Last year I solved the problem by giving her an extra closet to put all her clothes in. This year I'm thinking of giving Veronica her very own personal ATM machine.

Jughead was ecstatic last year when I gave him an alarm clock with a broken alarm... just so he could go on snoozing a little longer each school morning.

Archie is no problem. Last year I gave him a book of excuses for not handing in his homework on time. This year I'm giving him a book of lateness alibis. The one thing I never have to give Archie is sweets–he already has Betty and Veronica!

Chuck always gets drawing equipment to help further his cartooning talents. I only wish he'd stop drawing me with a big red nose. He must have me confused with one of my reindeer–the one with the big scarlet snout!

Since Archie formed his garage band, I give Mr. Lodge what he so desperately needs–a pair of earplugs!

Every Christmas I give Reggie a new, giant-sized mirror. Reggie is the only one I know who can actually wear out a mirror by over-using it.

And finally there's Betty. Dear wonderful Betty! I'm sorely tempted to give her what she really wants most for Christmas–ARCHIE! But there's a mischievous streak in me–I enjoy watching her and Veronica duke it out for carrot-top's affection. It's what makes life interesting.

And as the holidays approach, I'd like to leave you with this parting thought: what the world needs most during the Christmas season is peace and love...and oh yes, plenty of double-A, C and D batteries.

Merry Christmas and a
Happy New Year to one and all!

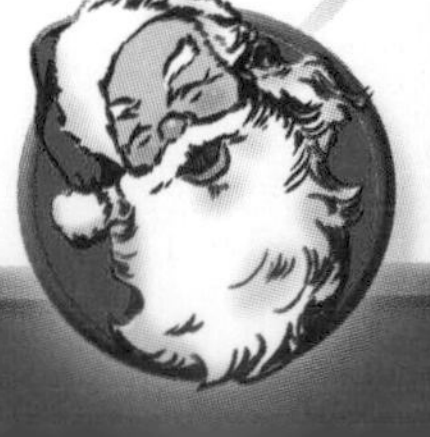

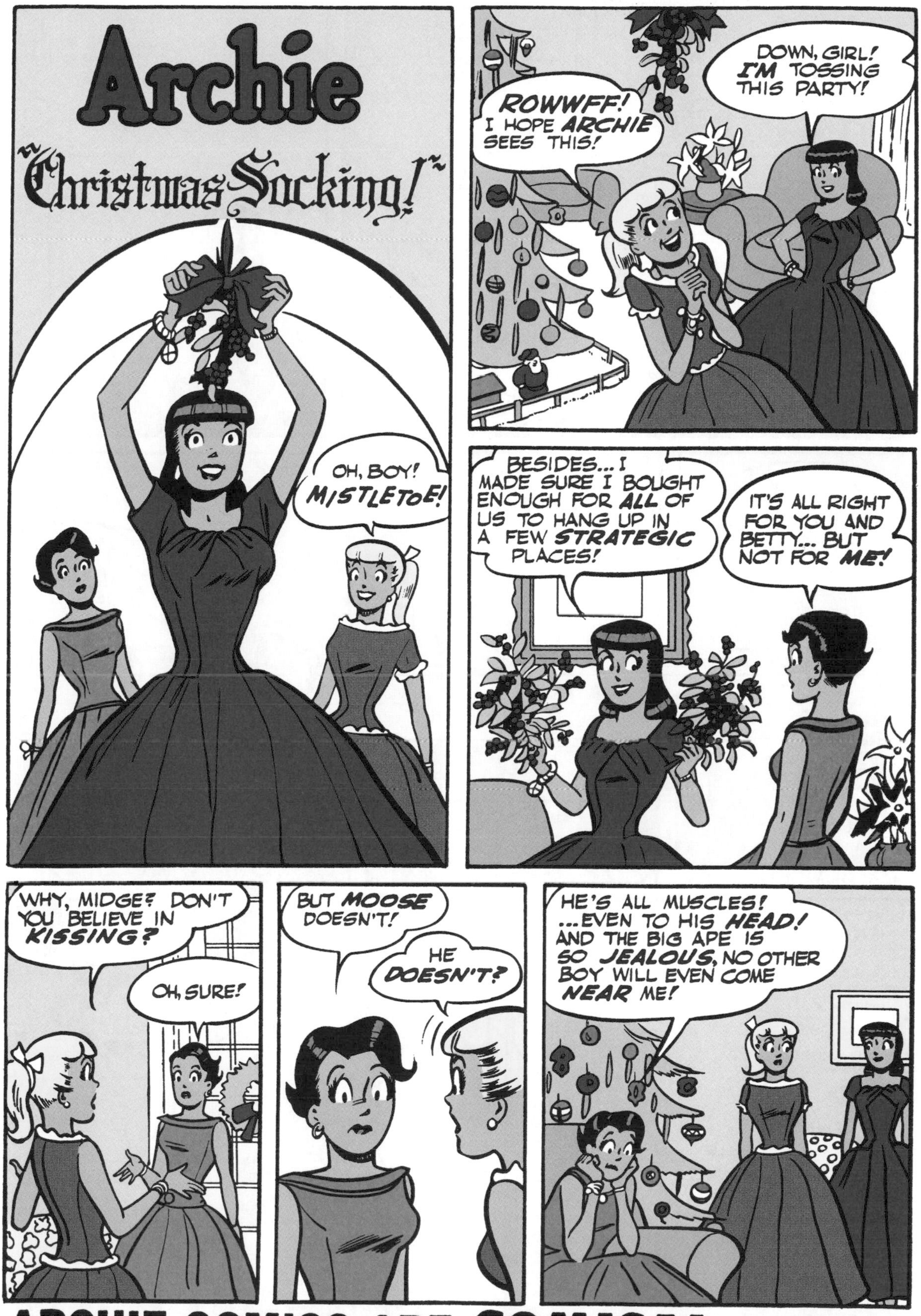
Archie
"Christmas Socking!"
OH, BOY! MISTLETOE!
ROWWFF! I HOPE ARCHIE SEES THIS!
DOWN, GIRL! I'M TOSSING THIS PARTY!
BESIDES... I MADE SURE I BOUGHT ENOUGH FOR ALL OF US TO HANG UP IN A FEW STRATEGIC PLACES!
IT'S ALL RIGHT FOR YOU AND BETTY... BUT NOT FOR ME!
WHY, MIDGE? DON'T YOU BELIEVE IN KISSING?
OH, SURE!
BUT MOOSE DOESN'T!
HE DOESN'T?
HE'S ALL MUSCLES! ...EVEN TO HIS HEAD! AND THE BIG APE IS SO JEALOUS, NO OTHER BOY WILL EVEN COME NEAR ME!

ARCHIE COMICS ARE COMICAL COMICS

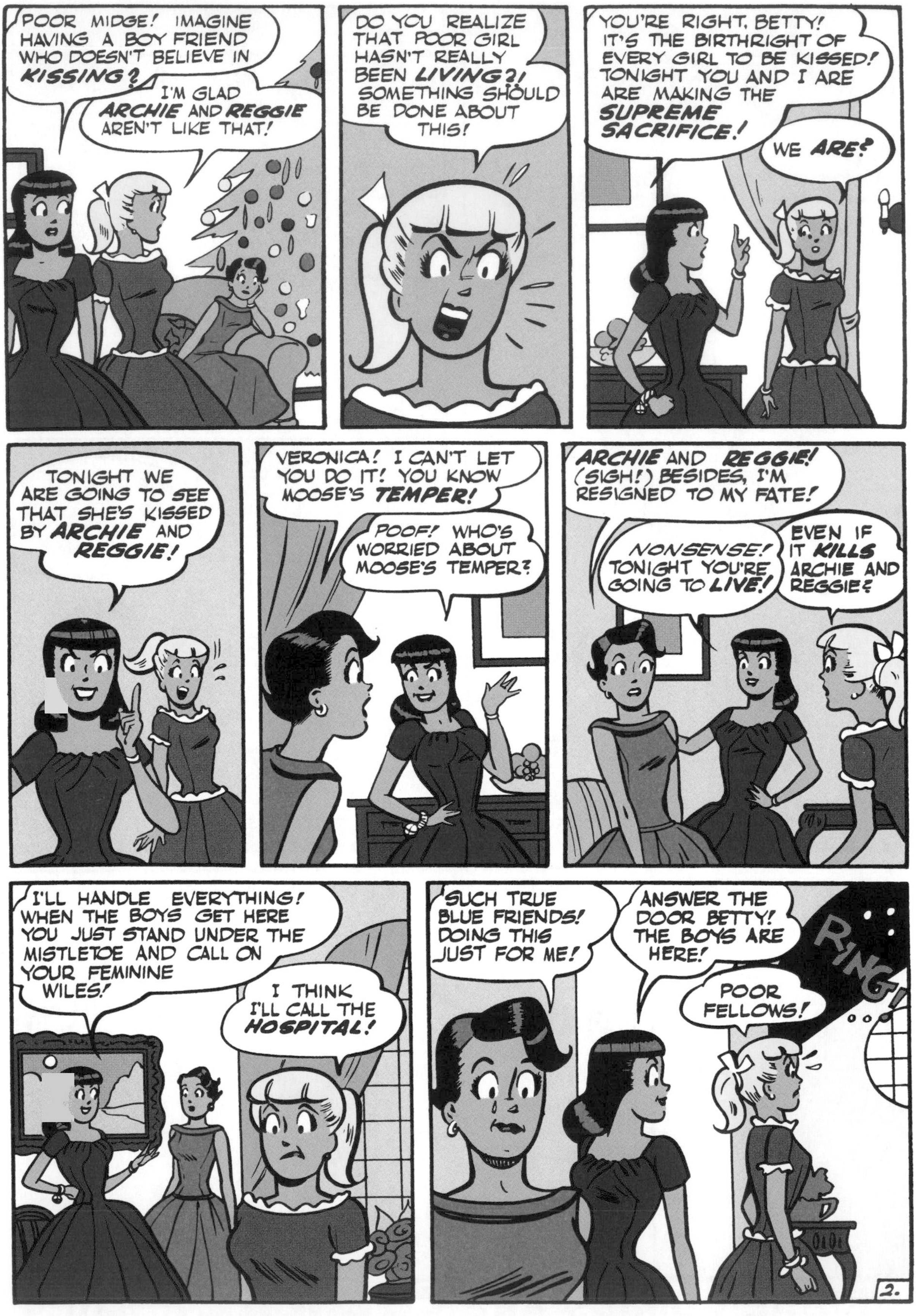
POOR MIDGE! IMAGINE HAVING A BOY FRIEND WHO DOESN'T BELIEVE IN KISSING?
I'M GLAD ARCHIE AND REGGIE AREN'T LIKE THAT!
DO YOU REALIZE THAT POOR GIRL HASN'T REALLY BEEN LIVING?! SOMETHING SHOULD BE DONE ABOUT THIS!
YOU'RE RIGHT, BETTY! IT'S THE BIRTHRIGHT OF EVERY GIRL TO BE KISSED! TONIGHT YOU AND I ARE ARE MAKING THE SUPREME SACRIFICE!
WE ARE?
TONIGHT WE ARE GOING TO SEE THAT SHE'S KISSED BY ARCHIE AND REGGIE!
VERONICA! I CAN'T LET YOU DO IT! YOU KNOW MOOSE'S TEMPER!
POOF! WHO'S WORRIED ABOUT MOOSE'S TEMPER?
ARCHIE AND REGGIE! (SIGH!) BESIDES, I'M RESIGNED TO MY FATE!
NONSENSE! TONIGHT YOU'RE GOING TO LIVE!
EVEN IF IT KILLS ARCHIE AND REGGIE?
I'LL HANDLE EVERYTHING! WHEN THE BOYS GET HERE YOU JUST STAND UNDER THE MISTLETOE AND CALL ON YOUR FEMININE WILES!
I THINK I'LL CALL THE HOSPITAL!
SUCH TRUE BLUE FRIENDS! DOING THIS JUST FOR ME!
ANSWER THE DOOR BETTY! THE BOYS ARE HERE!
POOR FELLOWS!
RING!
2.

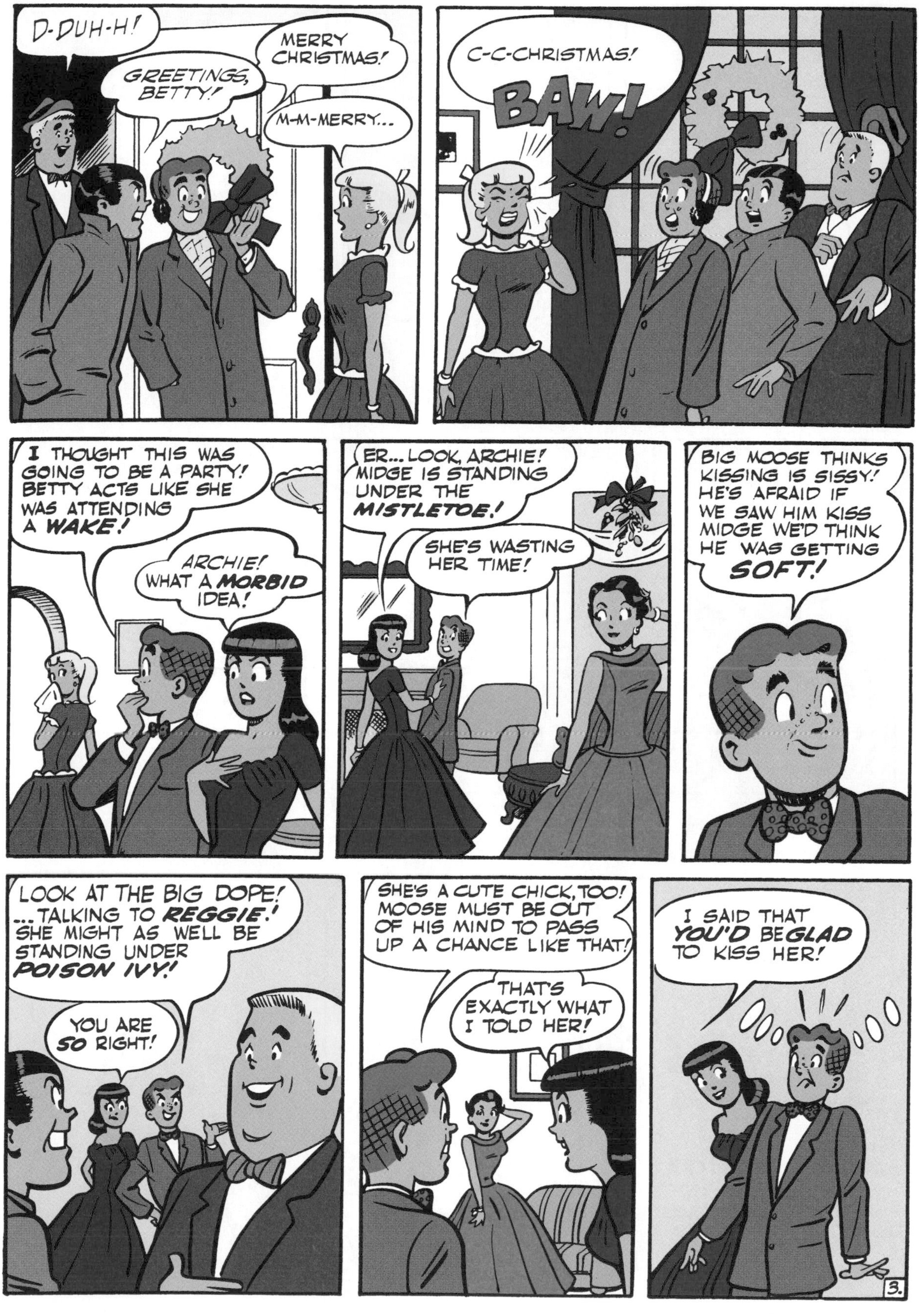
D-DUH-H!
GREETINGS, BETTY!
MERRY CHRISTMAS!
M-M-MERRY...
C-C-CHRISTMAS!
BAW!
I THOUGHT THIS WAS GOING TO BE A PARTY! BETTY ACTS LIKE SHE WAS ATTENDING A WAKE!
ARCHIE! WHAT A MORBID IDEA!
ER... LOOK, ARCHIE! MIDGE IS STANDING UNDER THE MISTLETOE!
SHE'S WASTING HER TIME!
BIG MOOSE THINKS KISSING IS SISSY! HE'S AFRAID IF WE SAW HIM KISS MIDGE WE'D THINK HE WAS GETTING SOFT!
LOOK AT THE BIG DOPE! ...TALKING TO REGGIE! SHE MIGHT AS WELL BE STANDING UNDER POISON IVY!
YOU ARE SO RIGHT!
SHE'S A CUTE CHICK, TOO! MOOSE MUST BE OUT OF HIS MIND TO PASS UP A CHANCE LIKE THAT!
THAT'S EXACTLY WHAT I TOLD HER!
I SAID THAT YOU'D BE GLAD TO KISS HER!
3.

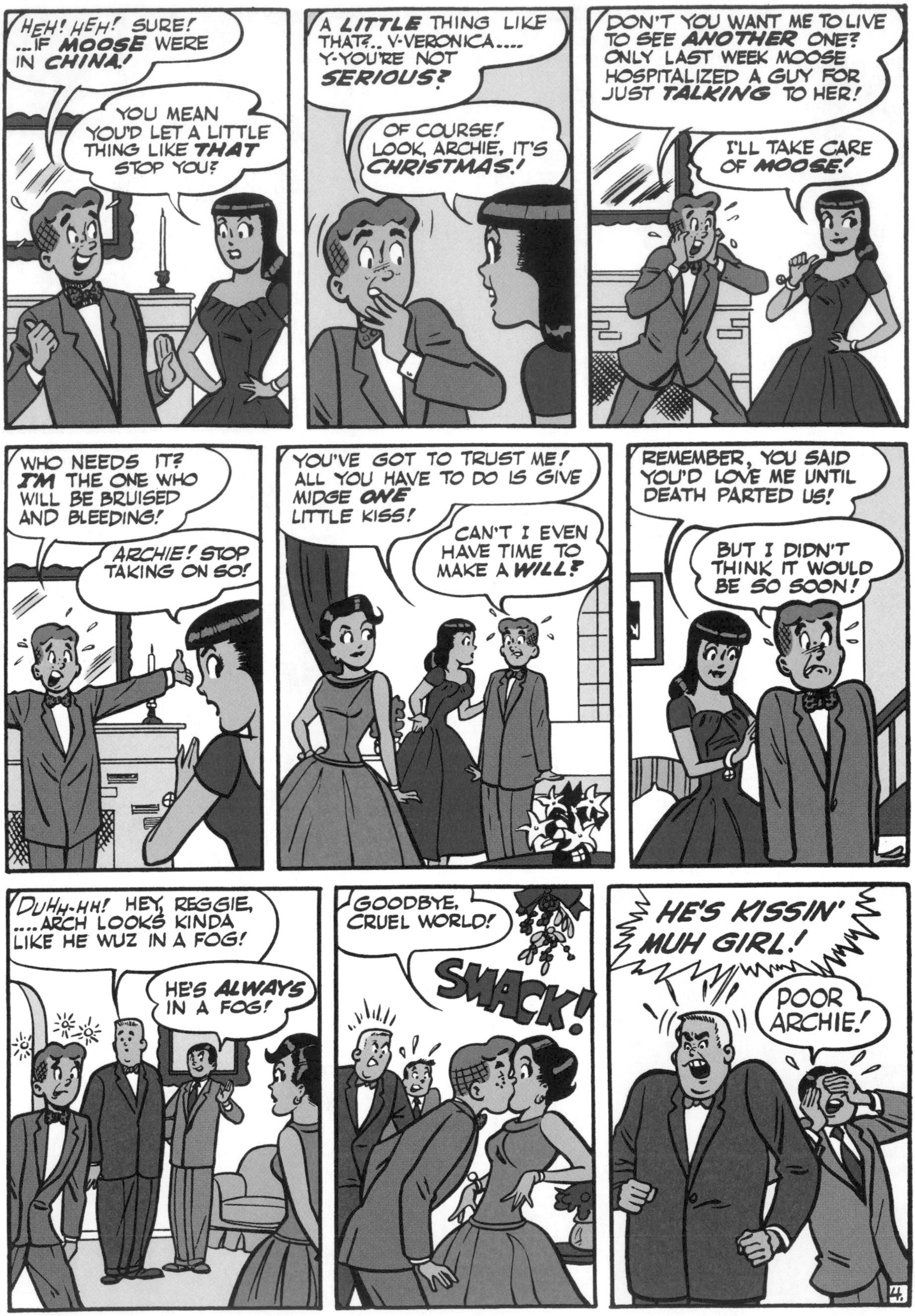
HEH! HEH! SURE! ...IF MOOSE WERE IN CHINA!
YOU MEAN YOU'D LET A LITTLE THING LIKE THAT STOP YOU?
A LITTLE THING LIKE THAT?.. V-VERONICA.... Y-YOU'RE NOT SERIOUS?
OF COURSE! LOOK, ARCHIE, IT'S CHRISTMAS!
DON'T YOU WANT ME TO LIVE TO SEE ANOTHER ONE? ONLY LAST WEEK MOOSE HOSPITALIZED A GUY FOR JUST TALKING TO HER!
I'LL TAKE CARE OF MOOSE!
WHO NEEDS IT? I'M THE ONE WHO WILL BE BRUISED AND BLEEDING!
ARCHIE! STOP TAKING ON SO!
YOU'VE GOT TO TRUST ME! ALL YOU HAVE TO DO IS GIVE MIDGE ONE LITTLE KISS!
CAN'T I EVEN HAVE TIME TO MAKE A WILL?
REMEMBER, YOU SAID YOU'D LOVE ME UNTIL DEATH PARTED US!
BUT I DIDN'T THINK IT WOULD BE SO SOON!
DUHH-HH! HEY, REGGIE, ...ARCH LOOKS KINDA LIKE HE WUZ IN A FOG!
HE'S ALWAYS IN A FOG!
GOODBYE, CRUEL WORLD!
SMACK!
HE'S KISSIN' MUH GIRL!
POOR ARCHIE!
4.

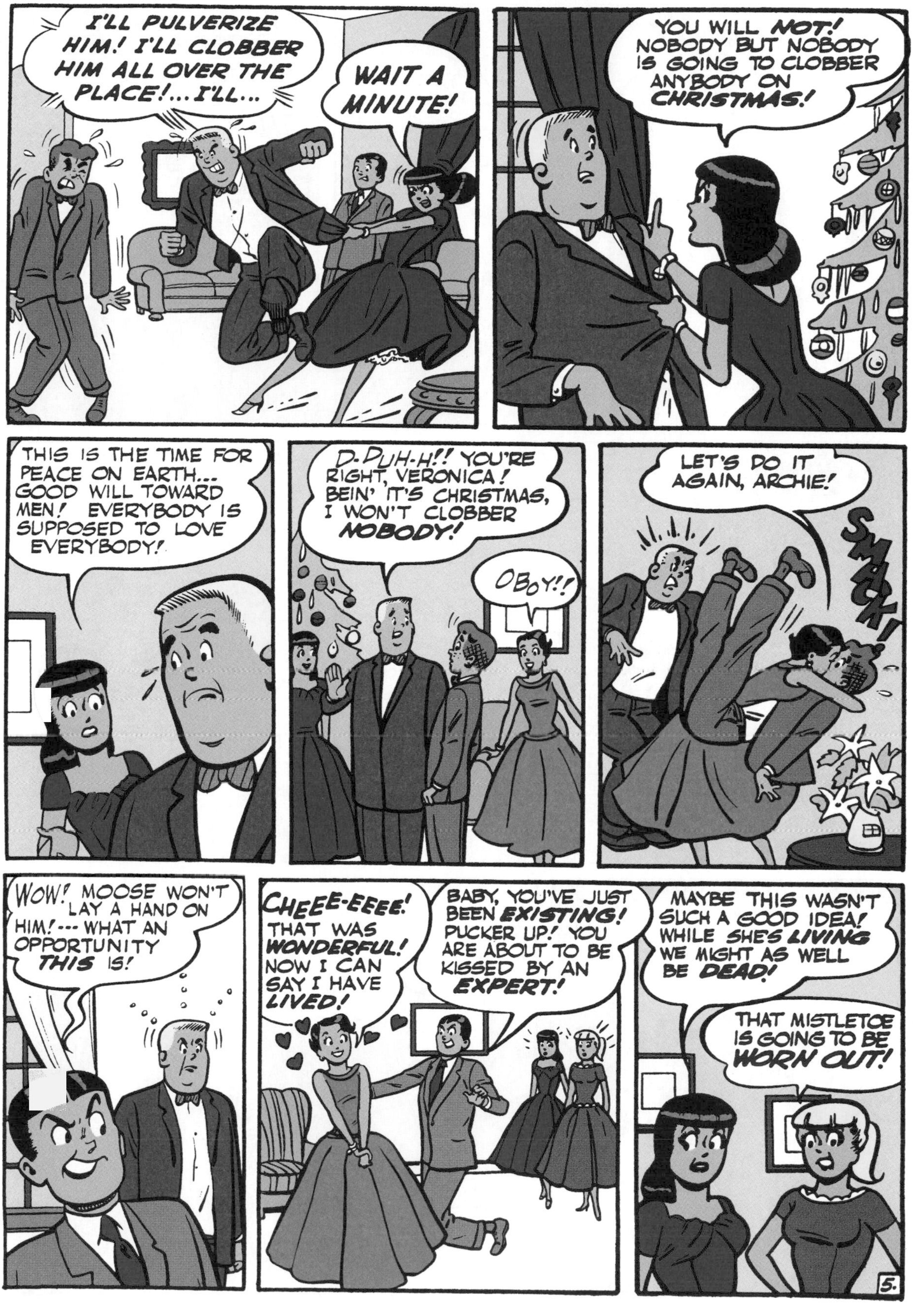
I'LL PULVERIZE HIM! I'LL CLOBBER HIM ALL OVER THE PLACE!... I'LL...
WAIT A MINUTE!
YOU WILL NOT! NOBODY BUT NOBODY IS GOING TO CLOBBER ANYBODY ON CHRISTMAS!
THIS IS THE TIME FOR PEACE ON EARTH... GOOD WILL TOWARD MEN! EVERYBODY IS SUPPOSED TO LOVE EVERYBODY!
D-DUH-H!! YOU'RE RIGHT, VERONICA! BEIN' IT'S CHRISTMAS, I WON'T CLOBBER NOBODY!
OBOY!!
LET'S DO IT AGAIN, ARCHIE!
SMACK!
WOW! MOOSE WON'T LAY A HAND ON HIM!--- WHAT AN OPPORTUNITY THIS IS!
CHEEE-EEEE! THAT WAS WONDERFUL! NOW I CAN SAY I HAVE LIVED!
BABY, YOU'VE JUST BEEN EXISTING! PUCKER UP! YOU ARE ABOUT TO BE KISSED BY AN EXPERT!
MAYBE THIS WASN'T SUCH A GOOD IDEA! WHILE SHE'S LIVING WE MIGHT AS WELL BE DEAD!
THAT MISTLETOE IS GOING TO BE WORN OUT!
5.

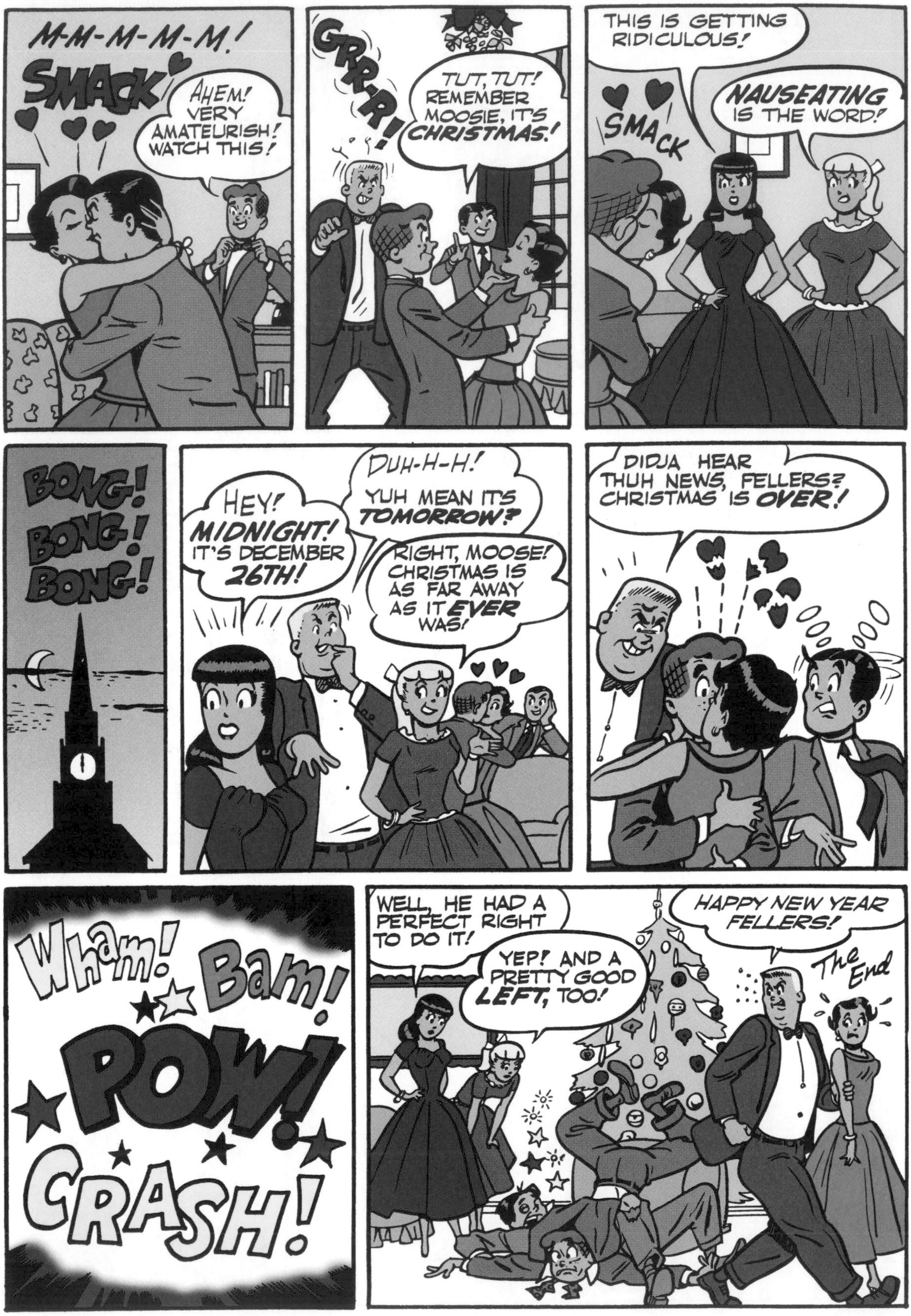
M-M-M-M-M!
SMACK
AHEM! VERY AMATEURISH! WATCH THIS!
GRR-R!
TUT, TUT! REMEMBER MOOSIE, IT'S CHRISTMAS!
THIS IS GETTING RIDICULOUS!
SMACK
NAUSEATING IS THE WORD!
BONG! BONG! BONG!
HEY! MIDNIGHT! IT'S DECEMBER 26TH!
DUH-H-H! YUH MEAN IT'S TOMORROW?
RIGHT, MOOSE! CHRISTMAS IS AS FAR AWAY AS IT EVER WAS!
DIDJA HEAR THUH NEWS, FELLERS? CHRISTMAS IS OVER!
Wham! Bam!
POW!
CRASH!
WELL, HE HAD A PERFECT RIGHT TO DO IT!
YEP! AND A PRETTY GOOD LEFT, TOO!
HAPPY NEW YEAR FELLERS!
The End

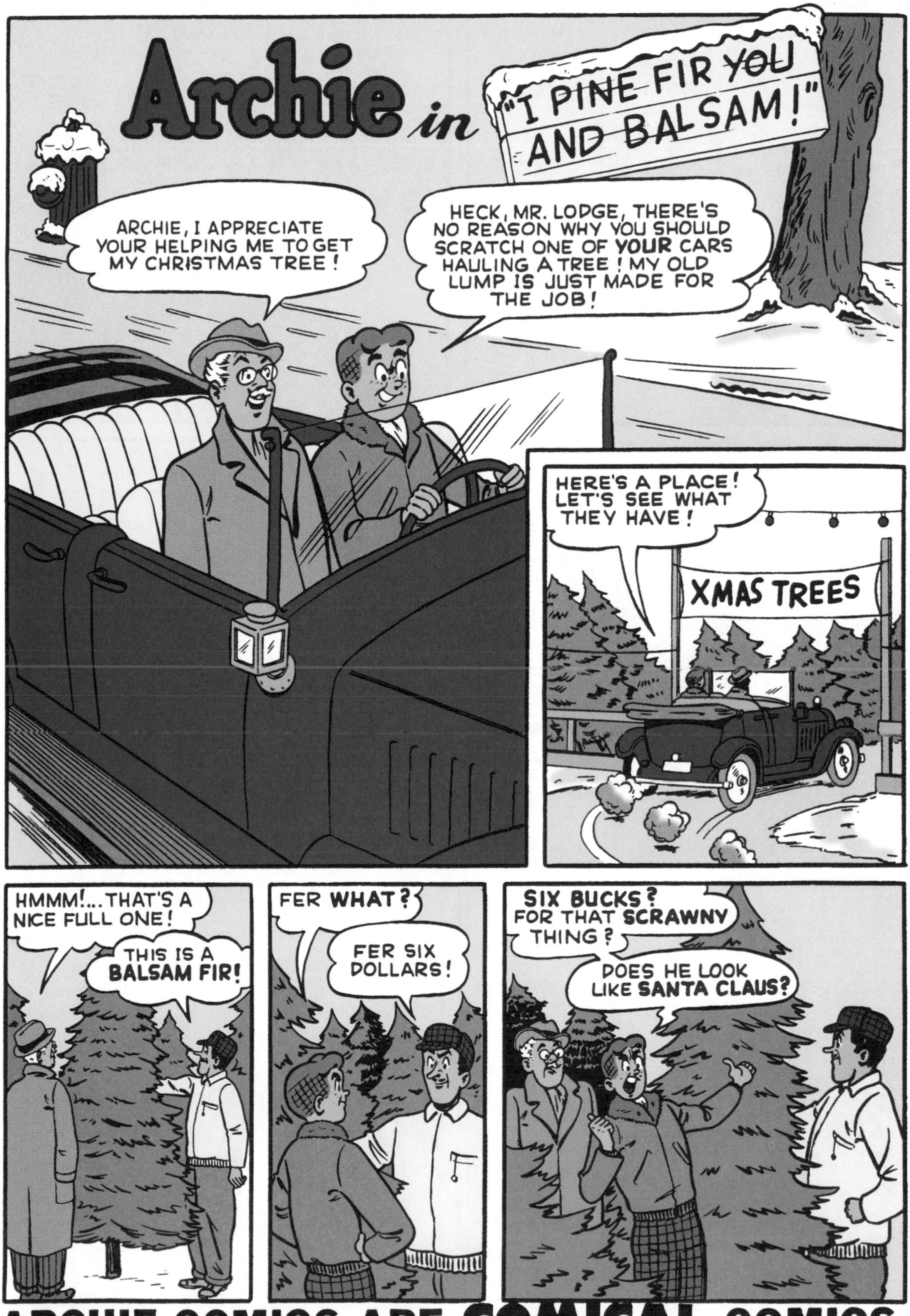
Archie in
"I PINE FIR YOU AND BALSAM!"
ARCHIE, I APPRECIATE YOUR HELPING ME TO GET MY CHRISTMAS TREE!
HECK, MR. LODGE, THERE'S NO REASON WHY YOU SHOULD SCRATCH ONE OF YOUR CARS HAULING A TREE! MY OLD LUMP IS JUST MADE FOR THE JOB!
HERE'S A PLACE! LET'S SEE WHAT THEY HAVE!
XMAS TREES
HMMM!... THAT'S A NICE FULL ONE!
THIS IS A BALSAM FIR!
FER WHAT?
FER SIX DOLLARS!
SIX BUCKS? FOR THAT SCRAWNY THING?
DOES HE LOOK LIKE SANTA CLAUS?

ARCHIE COMICS ARE COMICAL COMICS

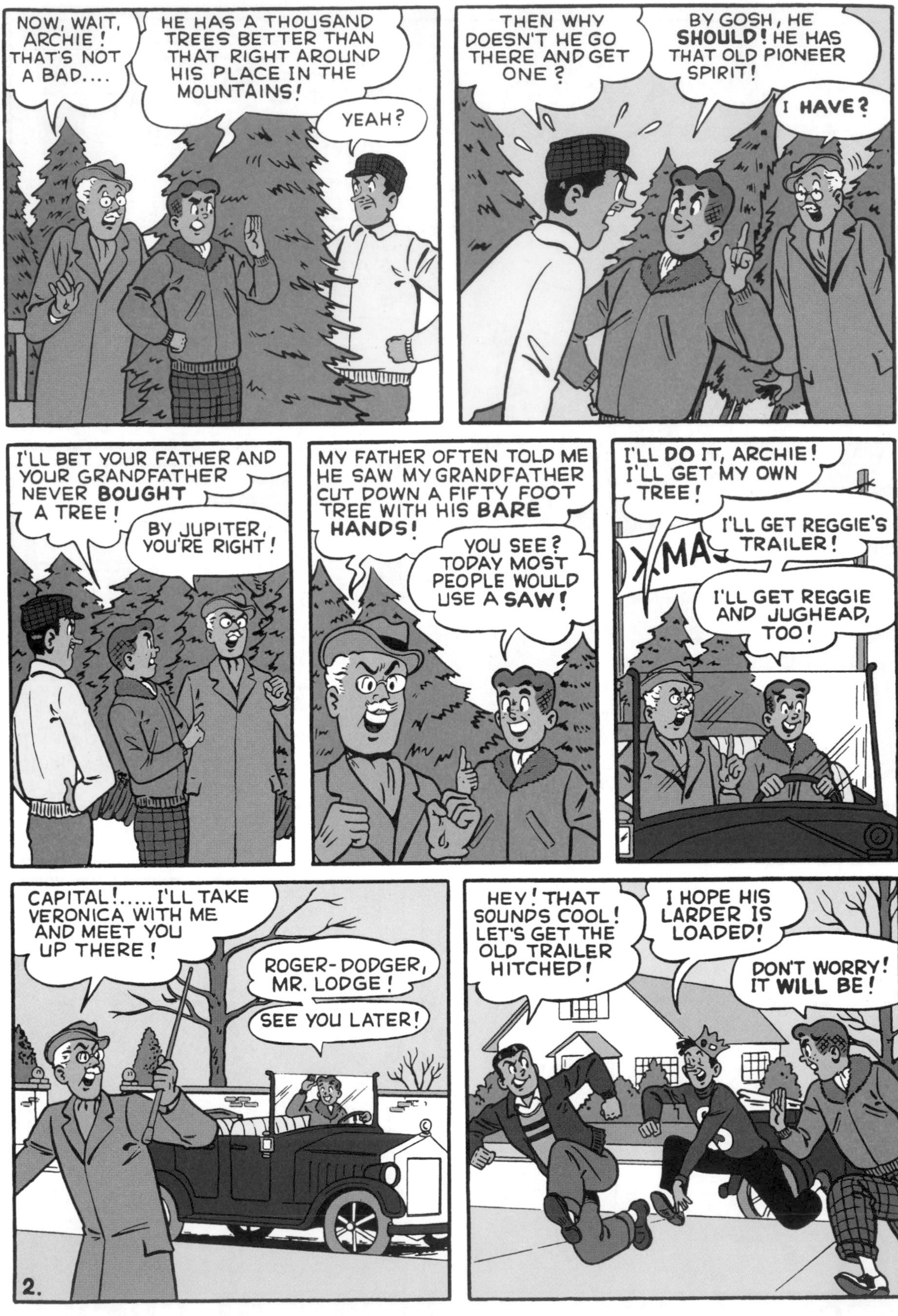
NOW, WAIT, ARCHIE! THAT'S NOT A BAD....
HE HAS A THOUSAND TREES BETTER THAN THAT RIGHT AROUND HIS PLACE IN THE MOUNTAINS!
YEAH?
THEN WHY DOESN'T HE GO THERE AND GET ONE?
BY GOSH, HE SHOULD! HE HAS THAT OLD PIONEER SPIRIT!
I HAVE?
I'LL BET YOUR FATHER AND YOUR GRANDFATHER NEVER BOUGHT A TREE!
BY JUPITER, YOU'RE RIGHT!
MY FATHER OFTEN TOLD ME HE SAW MY GRANDFATHER CUT DOWN A FIFTY FOOT TREE WITH HIS BARE HANDS!
YOU SEE? TODAY MOST PEOPLE WOULD USE A SAW!
I'LL DO IT, ARCHIE! I'LL GET MY OWN TREE!
I'LL GET REGGIE'S TRAILER!
I'LL GET REGGIE AND JUGHEAD, TOO!
XMA
CAPITAL!..... I'LL TAKE VERONICA WITH ME AND MEET YOU UP THERE!
ROGER-DODGER, MR. LODGE!
SEE YOU LATER!
2.
HEY! THAT SOUNDS COOL! LET'S GET THE OLD TRAILER HITCHED!
I HOPE HIS LARDER IS LOADED!
DON'T WORRY! IT WILL BE!

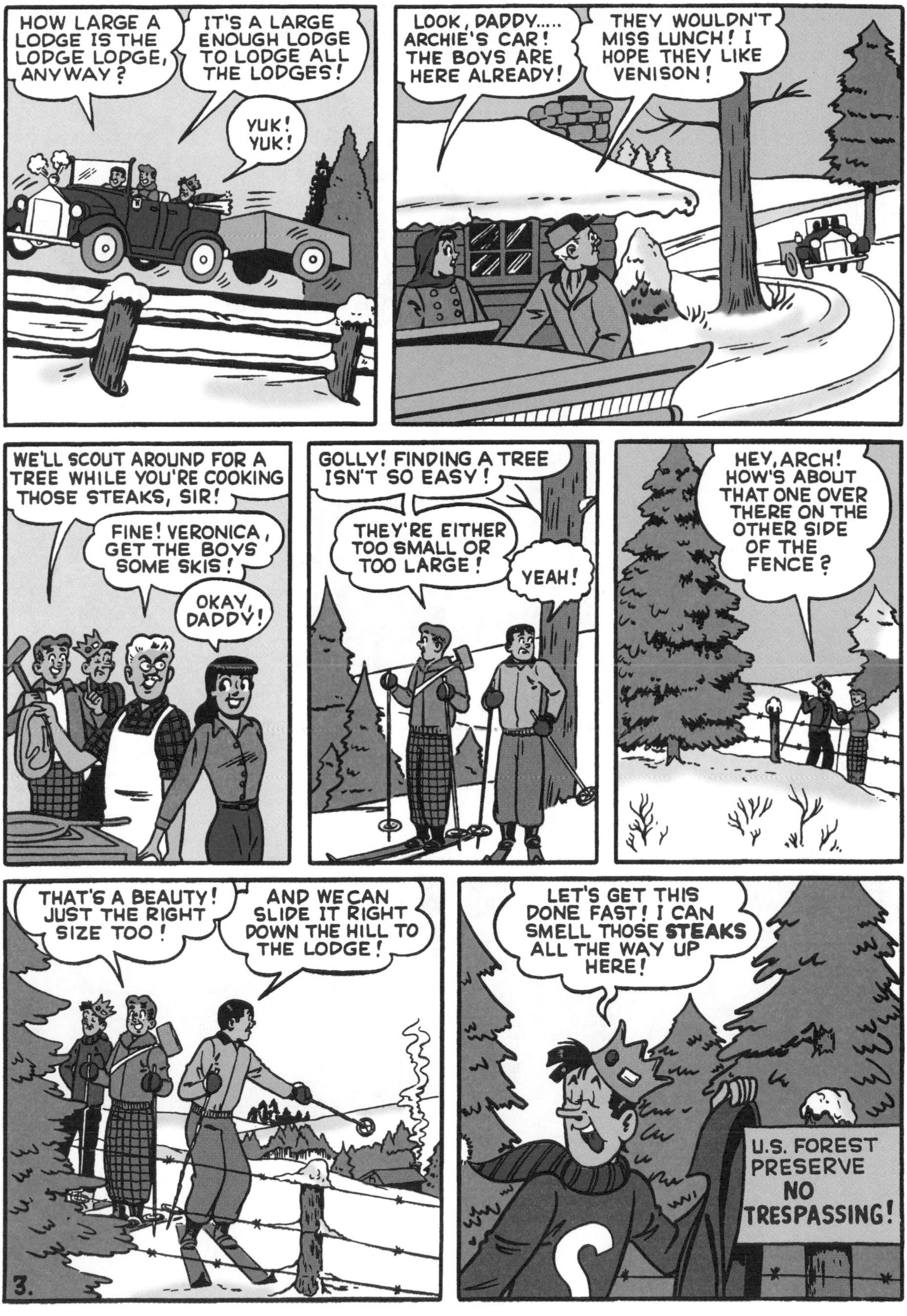
HOW LARGE A LODGE IS THE LODGE LODGE, ANYWAY?
IT'S A LARGE ENOUGH LODGE TO LODGE ALL THE LODGES!
YUK! YUK!
LOOK, DADDY..... ARCHIE'S CAR! THE BOYS ARE HERE ALREADY!
THEY WOULDN'T MISS LUNCH! I HOPE THEY LIKE VENISON!
WE'LL SCOUT AROUND FOR A TREE WHILE YOU'RE COOKING THOSE STEAKS, SIR!
FINE! VERONICA, GET THE BOYS SOME SKIS!
OKAY, DADDY!
GOLLY! FINDING A TREE ISN'T SO EASY!
THEY'RE EITHER TOO SMALL OR TOO LARGE!
YEAH!
HEY, ARCH! HOW'S ABOUT THAT ONE OVER THERE ON THE OTHER SIDE OF THE FENCE?
THAT'S A BEAUTY! JUST THE RIGHT SIZE TOO!
AND WE CAN SLIDE IT RIGHT DOWN THE HILL TO THE LODGE!
3.
LET'S GET THIS DONE FAST! I CAN SMELL THOSE STEAKS ALL THE WAY UP HERE!
U.S. FOREST PRESERVE NO TRESPASSING!

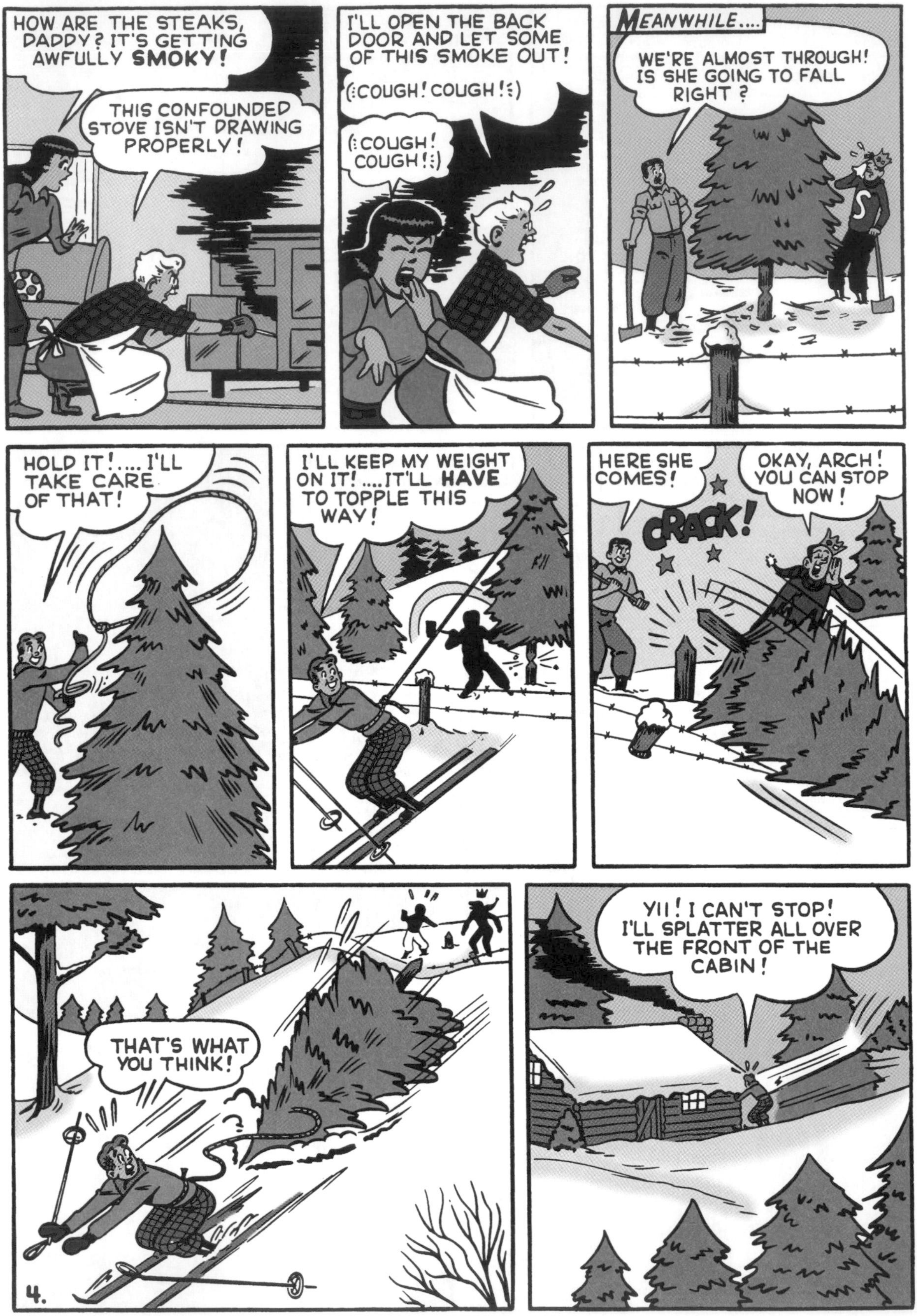
HOW ARE THE STEAKS, DADDY? IT'S GETTING AWFULLY SMOKY!
THIS CONFOUNDED STOVE ISN'T DRAWING PROPERLY!
I'LL OPEN THE BACK DOOR AND LET SOME OF THIS SMOKE OUT!
(COUGH! COUGH!)
(COUGH! COUGH!)
MEANWHILE....
WE'RE ALMOST THROUGH! IS SHE GOING TO FALL RIGHT?
HOLD IT!.... I'LL TAKE CARE OF THAT!
I'LL KEEP MY WEIGHT ON IT! ....IT'LL HAVE TO TOPPLE THIS WAY!
HERE SHE COMES!
CRACK!
OKAY, ARCH! YOU CAN STOP NOW!
THAT'S WHAT YOU THINK!
4.
YII! I CAN'T STOP! I'LL SPLATTER ALL OVER THE FRONT OF THE CABIN!

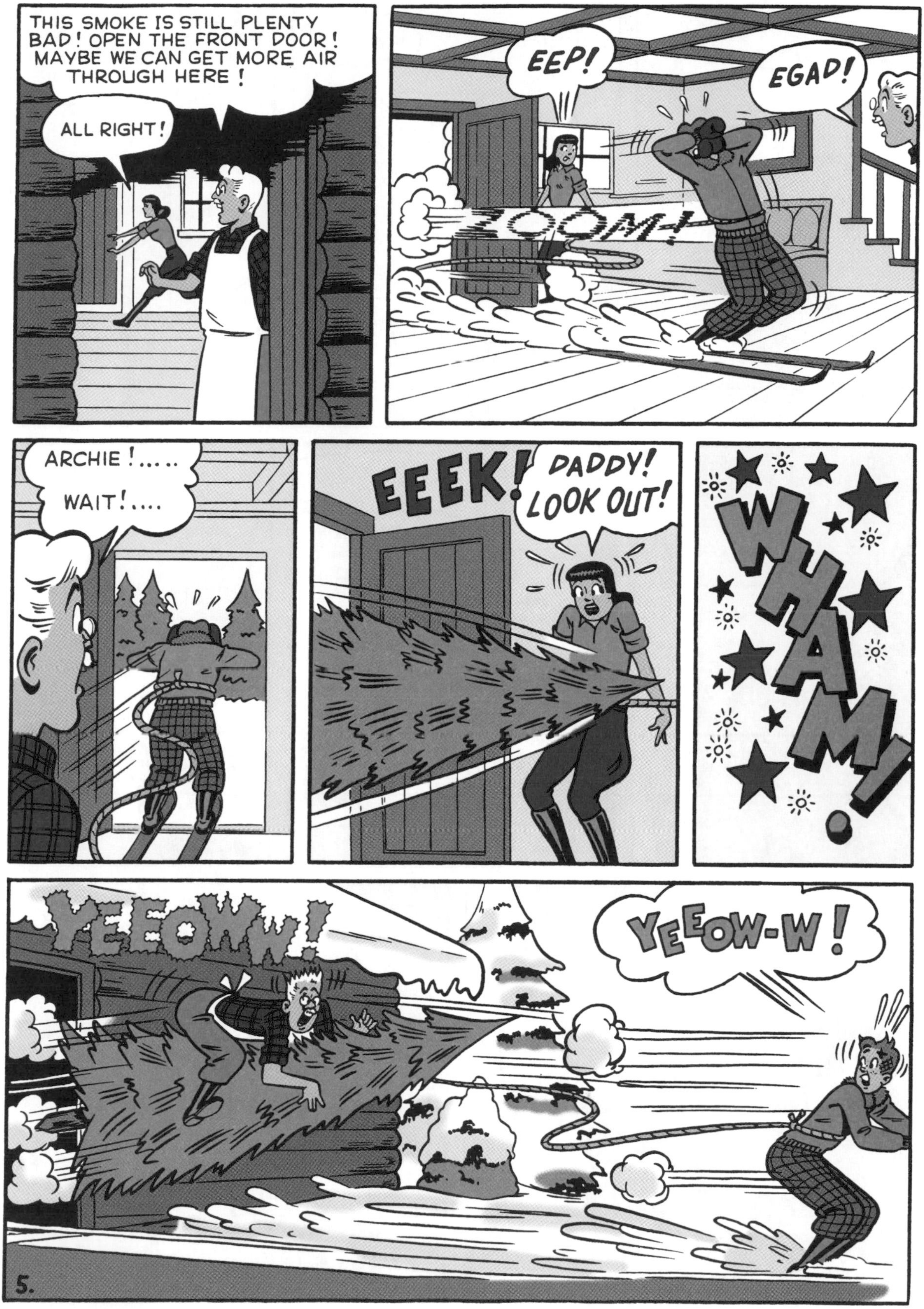
THIS SMOKE IS STILL PLENTY BAD! OPEN THE FRONT DOOR! MAYBE WE CAN GET MORE AIR THROUGH HERE!
ALL RIGHT!
EEP!
EGAD!
ZOOM!
ARCHIE!..... WAIT!....
EEEK!
DADDY! LOOK OUT!
WHAM!
YEEOWW!
YEEOW-W!
5.

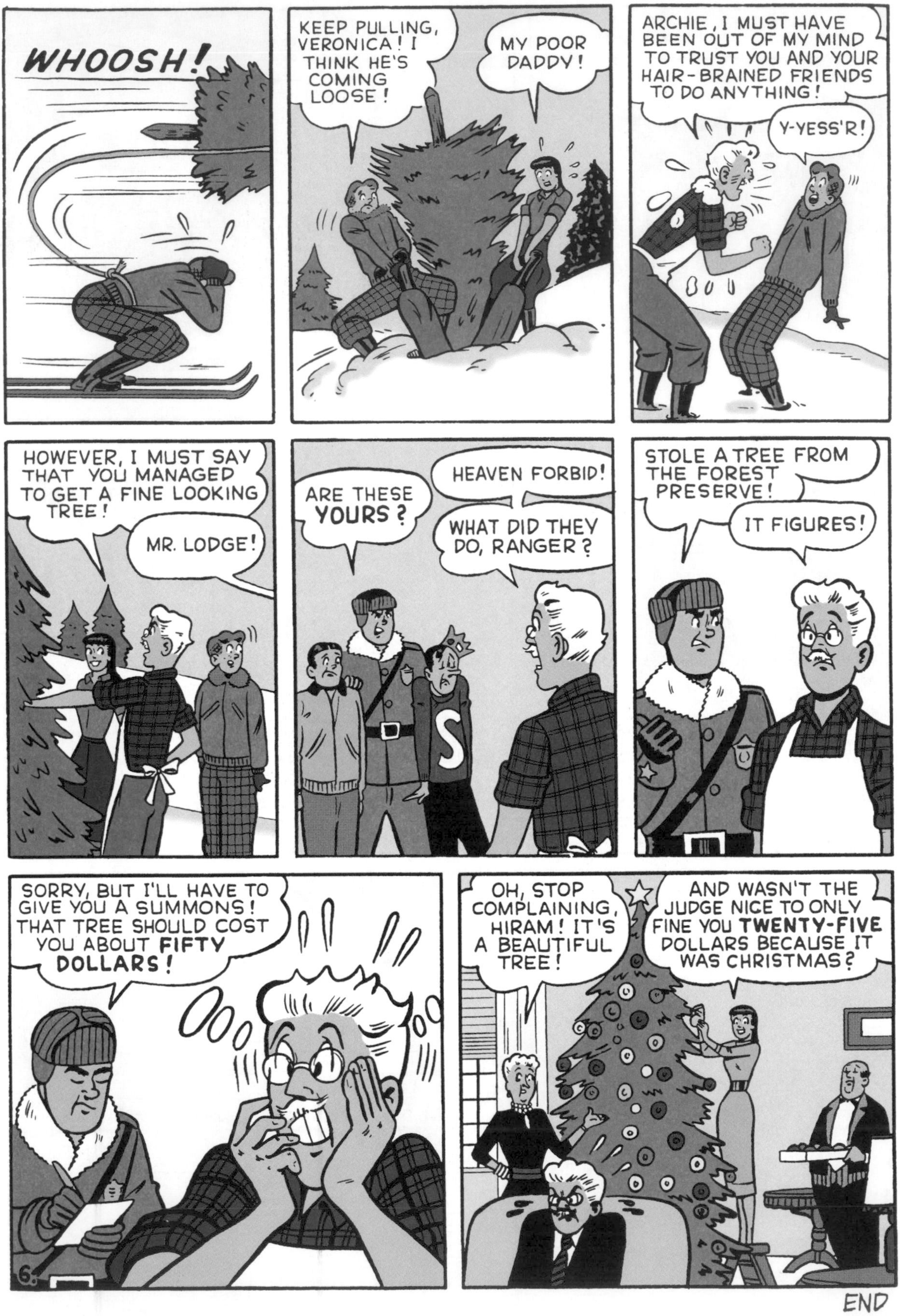
WHOOSH!
KEEP PULLING, VERONICA! I THINK HE'S COMING LOOSE!
MY POOR DADDY!
ARCHIE, I MUST HAVE BEEN OUT OF MY MIND TO TRUST YOU AND YOUR HAIR-BRAINED FRIENDS TO DO ANYTHING!
Y-YESS'R!
HOWEVER, I MUST SAY THAT YOU MANAGED TO GET A FINE LOOKING TREE!
MR. LODGE!
ARE THESE **YOURS**?
HEAVEN FORBID!
WHAT DID THEY DO, RANGER?
STOLE A TREE FROM THE FOREST PRESERVE!
IT FIGURES!
SORRY, BUT I'LL HAVE TO GIVE YOU A SUMMONS! THAT TREE SHOULD COST YOU ABOUT **FIFTY DOLLARS**!
6
OH, STOP COMPLAINING, HIRAM! IT'S A BEAUTIFUL TREE!
AND WASN'T THE JUDGE NICE TO ONLY FINE YOU **TWENTY-FIVE** DOLLARS BECAUSE IT WAS CHRISTMAS?
END

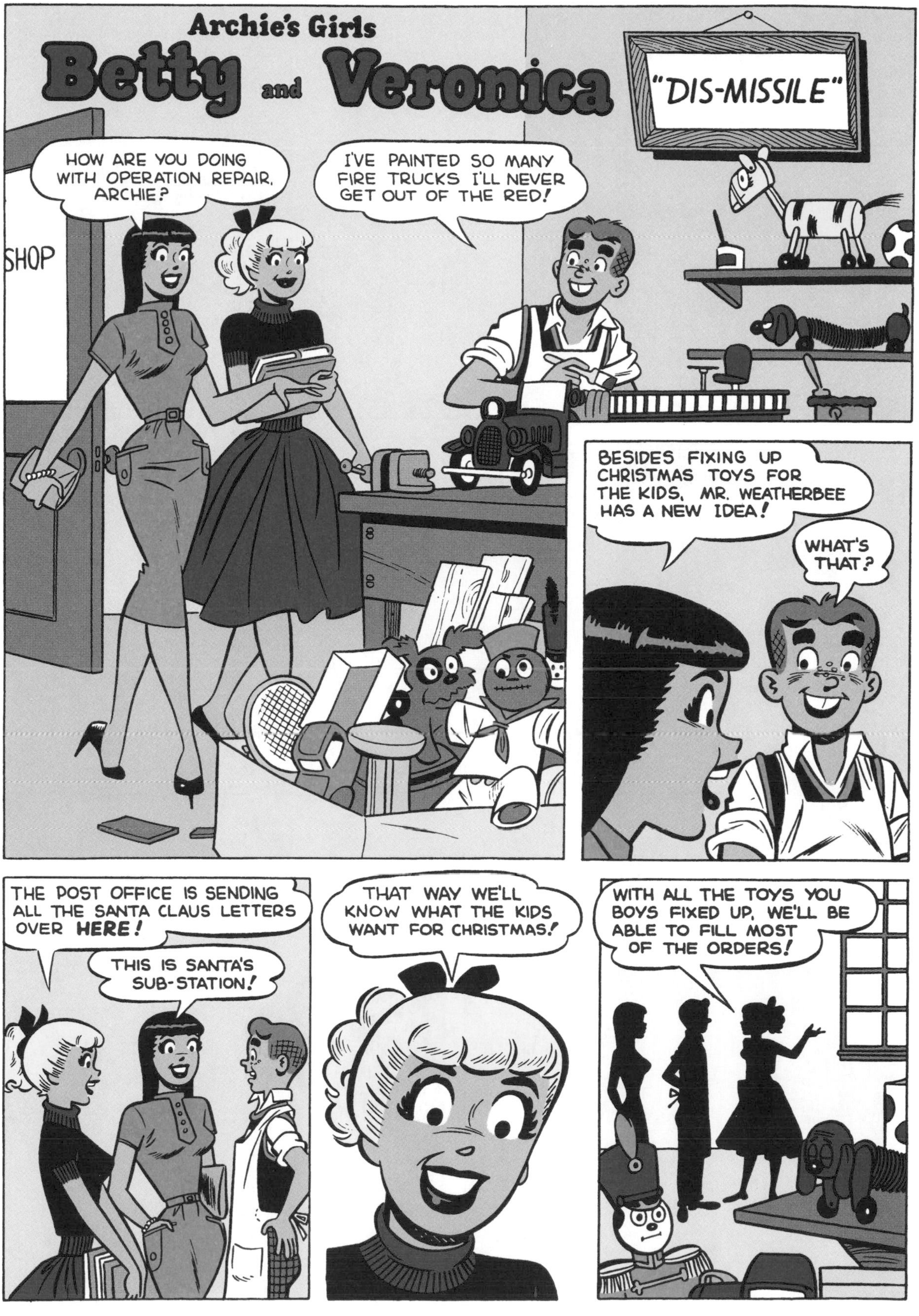
Archie's Girls
Betty and Veronica
"DIS-MISSILE"
SHOP
HOW ARE YOU DOING WITH OPERATION REPAIR, ARCHIE?
I'VE PAINTED SO MANY FIRE TRUCKS I'LL NEVER GET OUT OF THE RED!
BESIDES FIXING UP CHRISTMAS TOYS FOR THE KIDS, MR. WEATHERBEE HAS A NEW IDEA!
WHAT'S THAT?
THE POST OFFICE IS SENDING ALL THE SANTA CLAUS LETTERS OVER **HERE!**
THIS IS SANTA'S SUB-STATION!
THAT WAY WE'LL KNOW WHAT THE KIDS WANT FOR CHRISTMAS!
WITH ALL THE TOYS YOU BOYS FIXED UP, WE'LL BE ABLE TO FILL MOST OF THE ORDERS!

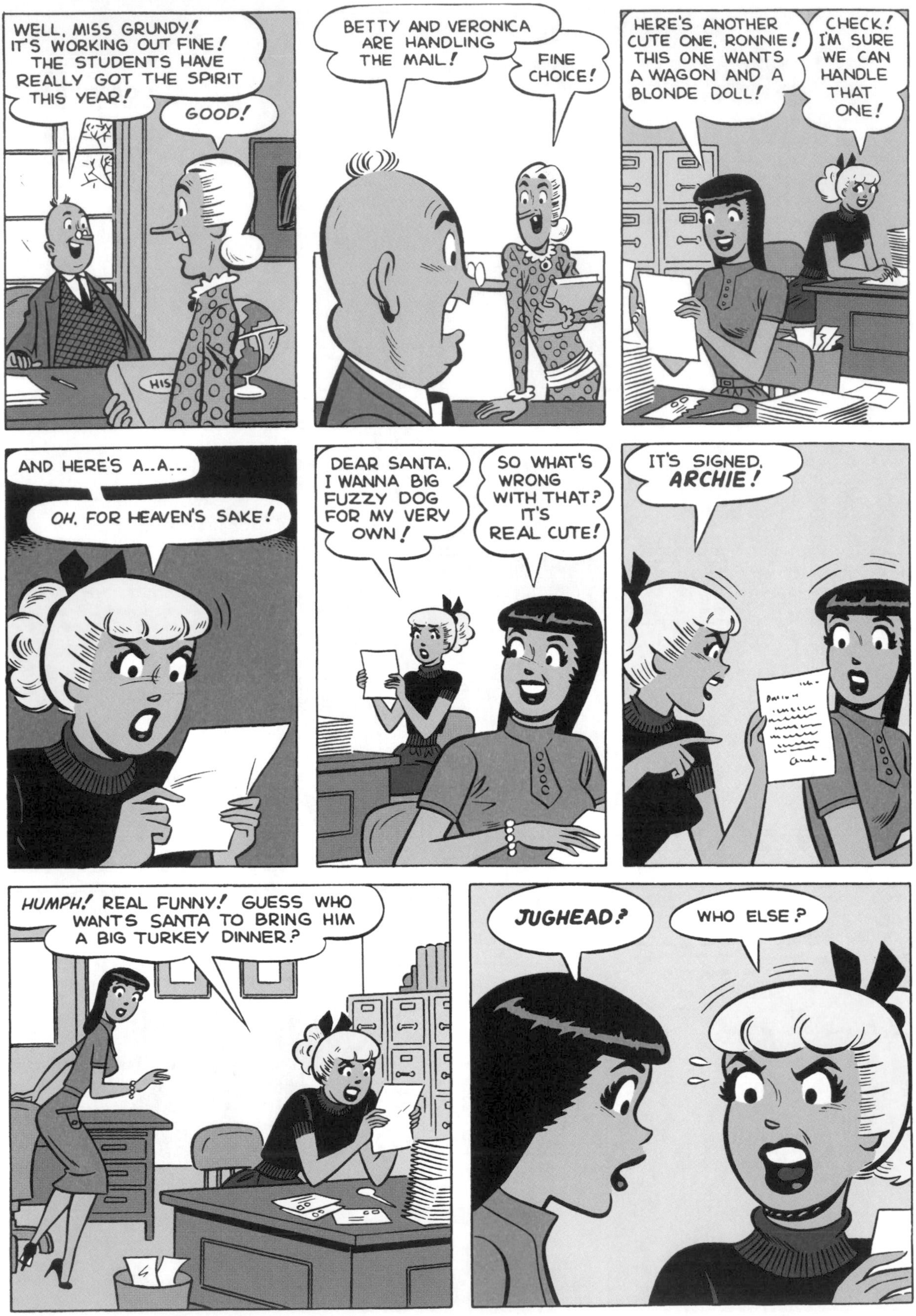
WELL, MISS GRUNDY! IT'S WORKING OUT FINE! THE STUDENTS HAVE REALLY GOT THE SPIRIT THIS YEAR!
GOOD!
BETTY AND VERONICA ARE HANDLING THE MAIL!
FINE CHOICE!
HERE'S ANOTHER CUTE ONE, RONNIE! THIS ONE WANTS A WAGON AND A BLONDE DOLL!
CHECK! I'M SURE WE CAN HANDLE THAT ONE!
AND HERE'S A..A...
OH, FOR HEAVEN'S SAKE!
DEAR SANTA, I WANNA BIG FUZZY DOG FOR MY VERY OWN!
SO WHAT'S WRONG WITH THAT? IT'S REAL CUTE!
IT'S SIGNED, ARCHIE!
HUMPH! REAL FUNNY! GUESS WHO WANTS SANTA TO BRING HIM A BIG TURKEY DINNER?
JUGHEAD?
WHO ELSE?

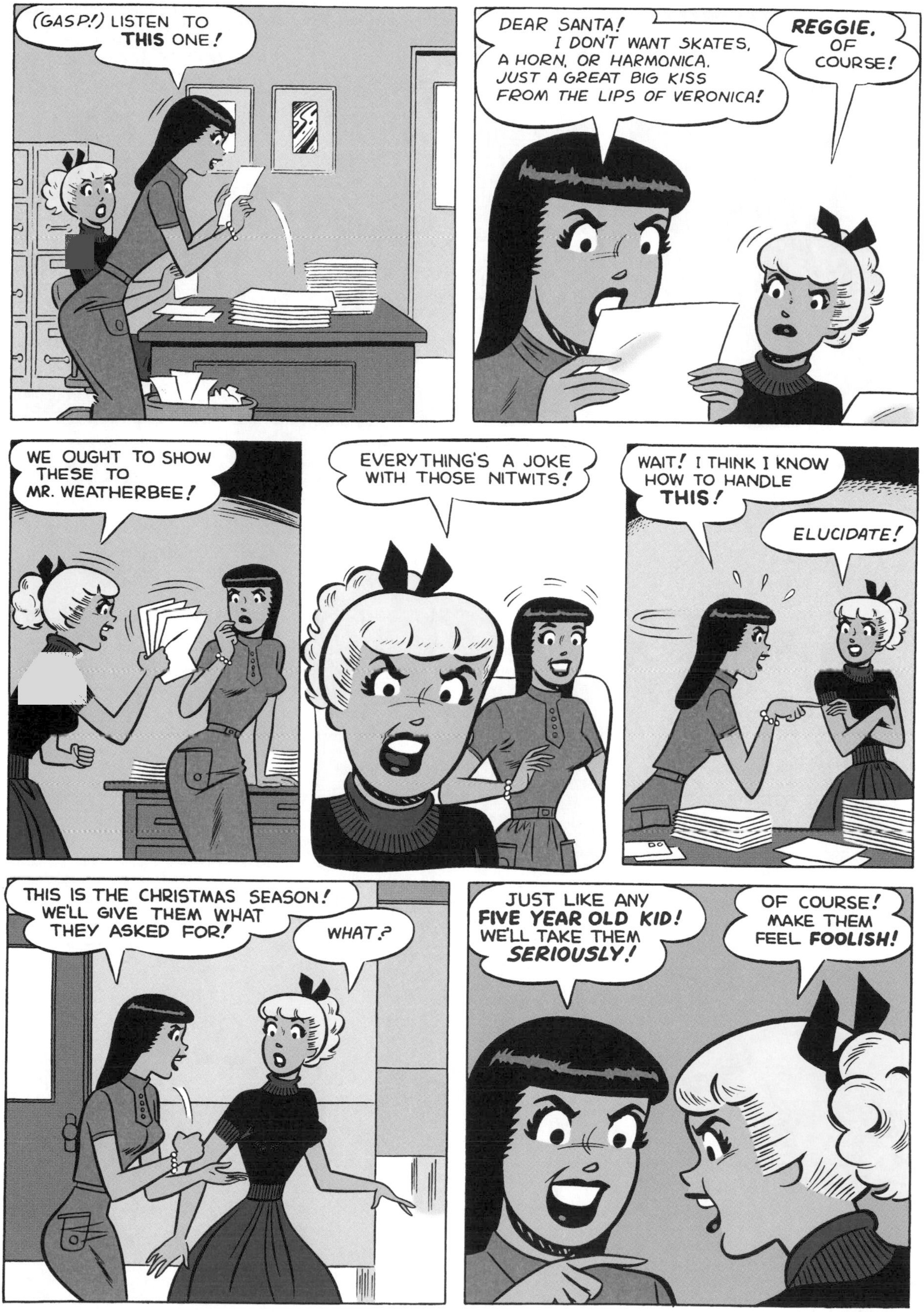
(GASP!) LISTEN TO THIS ONE!
DEAR SANTA! I DON'T WANT SKATES, A HORN, OR HARMONICA. JUST A GREAT BIG KISS FROM THE LIPS OF VERONICA!
REGGIE, OF COURSE!
WE OUGHT TO SHOW THESE TO MR. WEATHERBEE!
EVERYTHING'S A JOKE WITH THOSE NITWITS!
WAIT! I THINK I KNOW HOW TO HANDLE THIS!
ELUCIDATE!
THIS IS THE CHRISTMAS SEASON! WE'LL GIVE THEM WHAT THEY ASKED FOR!
WHAT?
JUST LIKE ANY FIVE YEAR OLD KID! WE'LL TAKE THEM SERIOUSLY!
OF COURSE! MAKE THEM FEEL FOOLISH!

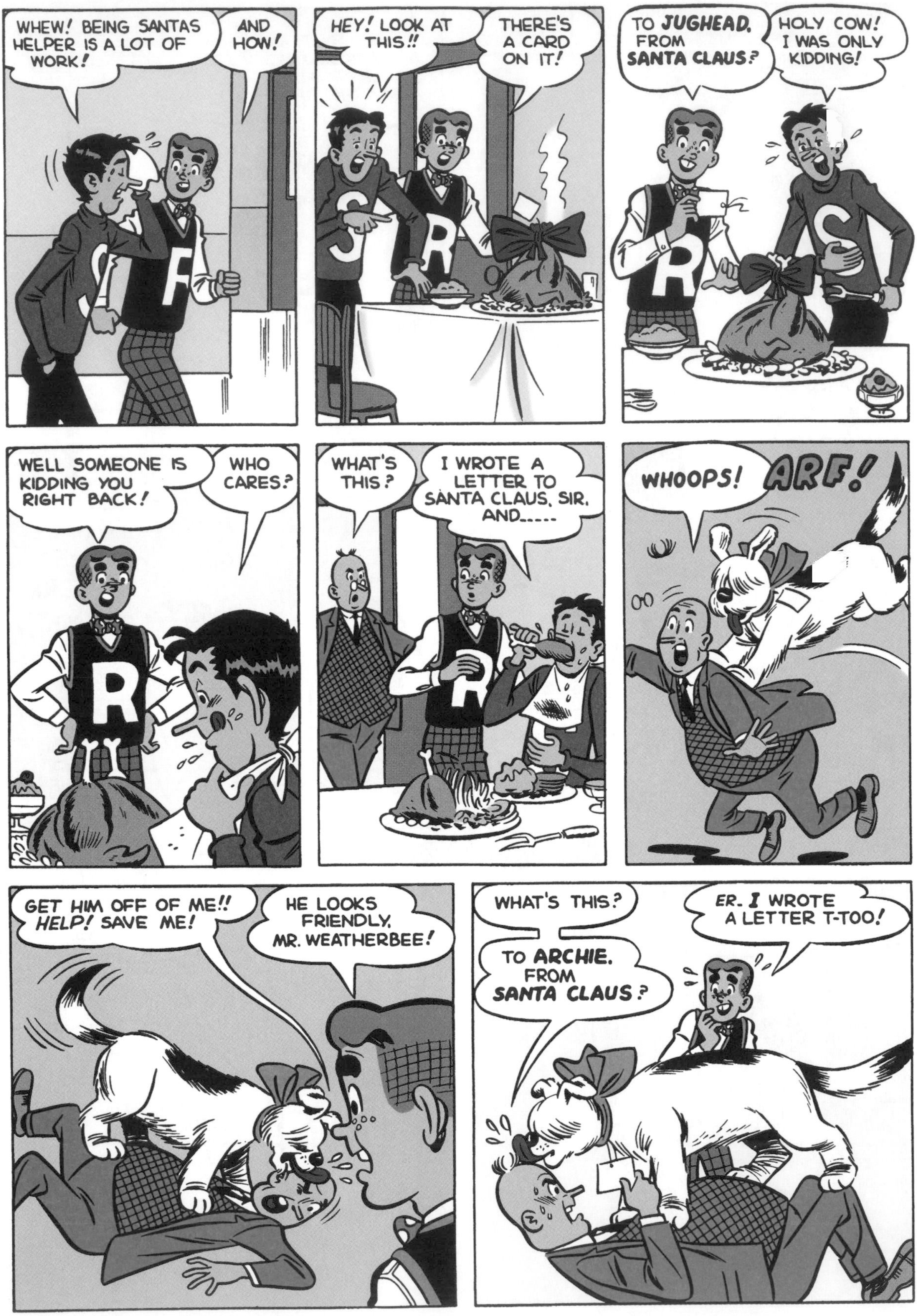
WHEW! BEING SANTAS HELPER IS A LOT OF WORK!
AND HOW!
HEY! LOOK AT THIS!!
THERE'S A CARD ON IT!
TO JUGHEAD, FROM SANTA CLAUS?
HOLY COW! I WAS ONLY KIDDING!
WELL SOMEONE IS KIDDING YOU RIGHT BACK!
WHO CARES?
WHAT'S THIS?
I WROTE A LETTER TO SANTA CLAUS, SIR, AND.....
WHOOPS!
ARF!
GET HIM OFF OF ME!! HELP! SAVE ME!
HE LOOKS FRIENDLY, MR. WEATHERBEE!
WHAT'S THIS?
TO ARCHIE, FROM SANTA CLAUS?
ER- I WROTE A LETTER T-TOO!

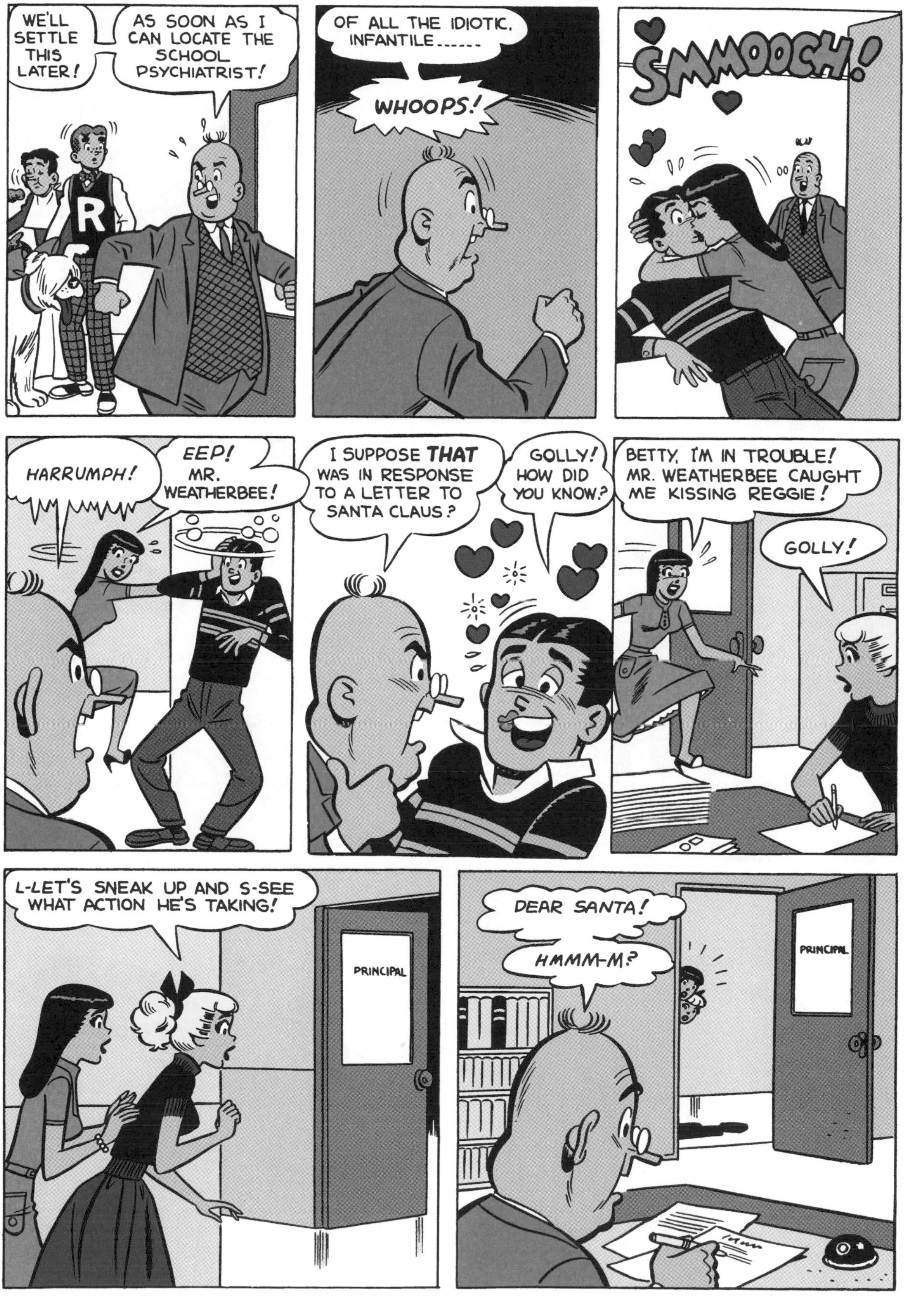
WE'LL SETTLE THIS LATER!
AS SOON AS I CAN LOCATE THE SCHOOL PSYCHIATRIST!
OF ALL THE IDIOTIC, INFANTILE ------
WHOOPS!
SMMOOCH!
HARRUMPH!
EEP! MR. WEATHERBEE!
I SUPPOSE THAT WAS IN RESPONSE TO A LETTER TO SANTA CLAUS?
GOLLY! HOW DID YOU KNOW?
BETTY, I'M IN TROUBLE! MR. WEATHERBEE CAUGHT ME KISSING REGGIE!
GOLLY!
L-LET'S SNEAK UP AND S-SEE WHAT ACTION HE'S TAKING!
PRINCIPAL
DEAR SANTA!
HMMM-M?
PRINCIPAL

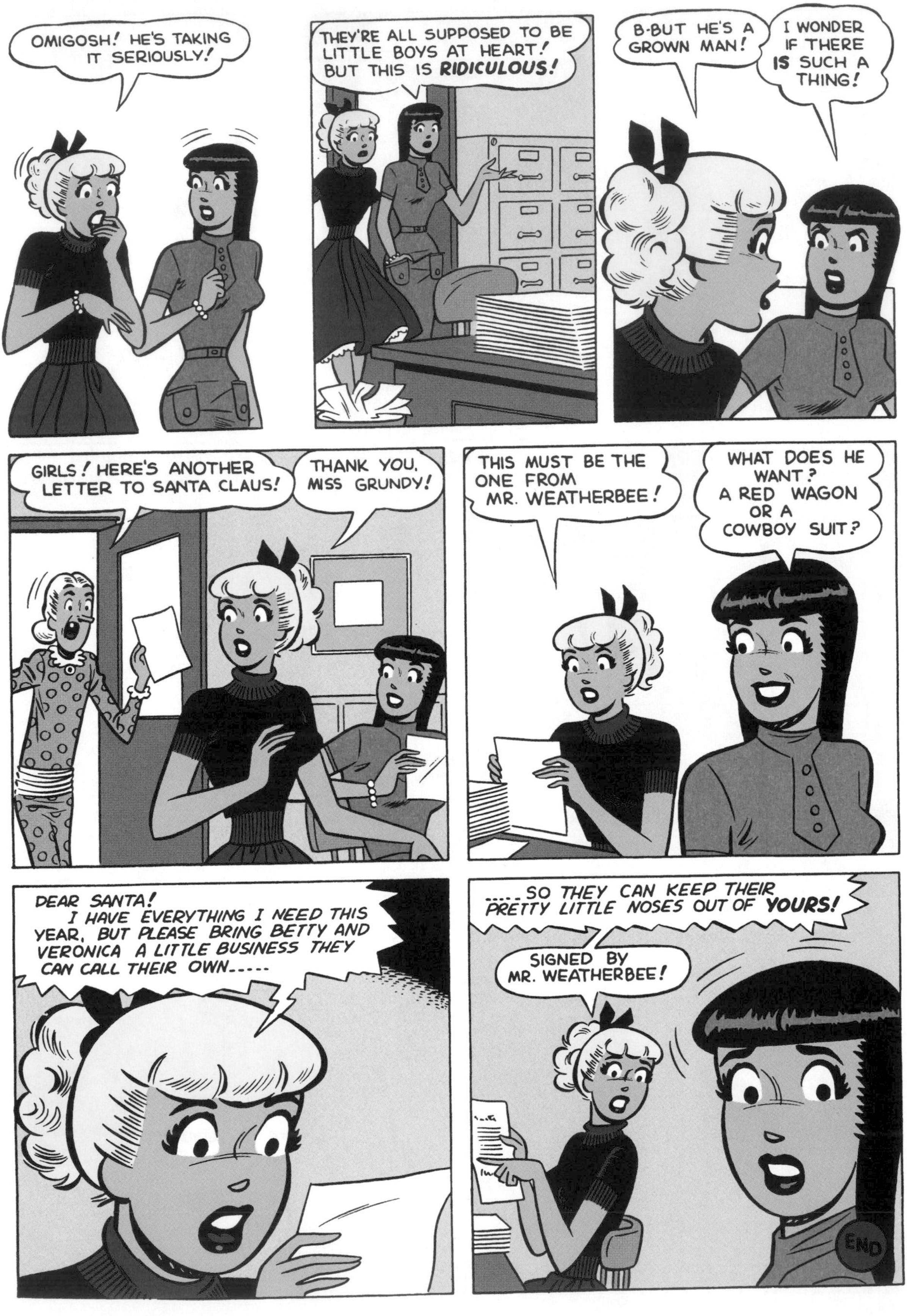
OMIGOSH! HE'S TAKING IT SERIOUSLY!
THEY'RE ALL SUPPOSED TO BE LITTLE BOYS AT HEART! BUT THIS IS RIDICULOUS!
B-BUT HE'S A GROWN MAN!
I WONDER IF THERE IS SUCH A THING!
GIRLS! HERE'S ANOTHER LETTER TO SANTA CLAUS!
THANK YOU, MISS GRUNDY!
THIS MUST BE THE ONE FROM MR. WEATHERBEE!
WHAT DOES HE WANT? A RED WAGON OR A COWBOY SUIT?
DEAR SANTA! I HAVE EVERYTHING I NEED THIS YEAR, BUT PLEASE BRING BETTY AND VERONICA A LITTLE BUSINESS THEY CAN CALL THEIR OWN-----
.....SO THEY CAN KEEP THEIR PRETTY LITTLE NOSES OUT OF YOURS!
SIGNED BY MR. WEATHERBEE!
END

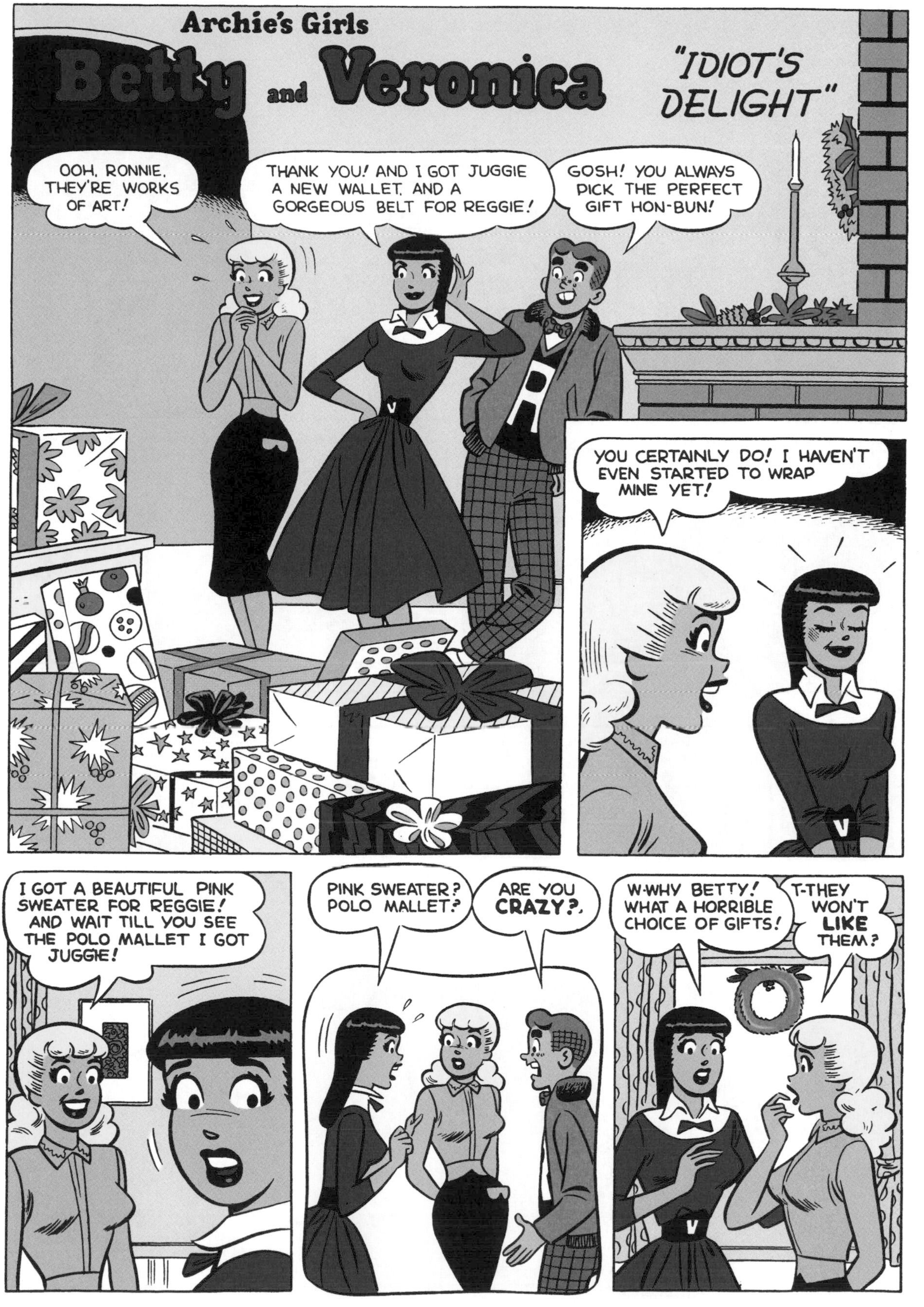
Archie's Girls
Betty and Veronica
"IDIOT'S DELIGHT"
OOH, RONNIE, THEY'RE WORKS OF ART!
THANK YOU! AND I GOT JUGGIE A NEW WALLET, AND A GORGEOUS BELT FOR REGGIE!
GOSH! YOU ALWAYS PICK THE PERFECT GIFT HON-BUN!
YOU CERTAINLY DO! I HAVEN'T EVEN STARTED TO WRAP MINE YET!
I GOT A BEAUTIFUL PINK SWEATER FOR REGGIE! AND WAIT TILL YOU SEE THE POLO MALLET I GOT JUGGIE!
PINK SWEATER? POLO MALLET?
ARE YOU CRAZY?
W-WHY BETTY! WHAT A HORRIBLE CHOICE OF GIFTS!
T-THEY WON'T LIKE THEM?

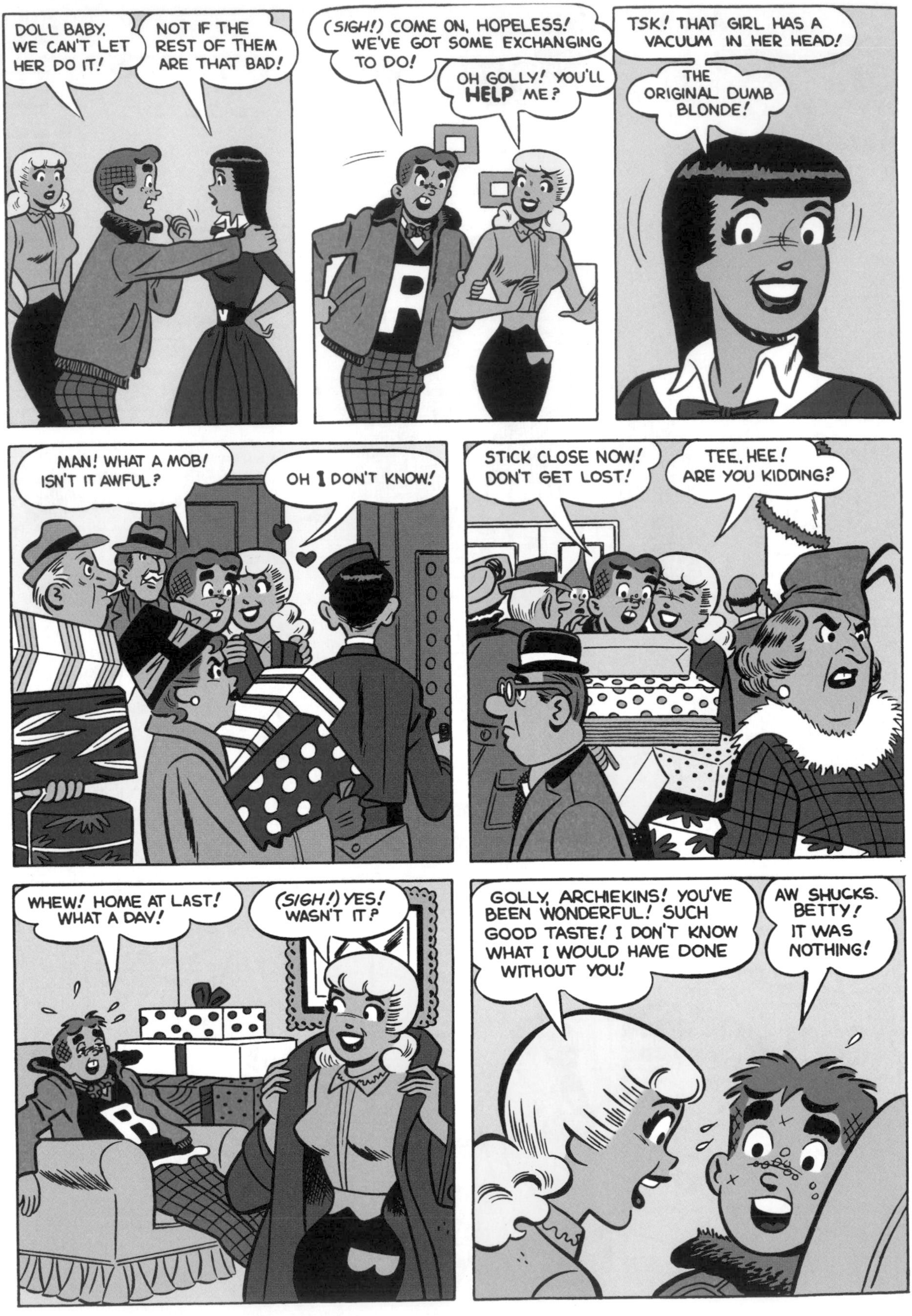
DOLL BABY, WE CAN'T LET HER DO IT!
NOT IF THE REST OF THEM ARE THAT BAD!
(SIGH!) COME ON, HOPELESS! WE'VE GOT SOME EXCHANGING TO DO!
OH GOLLY! YOU'LL HELP ME?
TSK! THAT GIRL HAS A VACUUM IN HER HEAD!
THE ORIGINAL DUMB BLONDE!
MAN! WHAT A MOB! ISN'T IT AWFUL?
OH I DON'T KNOW!
STICK CLOSE NOW! DON'T GET LOST!
TEE, HEE! ARE YOU KIDDING?
WHEW! HOME AT LAST! WHAT A DAY!
(SIGH!) YES! WASN'T IT?
GOLLY, ARCHIEKINS! YOU'VE BEEN WONDERFUL! SUCH GOOD TASTE! I DON'T KNOW WHAT I WOULD HAVE DONE WITHOUT YOU!
AW SHUCKS. BETTY! IT WAS NOTHING!

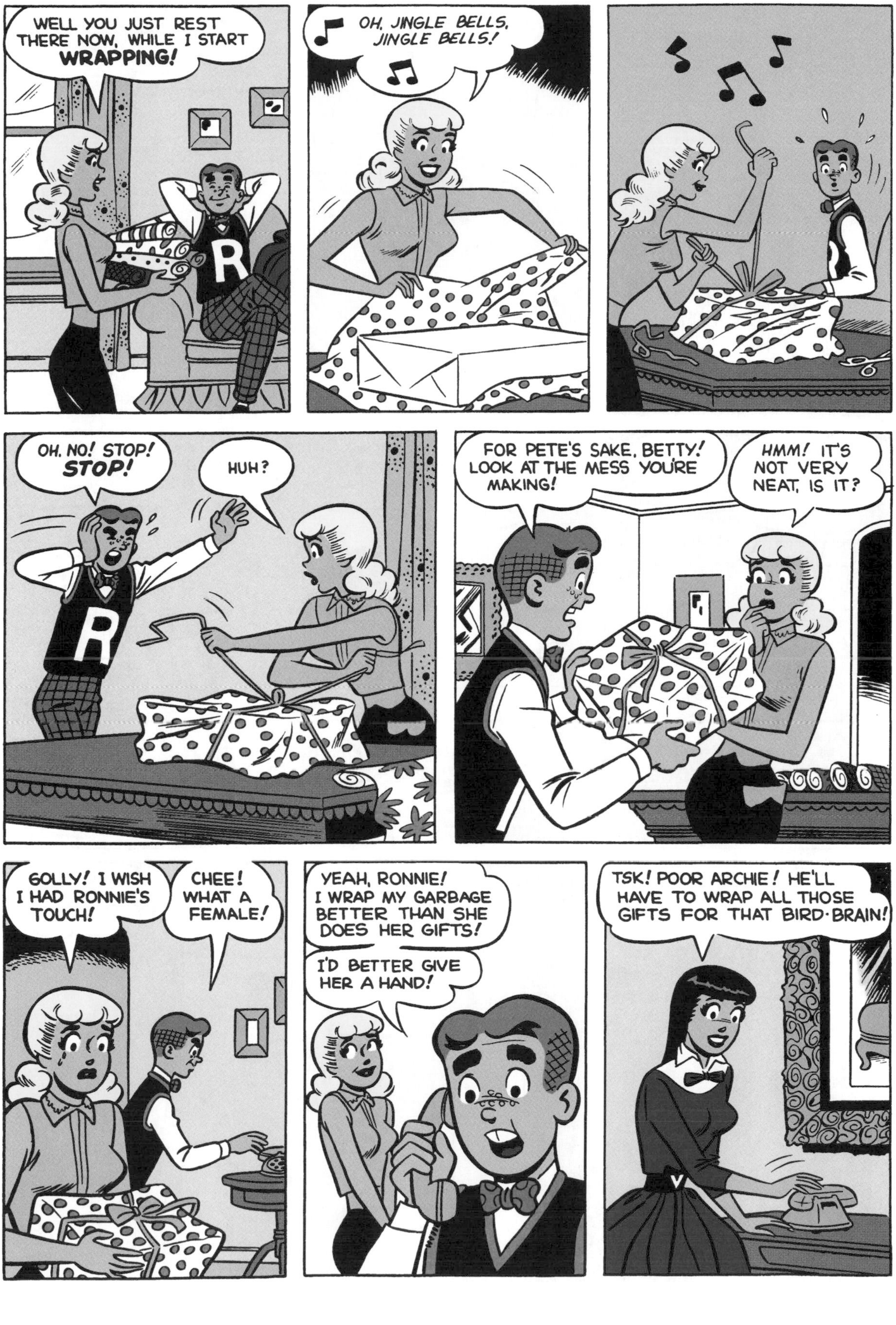
WELL YOU JUST REST THERE NOW, WHILE I START **WRAPPING!**
OH, JINGLE BELLS, JINGLE BELLS!
OH, NO! STOP! **STOP!**
HUH?
FOR PETE'S SAKE, BETTY! LOOK AT THE MESS YOU'RE MAKING!
HMM! IT'S NOT VERY NEAT, IS IT?
GOLLY! I WISH I HAD RONNIE'S TOUCH!
CHEE! WHAT A FEMALE!
YEAH, RONNIE! I WRAP MY GARBAGE BETTER THAN SHE DOES HER GIFTS!
I'D BETTER GIVE HER A HAND!
TSK! POOR ARCHIE! HE'LL HAVE TO WRAP ALL THOSE GIFTS FOR THAT BIRD-BRAIN!

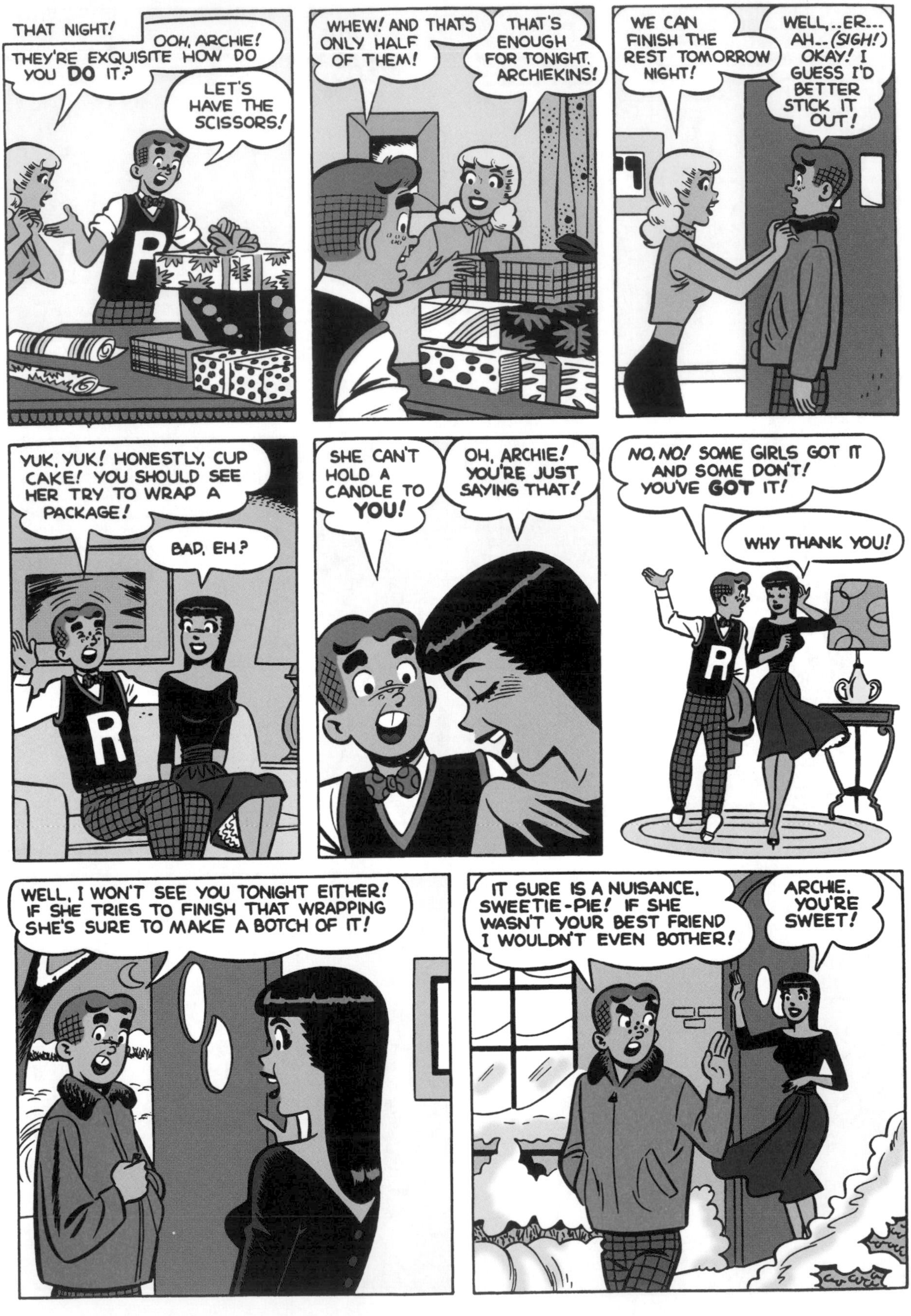
THAT NIGHT!
OOH, ARCHIE! THEY'RE EXQUISITE HOW DO YOU DO IT?
LET'S HAVE THE SCISSORS!
WHEW! AND THAT'S ONLY HALF OF THEM!
THAT'S ENOUGH FOR TONIGHT, ARCHIEKINS!
WE CAN FINISH THE REST TOMORROW NIGHT!
WELL,..ER... AH..(SIGH!) OKAY! I GUESS I'D BETTER STICK IT OUT!
YUK, YUK! HONESTLY, CUP CAKE! YOU SHOULD SEE HER TRY TO WRAP A PACKAGE!
BAD, EH?
SHE CAN'T HOLD A CANDLE TO YOU!
OH, ARCHIE! YOU'RE JUST SAYING THAT!
NO, NO! SOME GIRLS GOT IT AND SOME DON'T! YOU'VE GOT IT!
WHY THANK YOU!
WELL, I WON'T SEE YOU TONIGHT EITHER! IF SHE TRIES TO FINISH THAT WRAPPING SHE'S SURE TO MAKE A BOTCH OF IT!
IT SURE IS A NUISANCE, SWEETIE-PIE! IF SHE WASN'T YOUR BEST FRIEND I WOULDN'T EVEN BOTHER!
ARCHIE, YOU'RE SWEET!

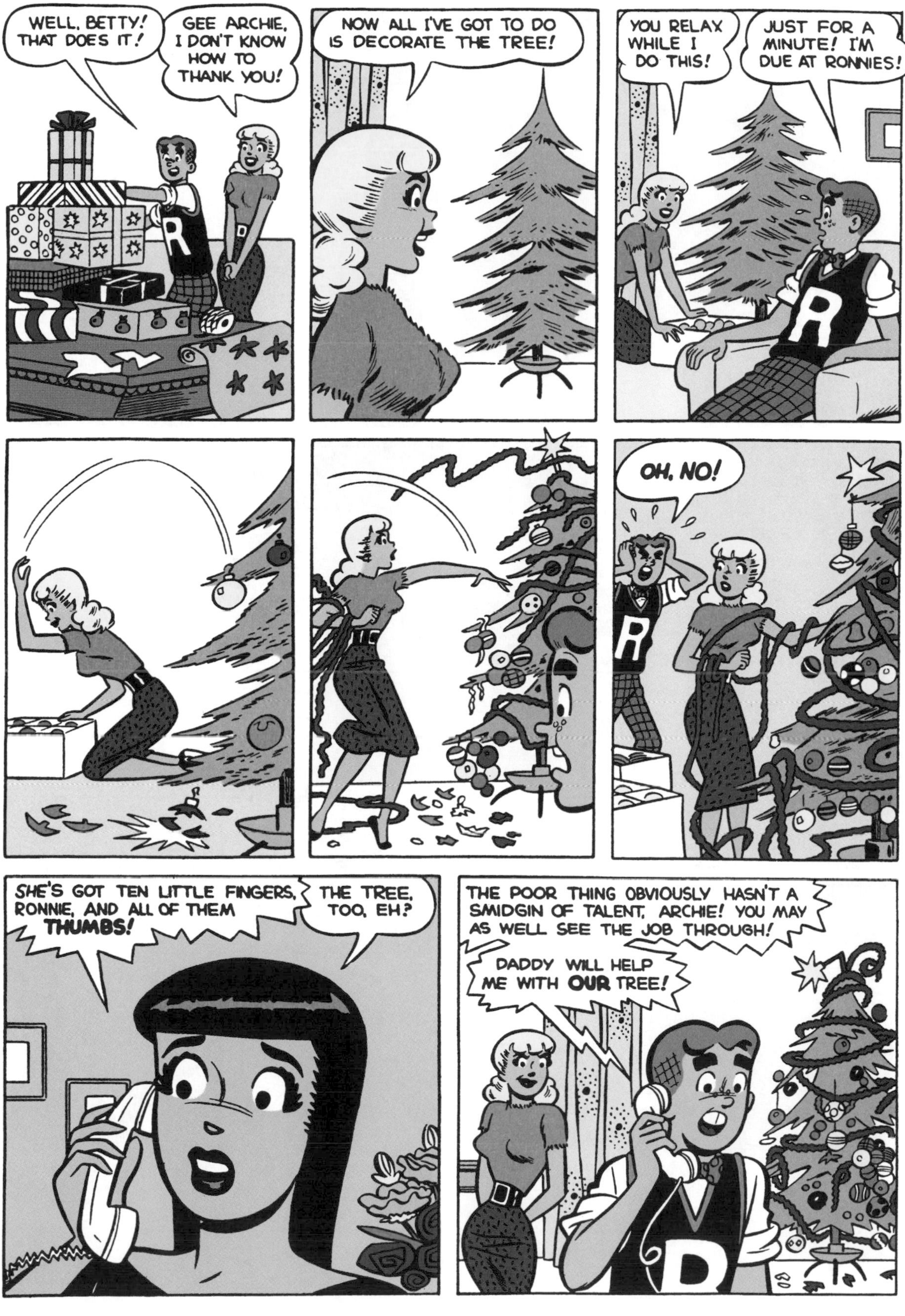
WELL, BETTY! THAT DOES IT!
GEE ARCHIE, I DON'T KNOW HOW TO THANK YOU!
NOW ALL I'VE GOT TO DO IS DECORATE THE TREE!
YOU RELAX WHILE I DO THIS!
JUST FOR A MINUTE! I'M DUE AT RONNIES!
OH, NO!
SHE'S GOT TEN LITTLE FINGERS, RONNIE, AND ALL OF THEM THUMBS!
THE TREE, TOO, EH?
THE POOR THING OBVIOUSLY HASN'T A SMIDGIN OF TALENT, ARCHIE! YOU MAY AS WELL SEE THE JOB THROUGH!
DADDY WILL HELP ME WITH OUR TREE!

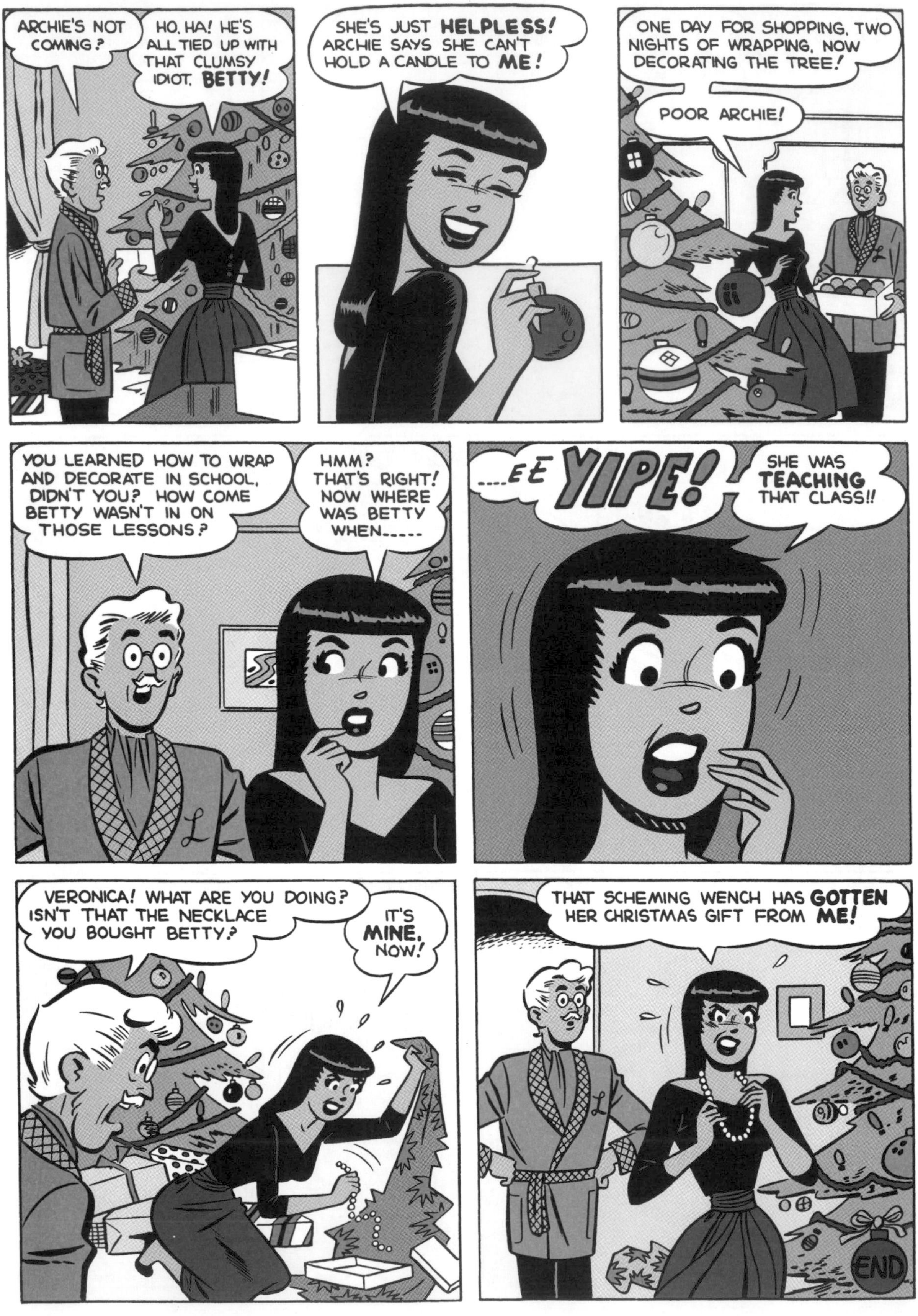
ARCHIE'S NOT COMING?
HO, HA! HE'S ALL TIED UP WITH THAT CLUMSY IDIOT, BETTY!
SHE'S JUST HELPLESS! ARCHIE SAYS SHE CAN'T HOLD A CANDLE TO ME!
ONE DAY FOR SHOPPING, TWO NIGHTS OF WRAPPING, NOW DECORATING THE TREE!
POOR ARCHIE!
YOU LEARNED HOW TO WRAP AND DECORATE IN SCHOOL, DIDN'T YOU? HOW COME BETTY WASN'T IN ON THOSE LESSONS?
HMM? THAT'S RIGHT! NOW WHERE WAS BETTY WHEN-----
----EE YIPE!
SHE WAS TEACHING THAT CLASS!!
VERONICA! WHAT ARE YOU DOING? ISN'T THAT THE NECKLACE YOU BOUGHT BETTY?
IT'S MINE, NOW!
THAT SCHEMING WENCH HAS GOTTEN HER CHRISTMAS GIFT FROM ME!
END

"DRESSED TO KILL"

GOLLY! THIS IS JUST GOING TO BE ABOUT THE WORST CHRISTMAS I'VE EVER HAD!

"OH Betty, I'm so thrilled," Veronica bubbled. "I got the most beautiful dress for your Christmas party. Would you like to see it?"

"I'd love to Veronica."

Veronica rushed to her closet and fished through the hundreds of garments she had hanging there. Mr. Lodge swore that she had more dresses in her closet than the dress shop had in stock. At last Veronica brought out her latest and flourished it proudly at Betty.

The eager smile on Betty's face suddenly vanished. It was replaced by pain and then anguish. "Veronica. You can't wear that dress to my party," she howled. "I bought one exactly like it that I was planning to wear."

"What . . . !" Veronica shrieked. "Don't you dare wear the same dress I do, Betty Cooper."

"But Veronica. You've got loads of dresses to pick from. I've only got this one new. I can't afford to buy another one."

"I don't care. I like this one. And if you wear yours, I just won't come to your party."

Betty stiffened. Her eyes shot sparks. "All right. Then don't come. I bought the dress first and I'm going to wear it. You're just plain mean, Veronica Lodge."

"All right. You can wear your old dress and I won't come. I'll have a Christmas party of my own and I'll invite Archie," Veronica seethed.

"Veronica. You wouldn't dare.

Archie has already accepted my invitation. He wouldn't turn me down now."

"Oh, wouldn't he? . . . We'll see about that."

Betty walked out of Veronica's house, her chin high. But it wasn't long before it fell. And what a fall. Clean down to the floor. Her eyes started to fill up as she realized what would happen. Veronica held the whip hand. Archie would never be able to refuse her. And without Archie, her own party would be ruined. She tried to tell herself that Archie wouldn't have the nerve to stand her up at this late date. Archie was too much a gentleman. Archie had too much character. Archie was too considerate. Then she suddenly had a vision of Veronica snuggling her beautiful head on Archie's shoulder, gazing at him soulfully with those big, blue eyes and trilling, "Archiekins, you'll come to my party, won't you lambie pie?"

"No," Betty moaned. "Archie is a dead duck. I'll have a perfectly miserable Christmas party this year without him." Betty ran into her

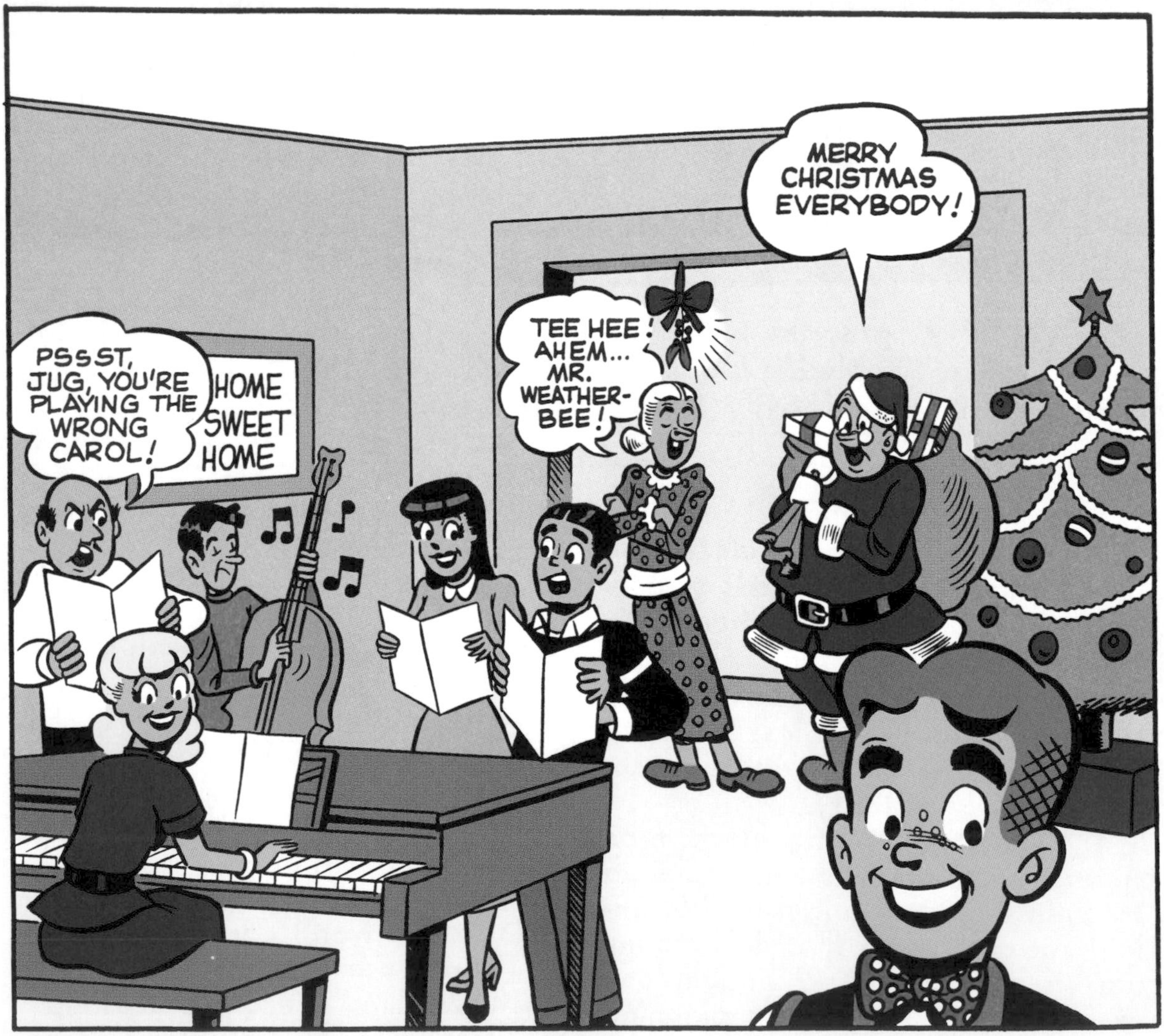
PSSST, JUG, YOU'RE PLAYING THE WRONG CAROL!
HOME SWEET HOME
TEE HEE! AHEM... MR. WEATHERBEE!
MERRY CHRISTMAS EVERYBODY!

house, threw herself on her bed and cried her heart out in her pillow.

Came the day of the party and Betty was trimming the Christmas tree and getting things ready for the big party that night. She was about as enthusiastic as a cow being led to the slaughter. Veronica hadn't phoned since their tiff. But worse still, neither had Archie. It was now a certainty that tonight was to be an Archie-less party. All week long, she had seen Archie trailing around with Veronica. He with that silly, love-sick look on his face and she hanging on to his arm like a drowning sailor to a life raft. Looking at him in that sultry way that made his adam's apple go up and down like a yo-yo and his eyeballs go "tilt."

Tonight was definitely going to be a complete and unadulterated washout.

If any last lingering hope had remained, it gradually grew smaller and smaller and finally disappeared completely when one by one all the gang arrived and still no Archie.

The kids were really whooping it up, dancing, singing, shouting, ex-

ARCHIE! YOU'VE COME TO MY PARTY!

SMACK

changing presents. But Betty might just as well have been on a desert island for all the people she saw.

Suddenly she felt a pair of lips on her cheek. Somebody was kissing her. She turned. Looked. Gasped. And almost fainted. There was a smiling Archie.

"Hiya, Betty. Mind my kissing you —I'm allowed to, you know. You're standing under the mistletoe."

"Oh, Archie," Betty said, her voice choked with relief. "You did come."

"Why sure I came. You invited me, didn't you?"

"'Of course. But Veronica, didn't she . . . that is . . . I mean . . ."

"Oh you mean that silly idea she had about making another party and inviting me. Sure she said something about that. But what kind of a heel do you think I am anyway, Betty? You didn't think I'd stand you up like that do you?"

"I—I—n-no. Of course not, Archie. I knew you wouldn't do that. But Veronica, well, she's not coming and . . ."

"Who said I'm not coming, Betty?"

Betty turned again. This time it was Veronica standing there. And wearing a different dress.

"Gee, I'm sorry I was so mean, Betty. Making such a fuss over a silly dress. I actually tried to take Archie away from your party. But he laced it into me. And I deserved it. You'll forgive me, won't you?"

"And you're still under the mistletoe, Betty," Archie said, and planted another kiss on her cheek.

All Betty could say between crying and laughing at the same time was, "There really is a Santa Claus."

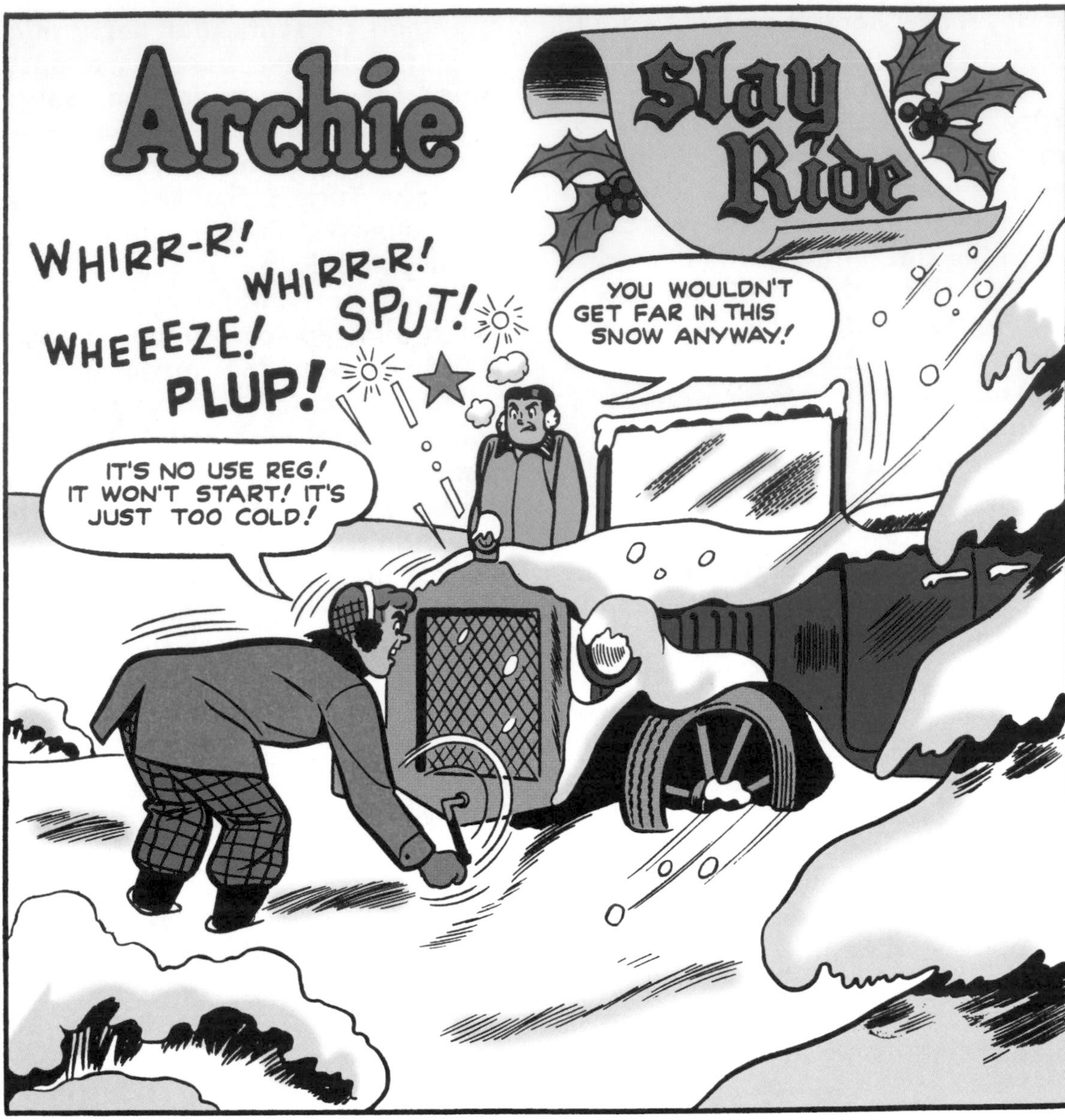
Archie
Slay Ride
WHIRR-R!
WHIRR-R!
WHEEEZE!
SPUT!
PLUP!
YOU WOULDN'T GET FAR IN THIS SNOW ANYWAY!
IT'S NO USE REG! IT WON'T START! IT'S JUST TOO COLD!

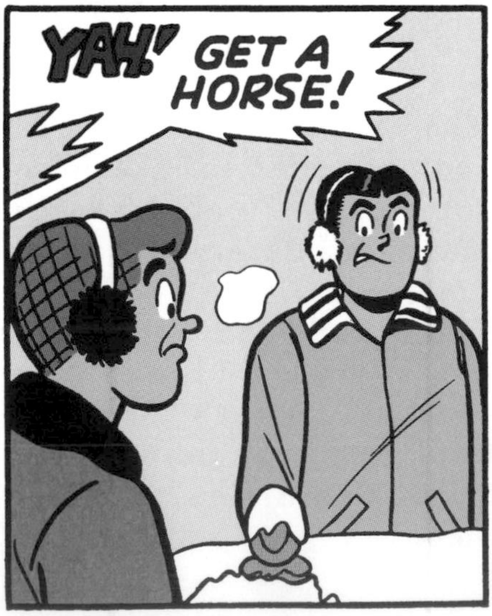
YAH! GET A HORSE!

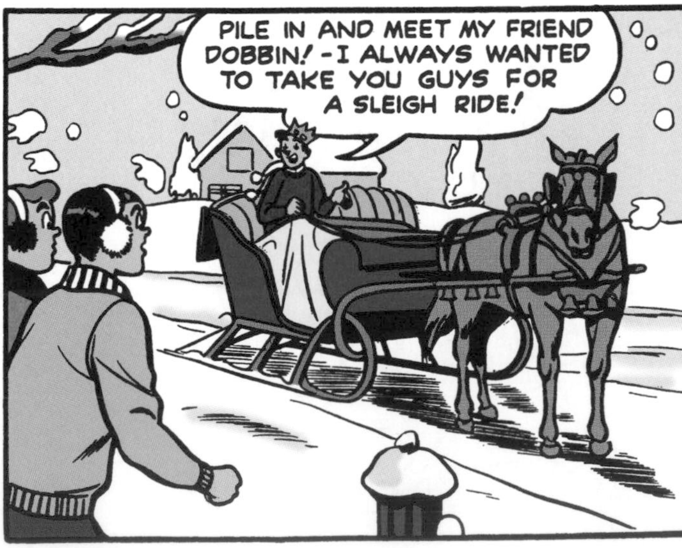
PILE IN AND MEET MY FRIEND DOBBIN! -I ALWAYS WANTED TO TAKE YOU GUYS FOR A SLEIGH RIDE!

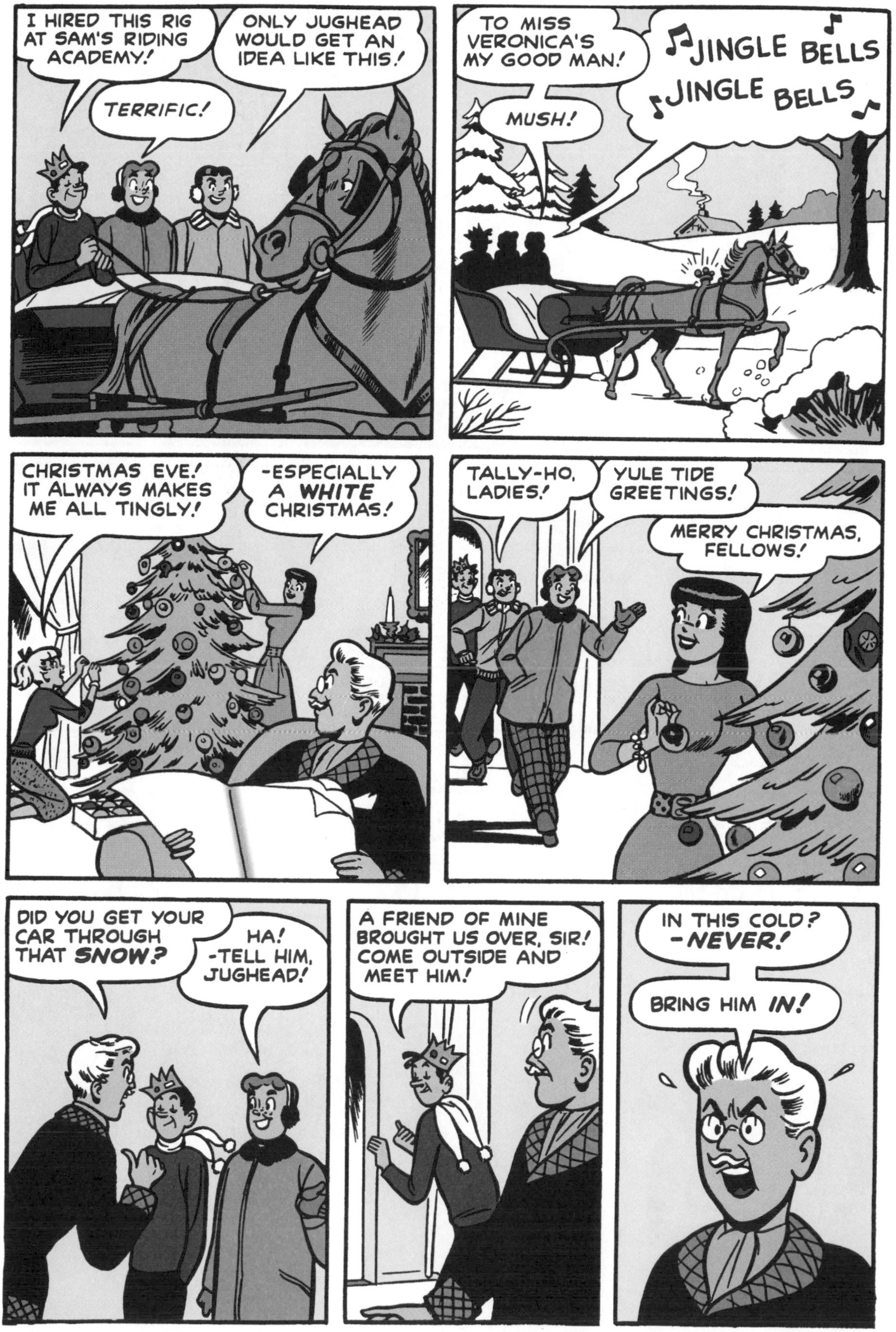
I HIRED THIS RIG AT SAM'S RIDING ACADEMY!
TERRIFIC!
ONLY JUGHEAD WOULD GET AN IDEA LIKE THIS!
TO MISS VERONICA'S MY GOOD MAN!
MUSH!
JINGLE BELLS
JINGLE BELLS
CHRISTMAS EVE! IT ALWAYS MAKES ME ALL TINGLY!
-ESPECIALLY A WHITE CHRISTMAS!
TALLY-HO, LADIES!
YULE TIDE GREETINGS!
MERRY CHRISTMAS, FELLOWS!
DID YOU GET YOUR CAR THROUGH THAT SNOW?
HA! -TELL HIM, JUGHEAD!
A FRIEND OF MINE BROUGHT US OVER, SIR! COME OUTSIDE AND MEET HIM!
IN THIS COLD? -NEVER!
BRING HIM IN!

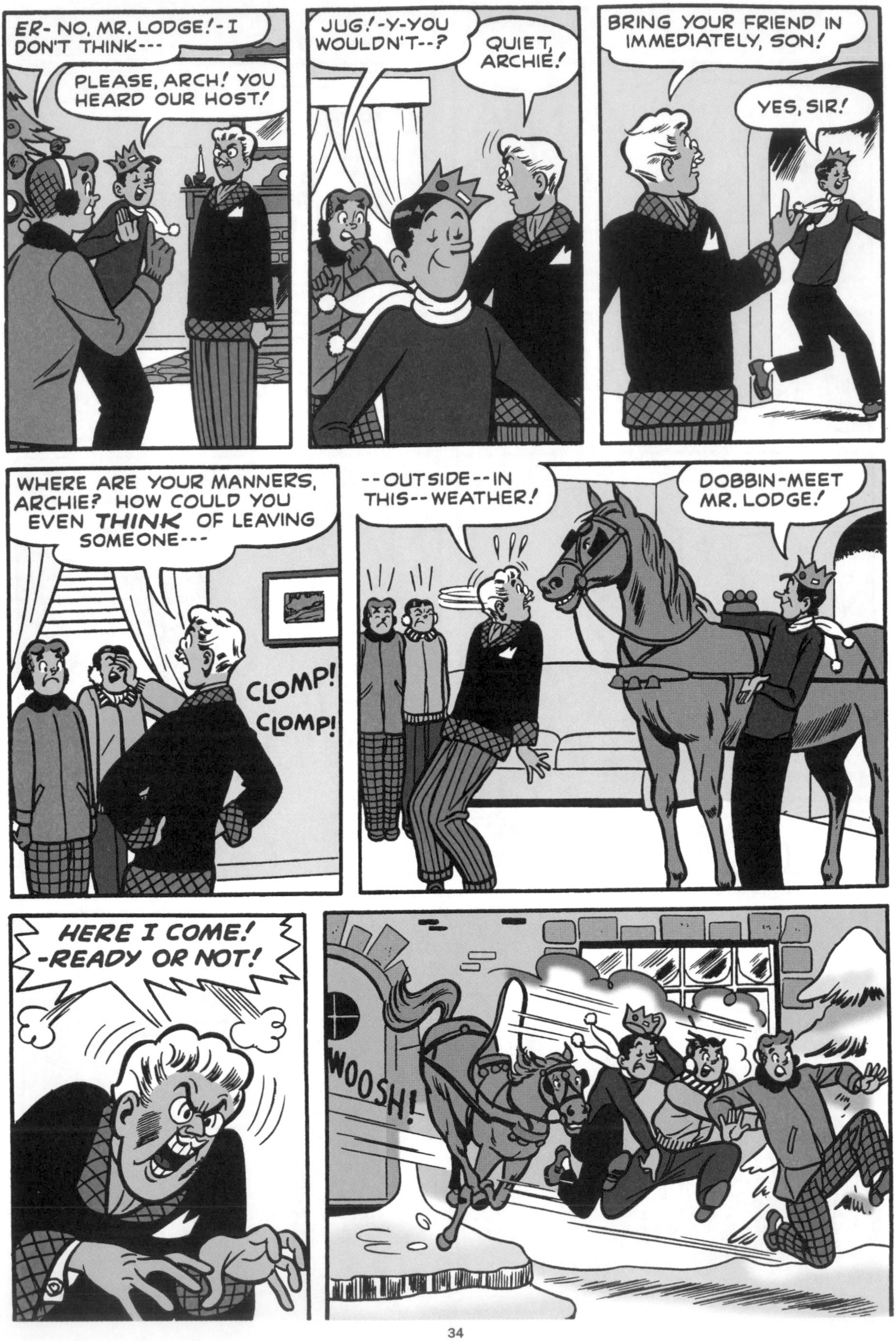
ER- NO, MR. LODGE!-I DON'T THINK---
PLEASE, ARCH! YOU HEARD OUR HOST!
JUG!-Y-YOU WOULDN'T--?
QUIET, ARCHIE!
BRING YOUR FRIEND IN IMMEDIATELY, SON!
YES, SIR!
WHERE ARE YOUR MANNERS, ARCHIE? HOW COULD YOU EVEN THINK OF LEAVING SOMEONE---
CLOMP! CLOMP!
--OUTSIDE--IN THIS--WEATHER!
DOBBIN-MEET MR. LODGE!
HERE I COME! -READY OR NOT!
WOOSH!

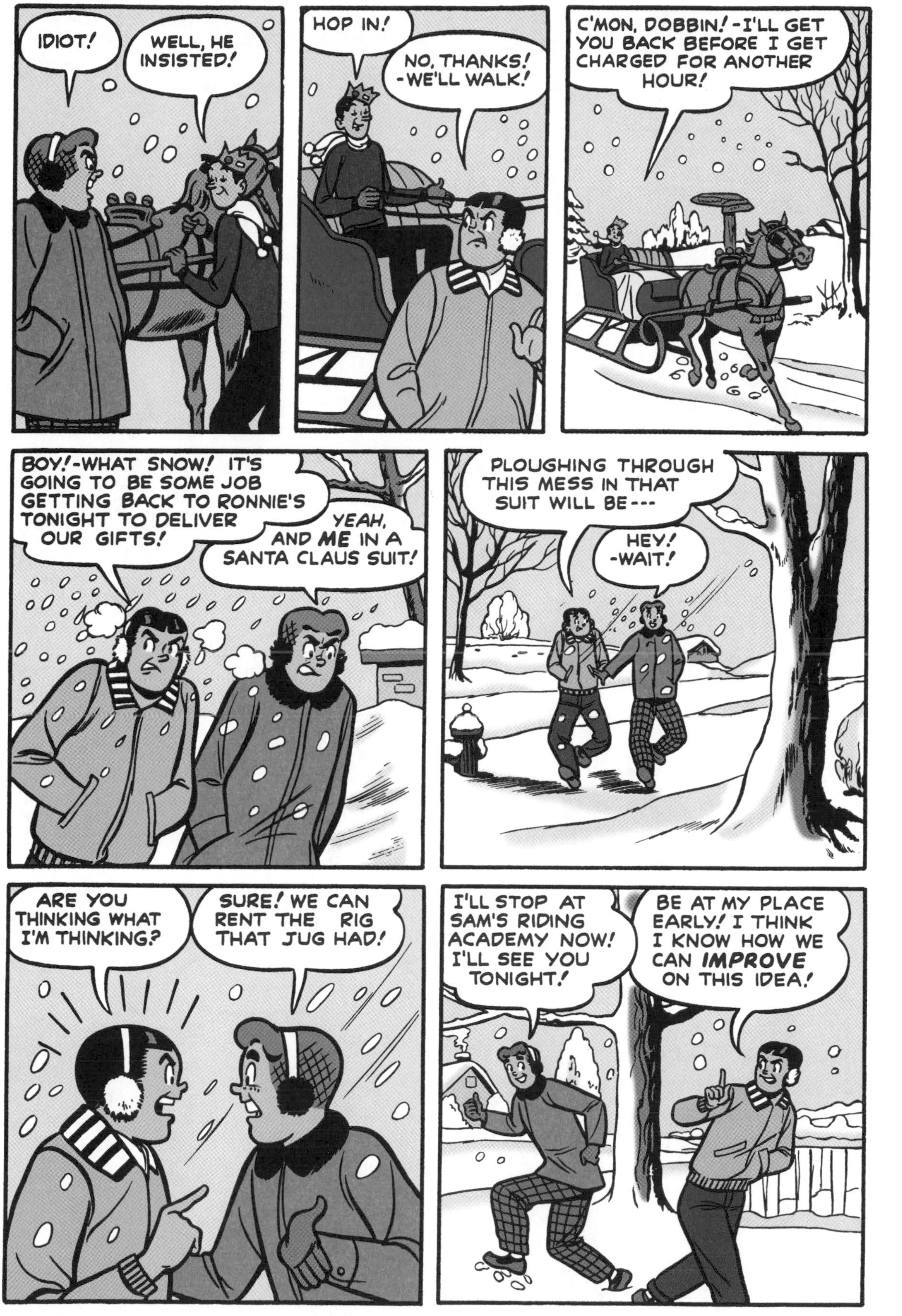
IDIOT!
WELL, HE INSISTED!
HOP IN!
NO, THANKS! -WE'LL WALK!
C'MON, DOBBIN! -I'LL GET YOU BACK BEFORE I GET CHARGED FOR ANOTHER HOUR!
BOY! -WHAT SNOW! IT'S GOING TO BE SOME JOB GETTING BACK TO RONNIE'S TONIGHT TO DELIVER OUR GIFTS!
YEAH, AND ME IN A SANTA CLAUS SUIT!
PLOUGHING THROUGH THIS MESS IN THAT SUIT WILL BE---
HEY! -WAIT!
ARE YOU THINKING WHAT I'M THINKING?
SURE! WE CAN RENT THE RIG THAT JUG HAD!
I'LL STOP AT SAM'S RIDING ACADEMY NOW! I'LL SEE YOU TONIGHT!
BE AT MY PLACE EARLY! I THINK I KNOW HOW WE CAN IMPROVE ON THIS IDEA!

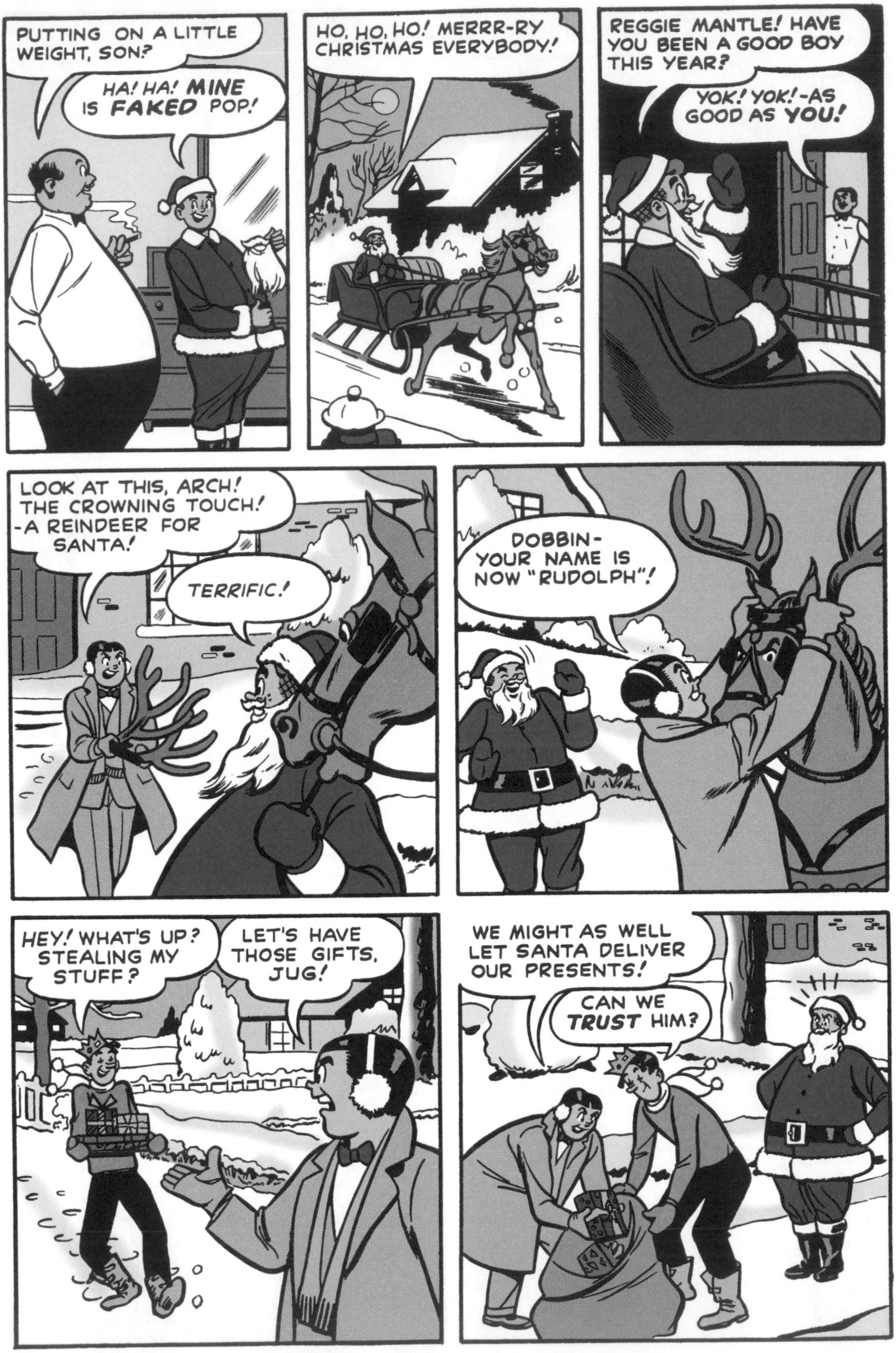
PUTTING ON A LITTLE WEIGHT, SON?
HA! HA! MINE IS FAKED POP!
HO, HO, HO! MERRR-RY CHRISTMAS EVERYBODY!
REGGIE MANTLE! HAVE YOU BEEN A GOOD BOY THIS YEAR?
YOK! YOK!-AS GOOD AS YOU!
LOOK AT THIS, ARCH! THE CROWNING TOUCH! -A REINDEER FOR SANTA!
TERRIFIC!
DOBBIN- YOUR NAME IS NOW "RUDOLPH"!
HEY! WHAT'S UP? STEALING MY STUFF?
LET'S HAVE THOSE GIFTS, JUG!
WE MIGHT AS WELL LET SANTA DELIVER OUR PRESENTS!
CAN WE TRUST HIM?

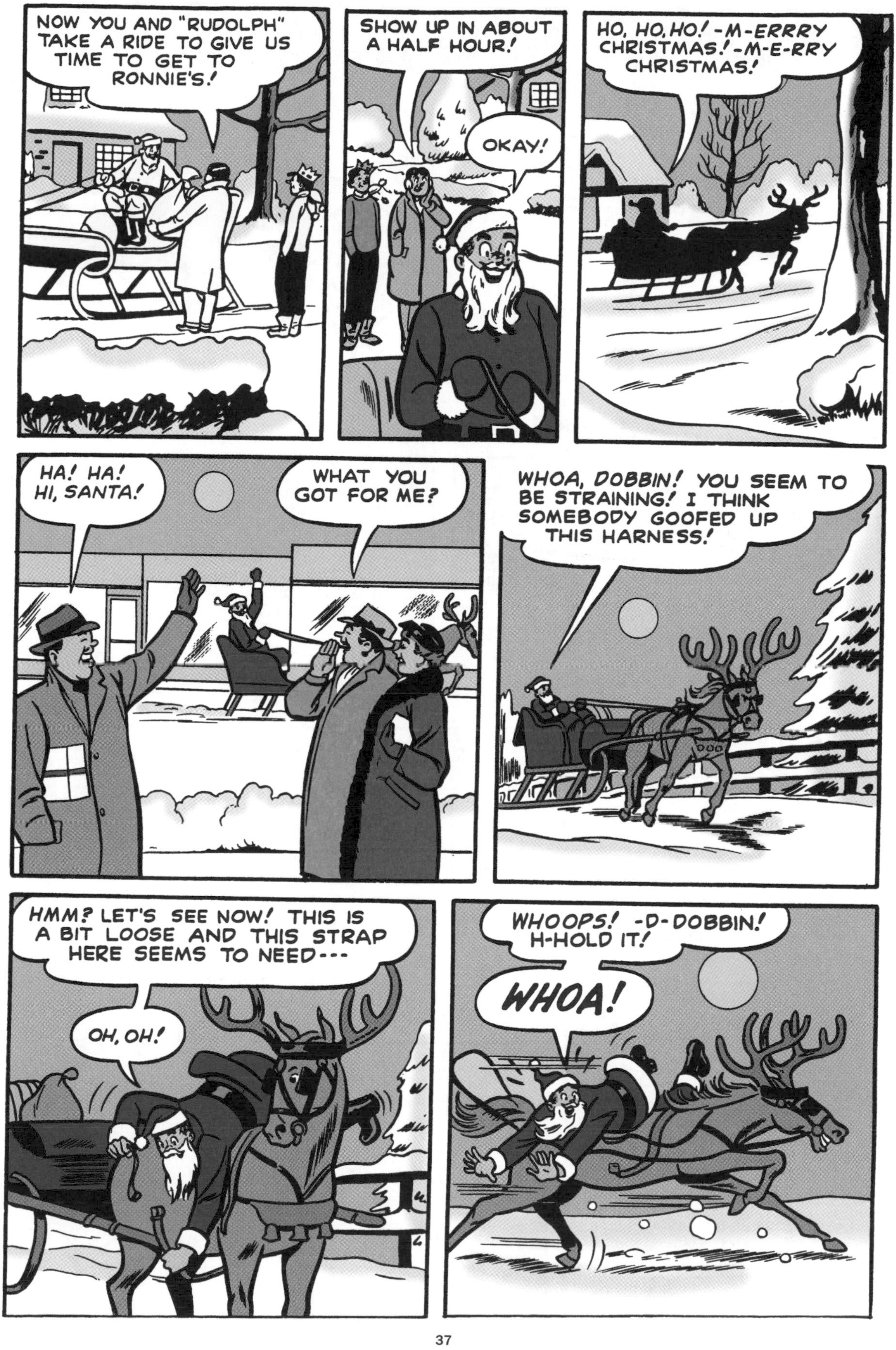
NOW YOU AND "RUDOLPH" TAKE A RIDE TO GIVE US TIME TO GET TO RONNIE'S!
SHOW UP IN ABOUT A HALF HOUR!
OKAY!
HO, HO, HO! -M-ERRRY CHRISTMAS! -M-E-RRY CHRISTMAS!
HA! HA! HI, SANTA!
WHAT YOU GOT FOR ME?
WHOA, DOBBIN! YOU SEEM TO BE STRAINING! I THINK SOMEBODY GOOFED UP THIS HARNESS!
HMM? LET'S SEE NOW! THIS IS A BIT LOOSE AND THIS STRAP HERE SEEMS TO NEED---
OH, OH!
WHOOPS! -D-DOBBIN! H-HOLD IT!
WHOA!

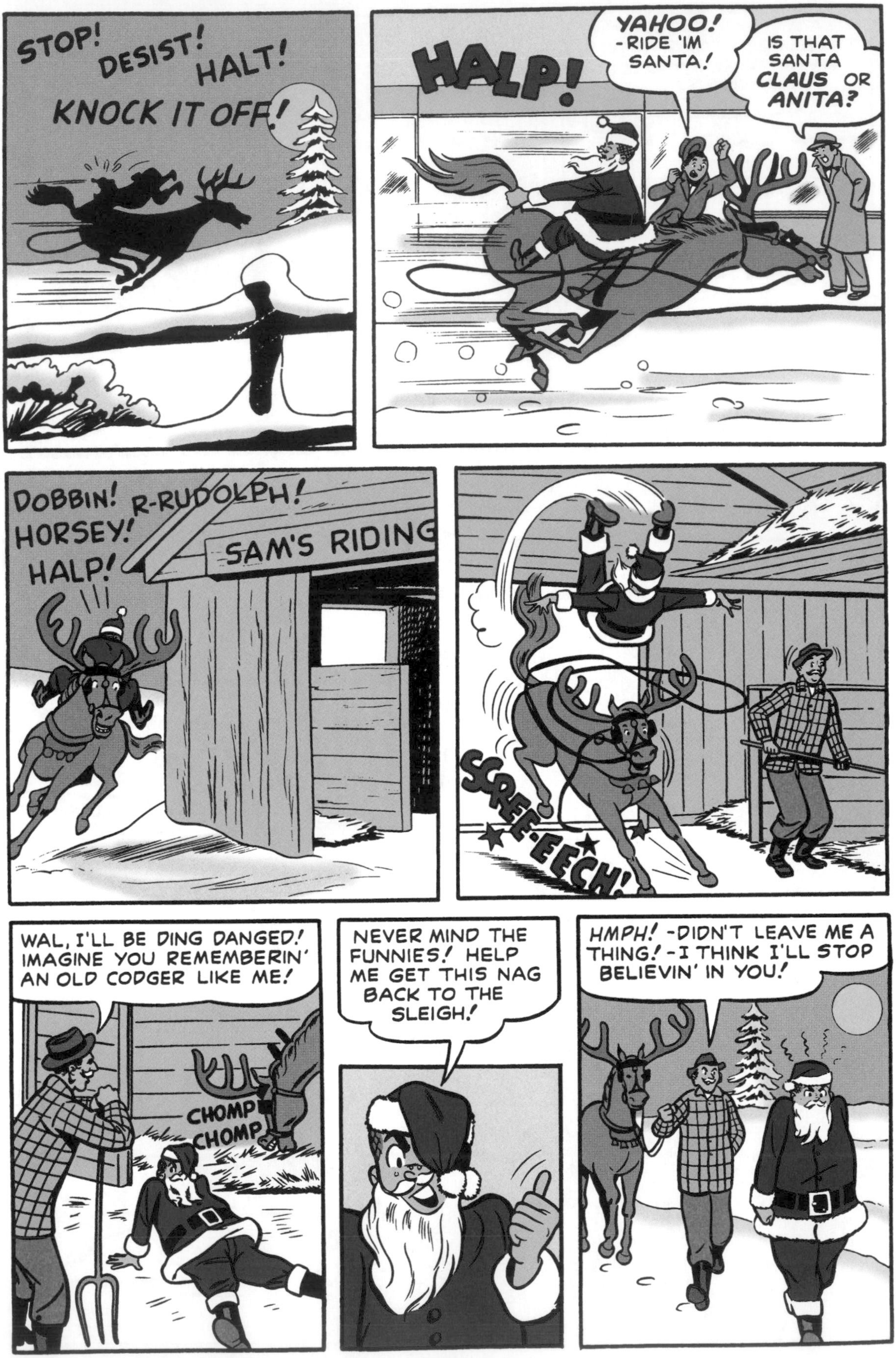
STOP! DESIST! HALT!
KNOCK IT OFF!
HALP!
YAHOO! -RIDE 'IM SANTA!
IS THAT SANTA CLAUS OR ANITA?
DOBBIN! HORSEY! HALP!
R-RUDOLPH!
SAM'S RIDING
SCREE-EECH!
WAL, I'LL BE DING DANGED! IMAGINE YOU REMEMBERIN' AN OLD CODGER LIKE ME!
CHOMP CHOMP
NEVER MIND THE FUNNIES! HELP ME GET THIS NAG BACK TO THE SLEIGH!
HMPH! -DIDN'T LEAVE ME A THING! -I THINK I'LL STOP BELIEVIN' IN YOU!

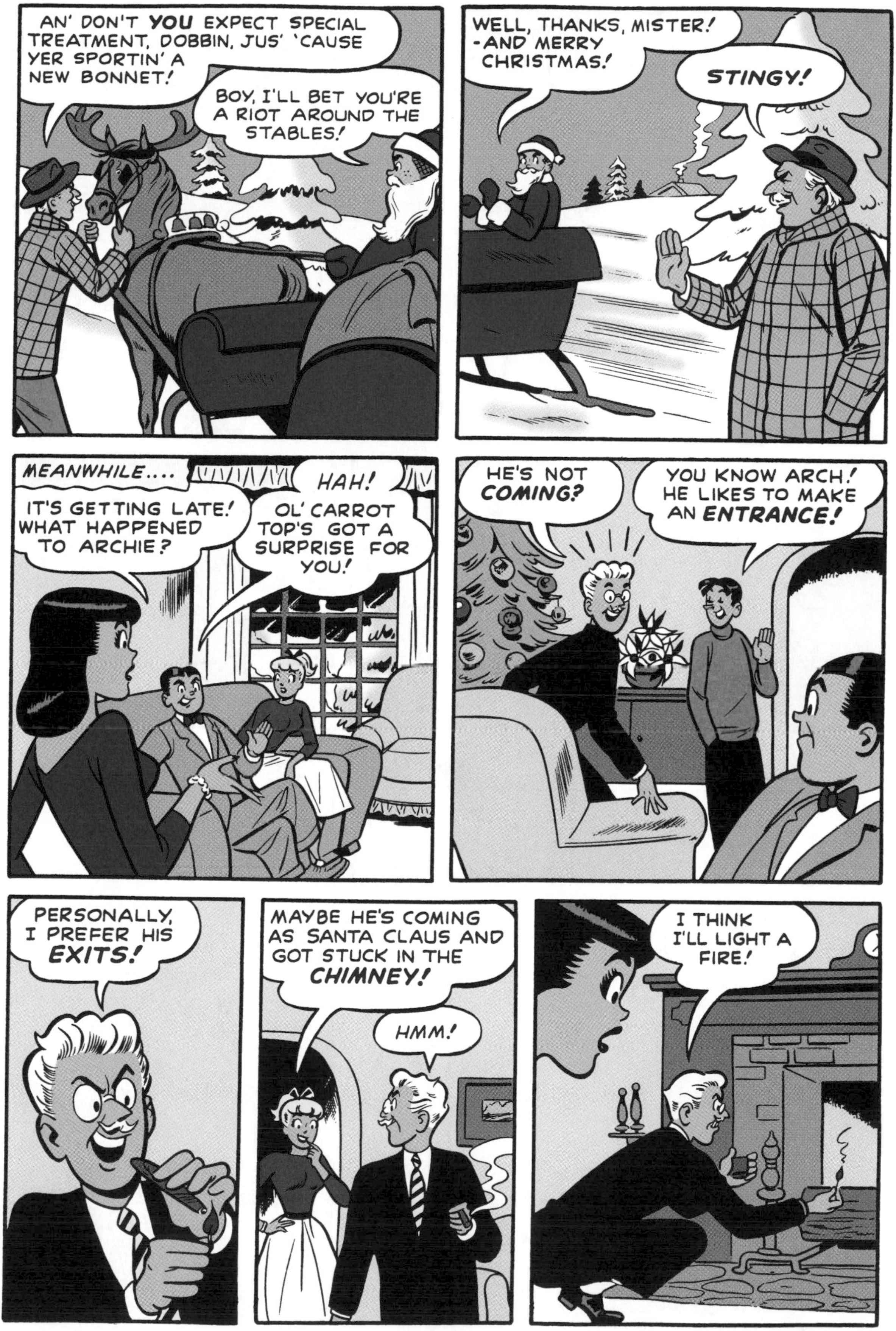
AN' DON'T YOU EXPECT SPECIAL TREATMENT, DOBBIN, JUS' 'CAUSE YER SPORTIN' A NEW BONNET!
BOY, I'LL BET YOU'RE A RIOT AROUND THE STABLES!
WELL, THANKS, MISTER! -AND MERRY CHRISTMAS!
STINGY!
MEANWHILE....
IT'S GETTING LATE! WHAT HAPPENED TO ARCHIE?
HAH! OL' CARROT TOP'S GOT A SURPRISE FOR YOU!
HE'S NOT COMING?
YOU KNOW ARCH! HE LIKES TO MAKE AN ENTRANCE!
PERSONALLY, I PREFER HIS EXITS!
MAYBE HE'S COMING AS SANTA CLAUS AND GOT STUCK IN THE CHIMNEY!
HMM!
I THINK I'LL LIGHT A FIRE!

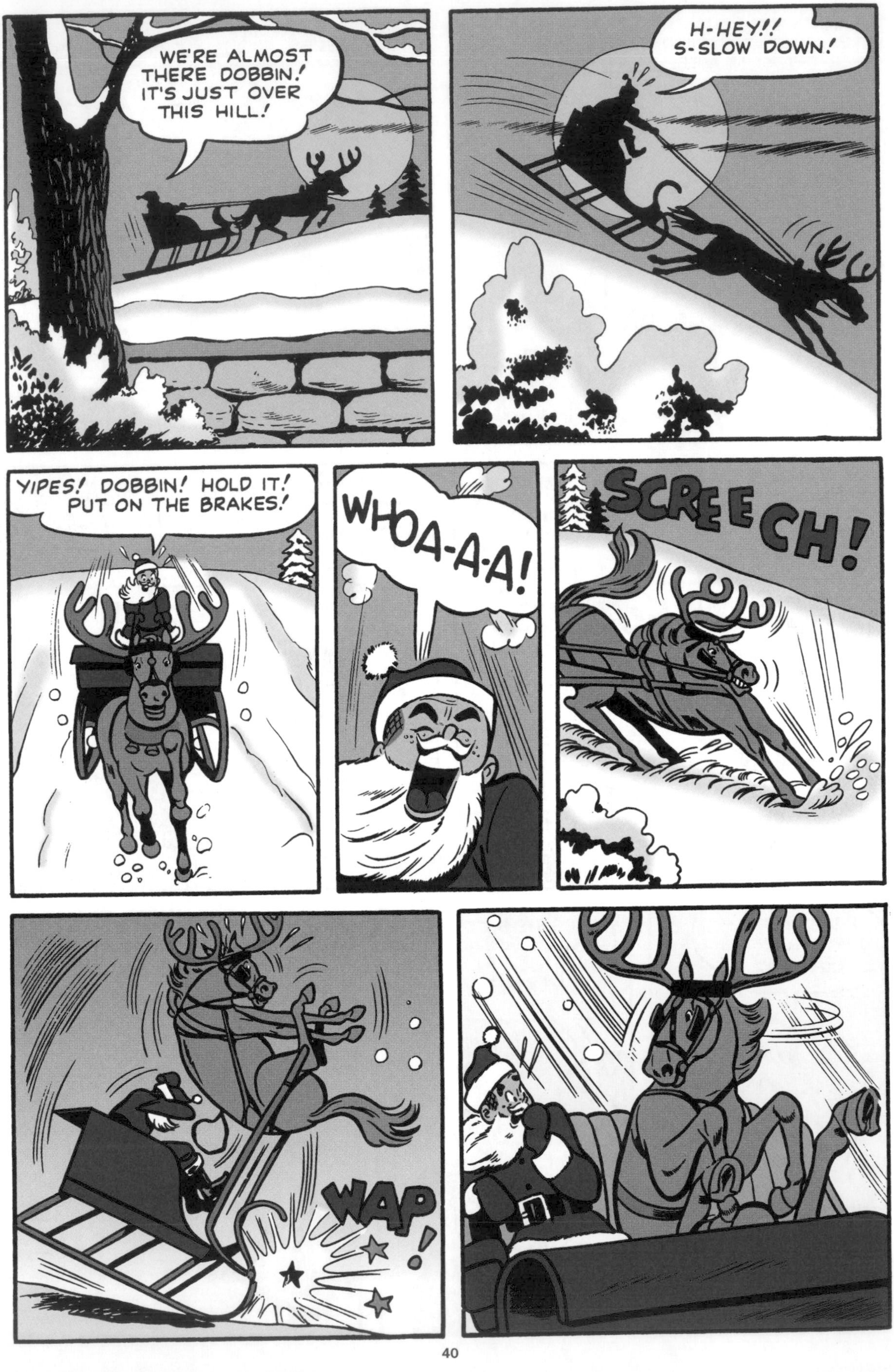
WE'RE ALMOST THERE DOBBIN! IT'S JUST OVER THIS HILL!
H-HEY!! S-SLOW DOWN!
YIPES! DOBBIN! HOLD IT! PUT ON THE BRAKES!
WHOA-A-A!
SCREECH!
WAP!

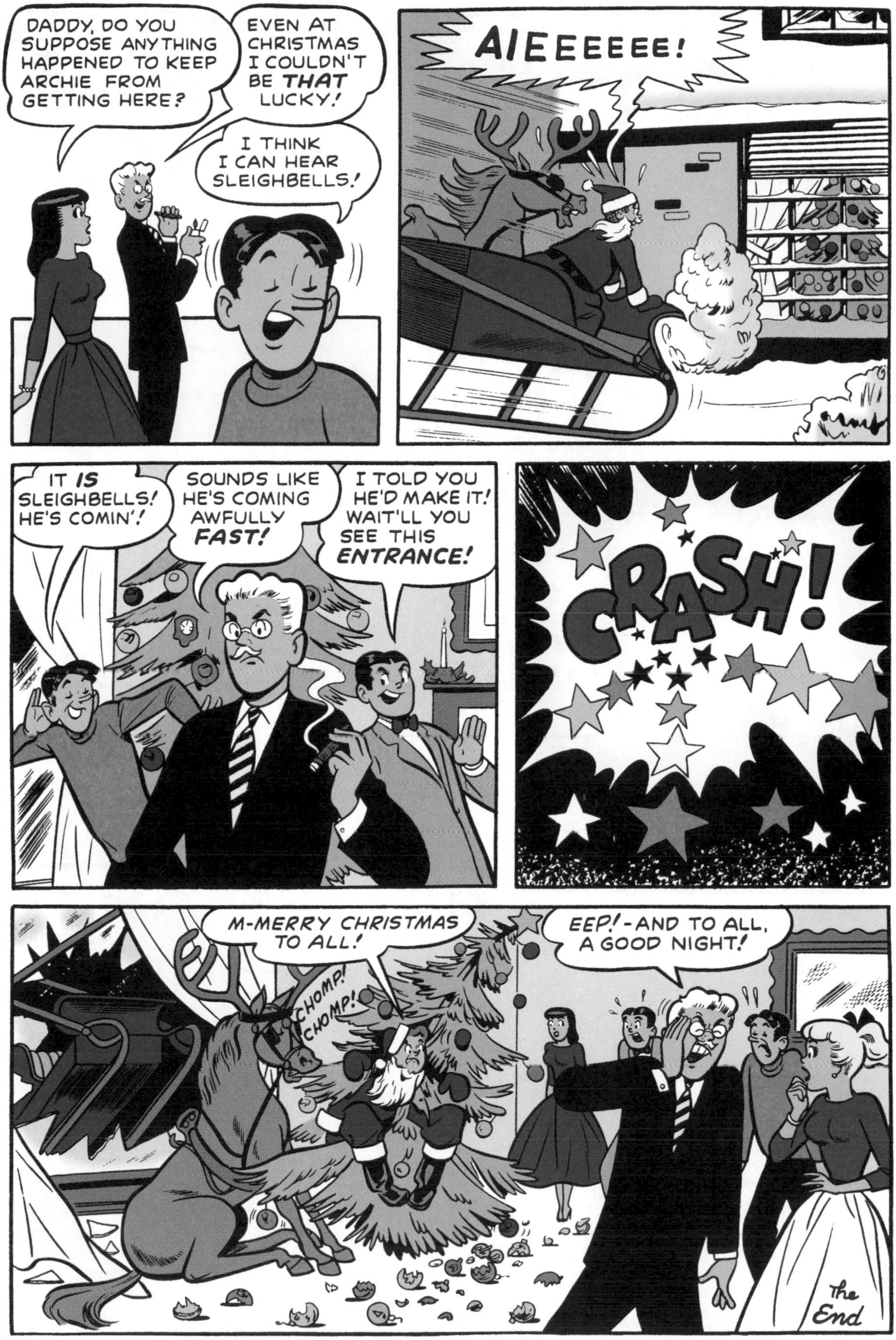
DADDY, DO YOU SUPPOSE ANYTHING HAPPENED TO KEEP ARCHIE FROM GETTING HERE?
EVEN AT CHRISTMAS I COULDN'T BE THAT LUCKY!
I THINK I CAN HEAR SLEIGHBELLS!
AIEEEEEE!
IT IS SLEIGHBELLS! HE'S COMIN'!
SOUNDS LIKE HE'S COMING AWFULLY FAST!
I TOLD YOU HE'D MAKE IT! WAIT'LL YOU SEE THIS ENTRANCE!
CRASH!
M-MERRY CHRISTMAS TO ALL!
CHOMP! CHOMP!
EEP! - AND TO ALL, A GOOD NIGHT!
The End

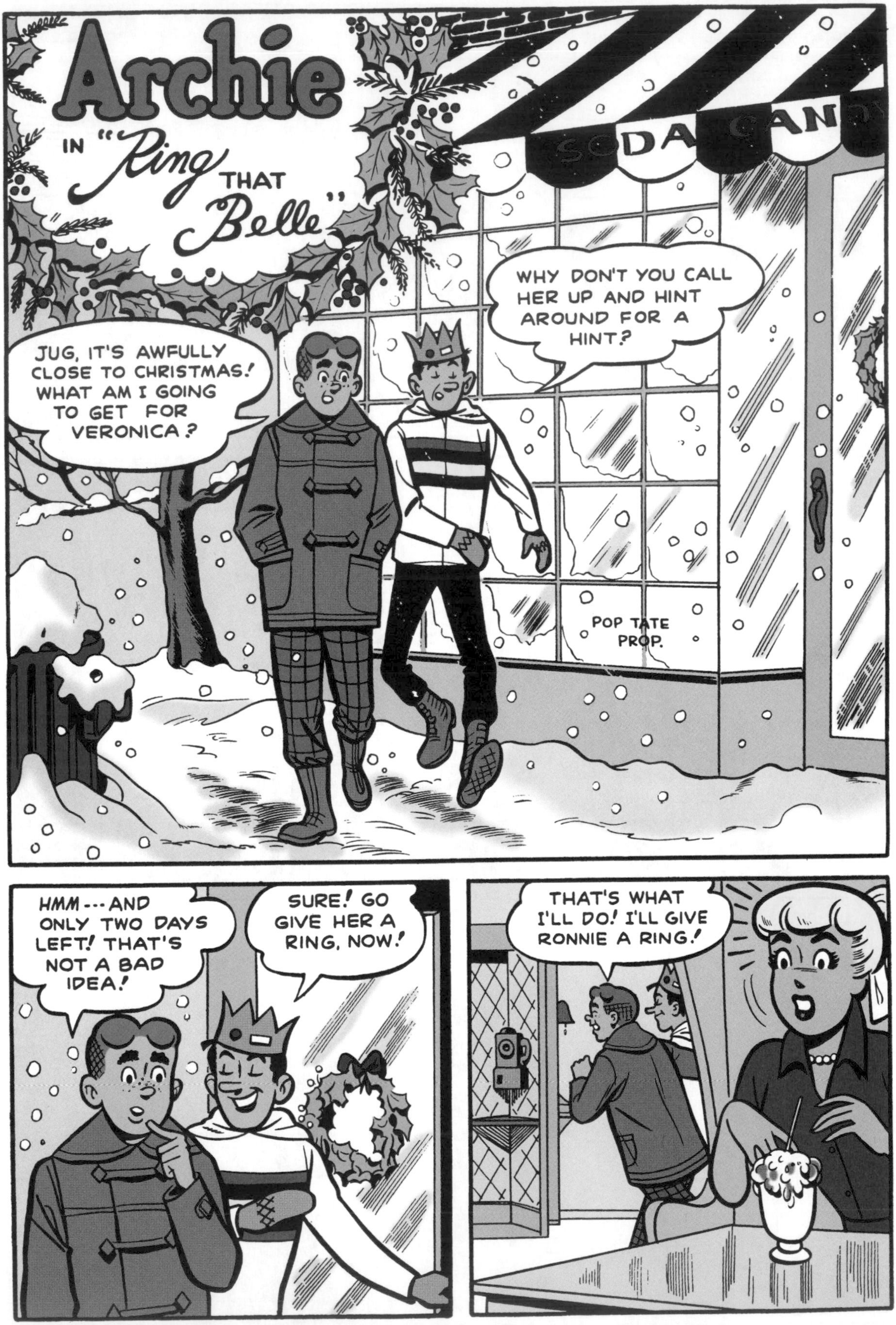
Archie
IN "Ring THAT Belle"
SODA CANDY
JUG, IT'S AWFULLY CLOSE TO CHRISTMAS! WHAT AM I GOING TO GET FOR VERONICA?
WHY DON'T YOU CALL HER UP AND HINT AROUND FOR A HINT?
POP TATE PROP.
HMM --- AND ONLY TWO DAYS LEFT! THAT'S NOT A BAD IDEA!
SURE! GO GIVE HER A RING, NOW!
THAT'S WHAT I'LL DO! I'LL GIVE RONNIE A RING!

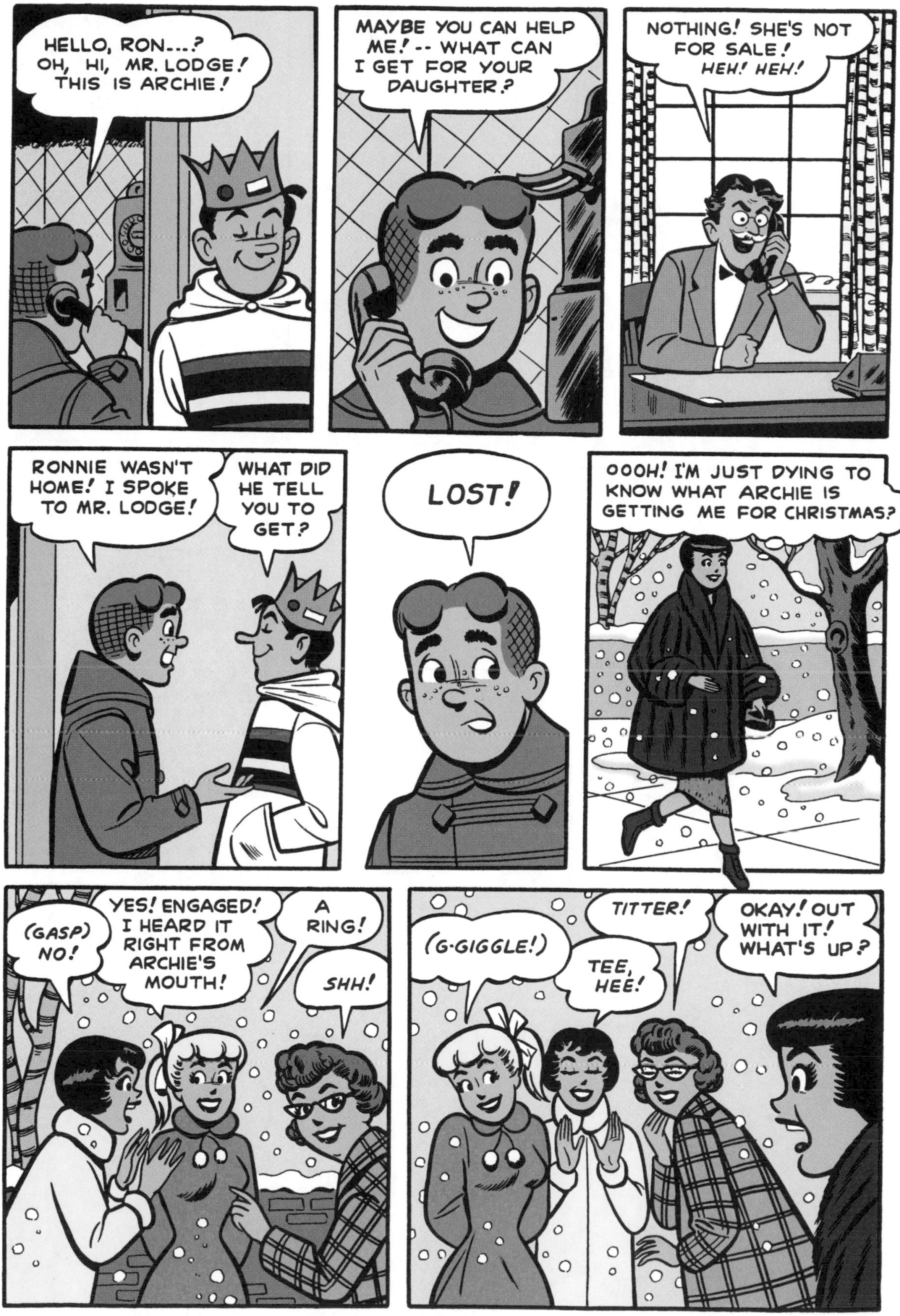
HELLO, RON...? OH, HI, MR. LODGE! THIS IS ARCHIE!
MAYBE YOU CAN HELP ME! -- WHAT CAN I GET FOR YOUR DAUGHTER?
NOTHING! SHE'S NOT FOR SALE! HEH! HEH!
RONNIE WASN'T HOME! I SPOKE TO MR. LODGE!
WHAT DID HE TELL YOU TO GET?
LOST!
OOOH! I'M JUST DYING TO KNOW WHAT ARCHIE IS GETTING ME FOR CHRISTMAS?
(GASP) NO!
YES! ENGAGED! I HEARD IT RIGHT FROM ARCHIE'S MOUTH!
A RING!
SHH!
(G-GIGGLE!)
TEE, HEE!
TITTER!
OKAY! OUT WITH IT! WHAT'S UP?

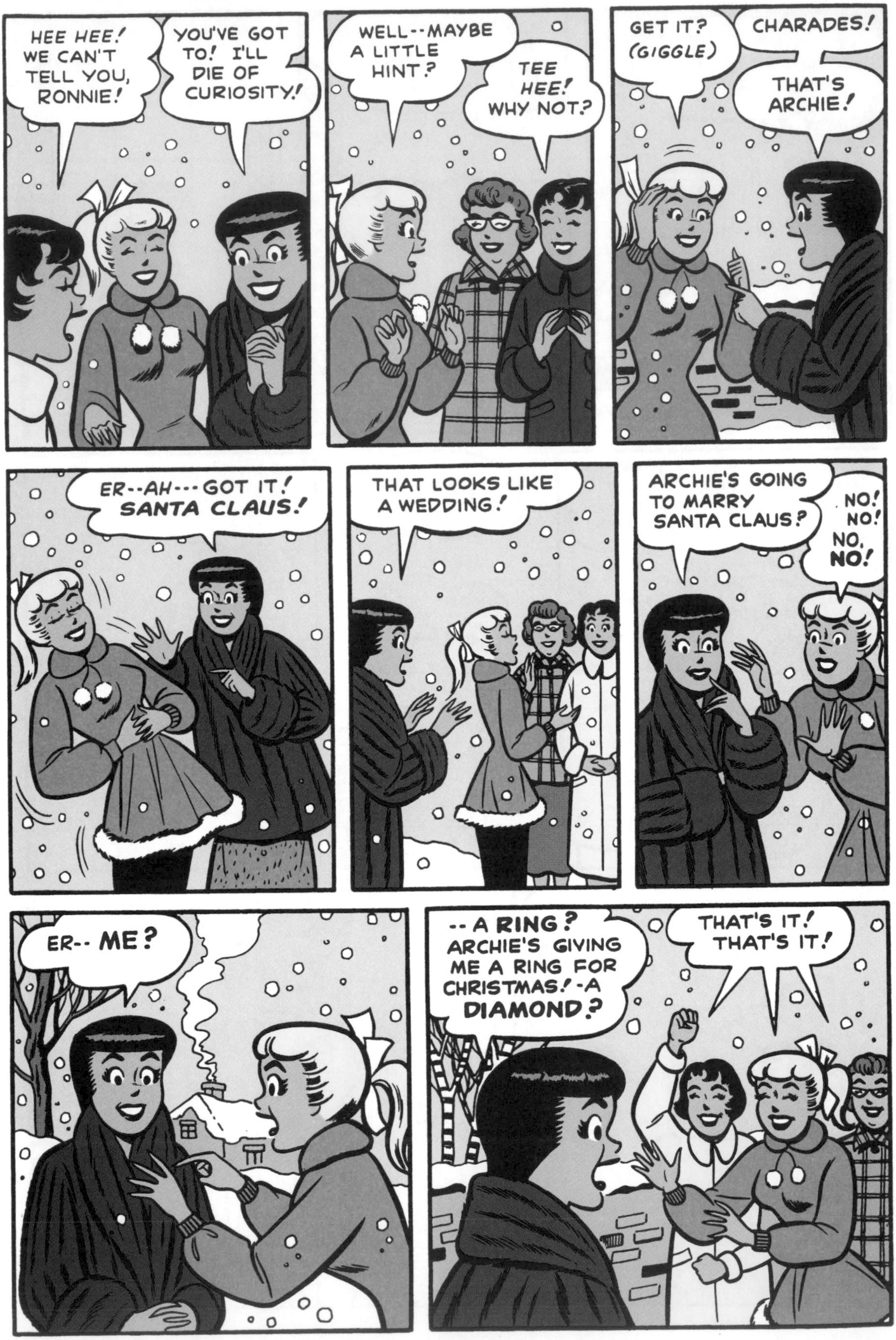

HEE HEE! WE CAN'T TELL YOU, RONNIE!
YOU'VE GOT TO! I'LL DIE OF CURIOSITY!
WELL--MAYBE A LITTLE HINT?
TEE HEE! WHY NOT?
GET IT? (GIGGLE)
CHARADES!
THAT'S ARCHIE!
ER--AH---GOT IT! SANTA CLAUS!
THAT LOOKS LIKE A WEDDING!
ARCHIE'S GOING TO MARRY SANTA CLAUS?
NO! NO! NO, NO!
ER-- ME?
--A RING? ARCHIE'S GIVING ME A RING FOR CHRISTMAS! -A DIAMOND?
THAT'S IT! THAT'S IT!

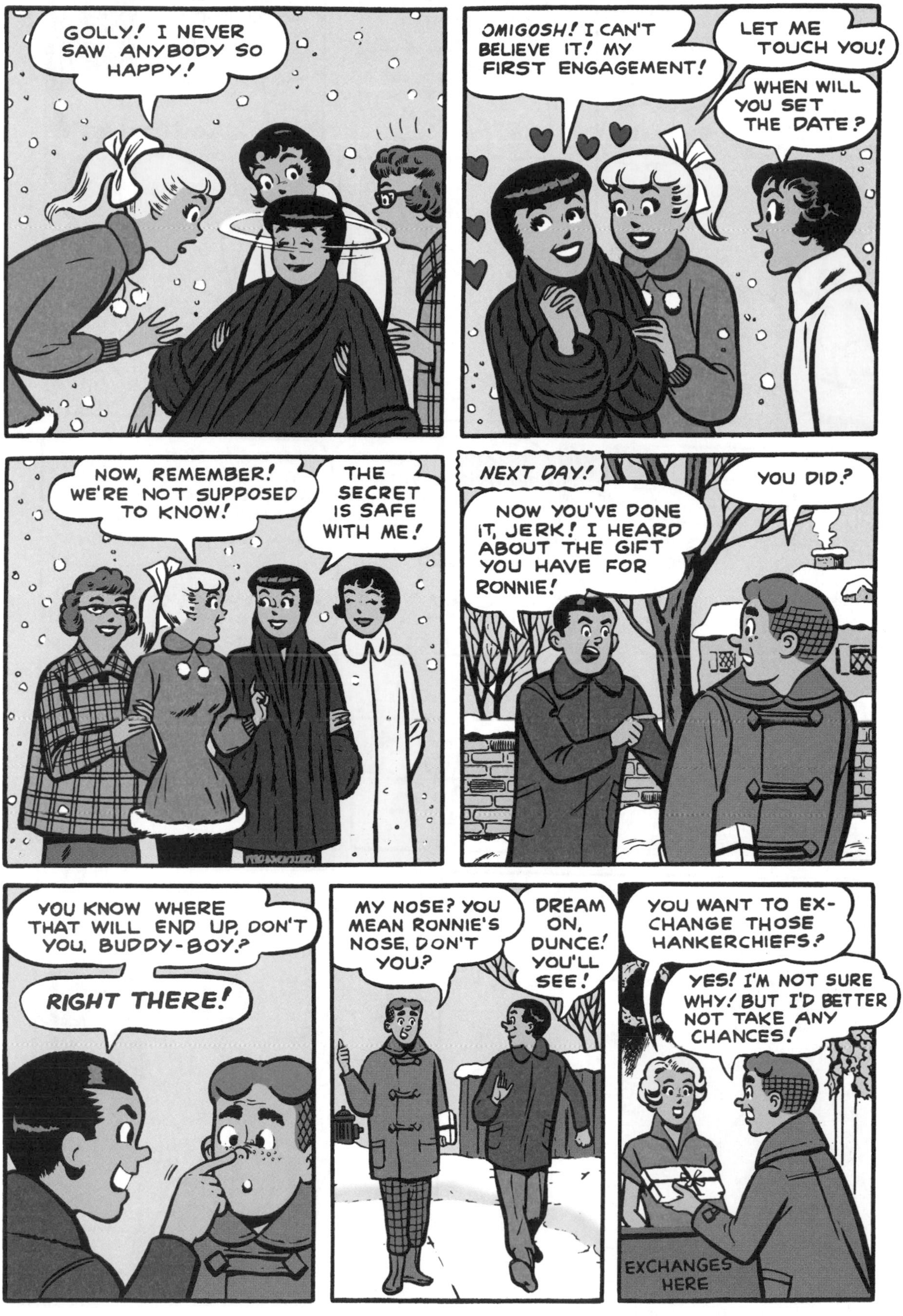
GOLLY! I NEVER SAW ANYBODY SO HAPPY!
OMIGOSH! I CAN'T BELIEVE IT! MY FIRST ENGAGEMENT!
LET ME TOUCH YOU!
WHEN WILL YOU SET THE DATE?
NOW, REMEMBER! WE'RE NOT SUPPOSED TO KNOW!
THE SECRET IS SAFE WITH ME!
NEXT DAY!
NOW YOU'VE DONE IT, JERK! I HEARD ABOUT THE GIFT YOU HAVE FOR RONNIE!
YOU DID?
YOU KNOW WHERE THAT WILL END UP, DON'T YOU, BUDDY-BOY?
RIGHT THERE!
MY NOSE? YOU MEAN RONNIE'S NOSE, DON'T YOU?
DREAM ON, DUNCE! YOU'LL SEE!
YOU WANT TO EX-CHANGE THOSE HANKERCHIEFS?
YES! I'M NOT SURE WHY! BUT I'D BETTER NOT TAKE ANY CHANCES!
EXCHANGES HERE

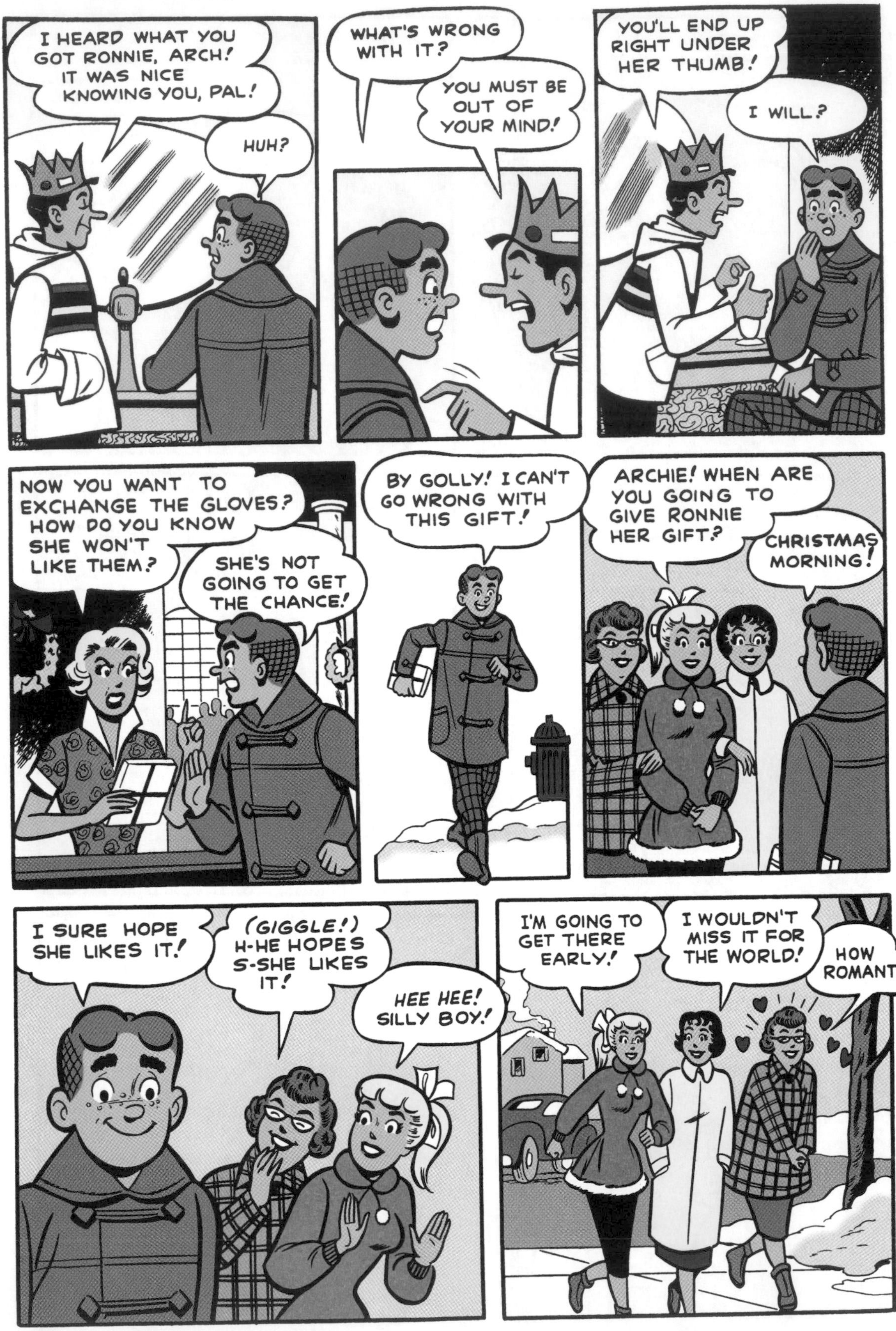
I HEARD WHAT YOU GOT RONNIE, ARCH! IT WAS NICE KNOWING YOU, PAL!
HUH?
WHAT'S WRONG WITH IT?
YOU MUST BE OUT OF YOUR MIND!
YOU'LL END UP RIGHT UNDER HER THUMB!
I WILL?
NOW YOU WANT TO EXCHANGE THE GLOVES? HOW DO YOU KNOW SHE WON'T LIKE THEM?
SHE'S NOT GOING TO GET THE CHANCE!
BY GOLLY! I CAN'T GO WRONG WITH THIS GIFT!
ARCHIE! WHEN ARE YOU GOING TO GIVE RONNIE HER GIFT?
CHRISTMAS MORNING!
I SURE HOPE SHE LIKES IT!
(GIGGLE!) H-HE HOPES S-SHE LIKES IT!
HEE HEE! SILLY BOY!
I'M GOING TO GET THERE EARLY!
I WOULDN'T MISS IT FOR THE WORLD!
HOW ROMANTIC!

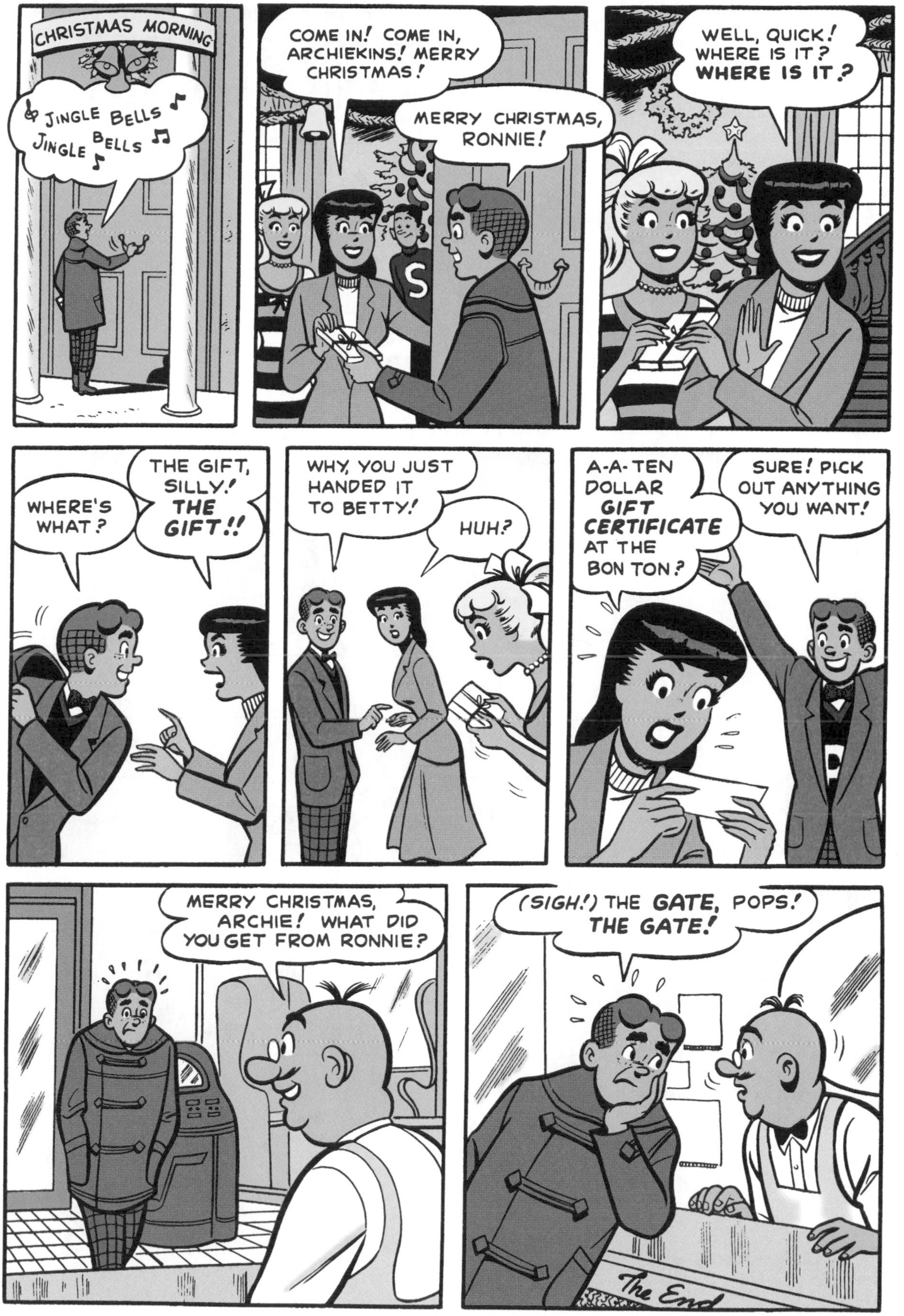
CHRISTMAS MORNING
JINGLE BELLS JINGLE BELLS
COME IN! COME IN, ARCHIEKINS! MERRY CHRISTMAS!
MERRY CHRISTMAS, RONNIE!
WELL, QUICK! WHERE IS IT? WHERE IS IT?
WHERE'S WHAT?
THE GIFT, SILLY! THE GIFT!!
WHY, YOU JUST HANDED IT TO BETTY!
HUH?
A-A-TEN DOLLAR GIFT CERTIFICATE AT THE BON TON?
SURE! PICK OUT ANYTHING YOU WANT!
MERRY CHRISTMAS, ARCHIE! WHAT DID YOU GET FROM RONNIE?
(SIGH!) THE GATE, POPS! THE GATE!
The End

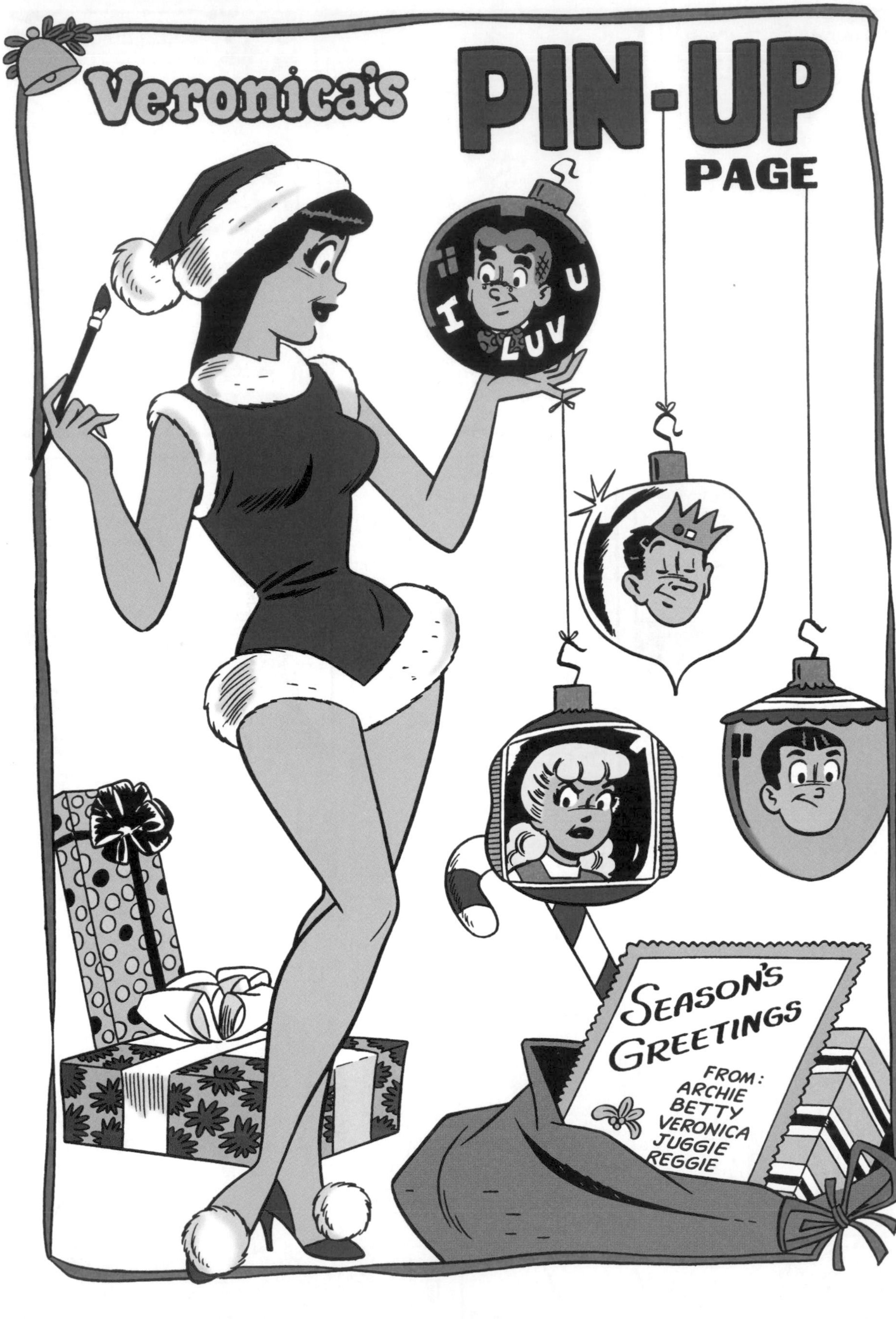
Veronica's PIN-UP PAGE
I LUV U
SEASON'S GREETINGS
FROM:
ARCHIE
BETTY
VERONICA
JUGGIE
REGGIE

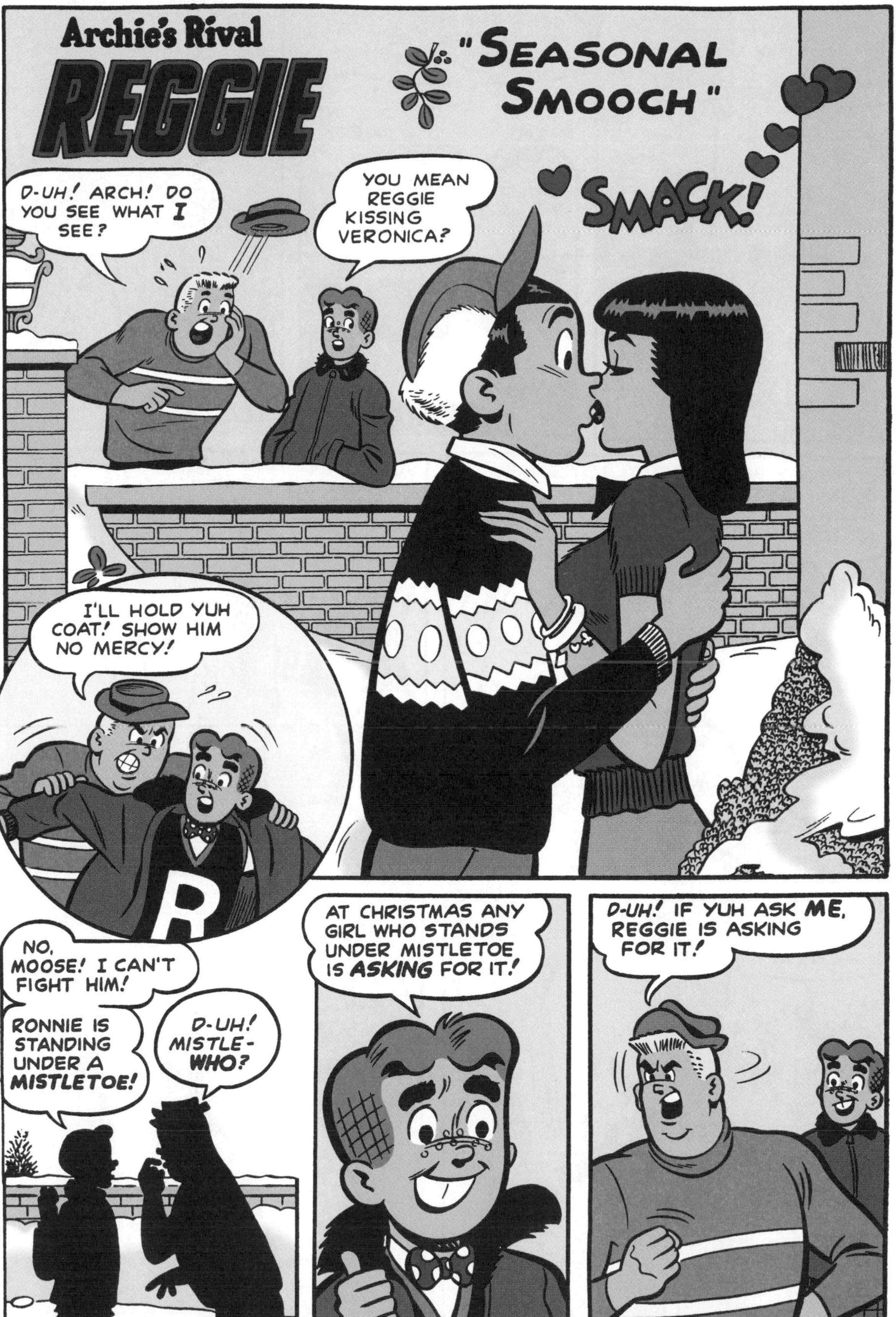
Archie's Rival
REGGIE
"SEASONAL SMOOCH"
D-UH! ARCH! DO YOU SEE WHAT I SEE?
YOU MEAN REGGIE KISSING VERONICA?
SMACK!
I'LL HOLD YUH COAT! SHOW HIM NO MERCY!
NO, MOOSE! I CAN'T FIGHT HIM!
RONNIE IS STANDING UNDER A MISTLETOE!
D-UH! MISTLE-WHO?
AT CHRISTMAS ANY GIRL WHO STANDS UNDER MISTLETOE IS ASKING FOR IT!
D-UH! IF YUH ASK ME, REGGIE IS ASKING FOR IT!

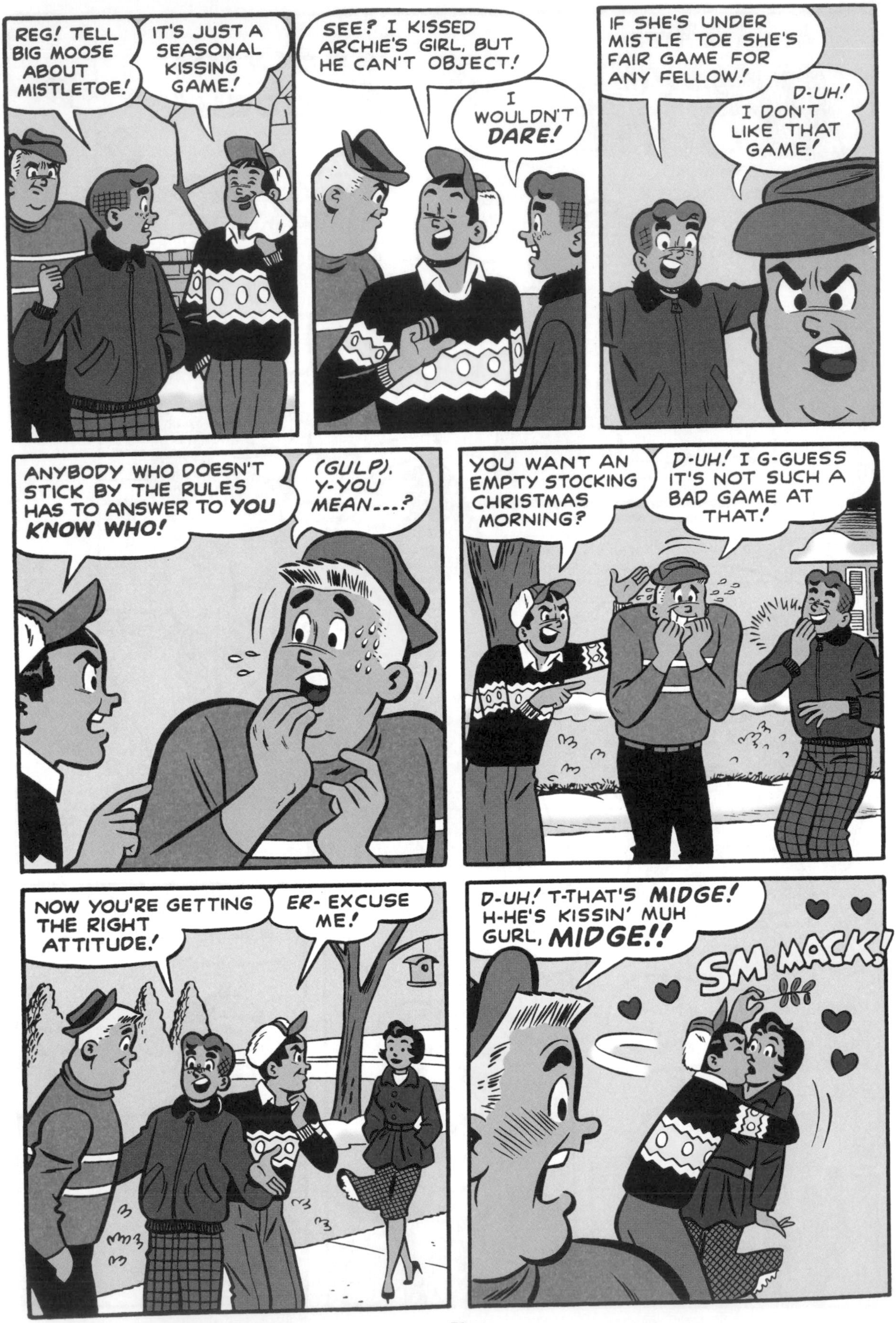
REG! TELL BIG MOOSE ABOUT MISTLETOE!
IT'S JUST A SEASONAL KISSING GAME!
SEE? I KISSED ARCHIE'S GIRL, BUT HE CAN'T OBJECT!
I WOULDN'T DARE!
IF SHE'S UNDER MISTLE TOE SHE'S FAIR GAME FOR ANY FELLOW!
D-UH! I DON'T LIKE THAT GAME!
ANYBODY WHO DOESN'T STICK BY THE RULES HAS TO ANSWER TO YOU KNOW WHO!
(GULP). Y-YOU MEAN...?
YOU WANT AN EMPTY STOCKING CHRISTMAS MORNING?
D-UH! I G-GUESS IT'S NOT SUCH A BAD GAME AT THAT!
NOW YOU'RE GETTING THE RIGHT ATTITUDE!
ER- EXCUSE ME!
D-UH! T-THAT'S MIDGE! H-HE'S KISSIN' MUH GURL, MIDGE!!
SM-MACK!

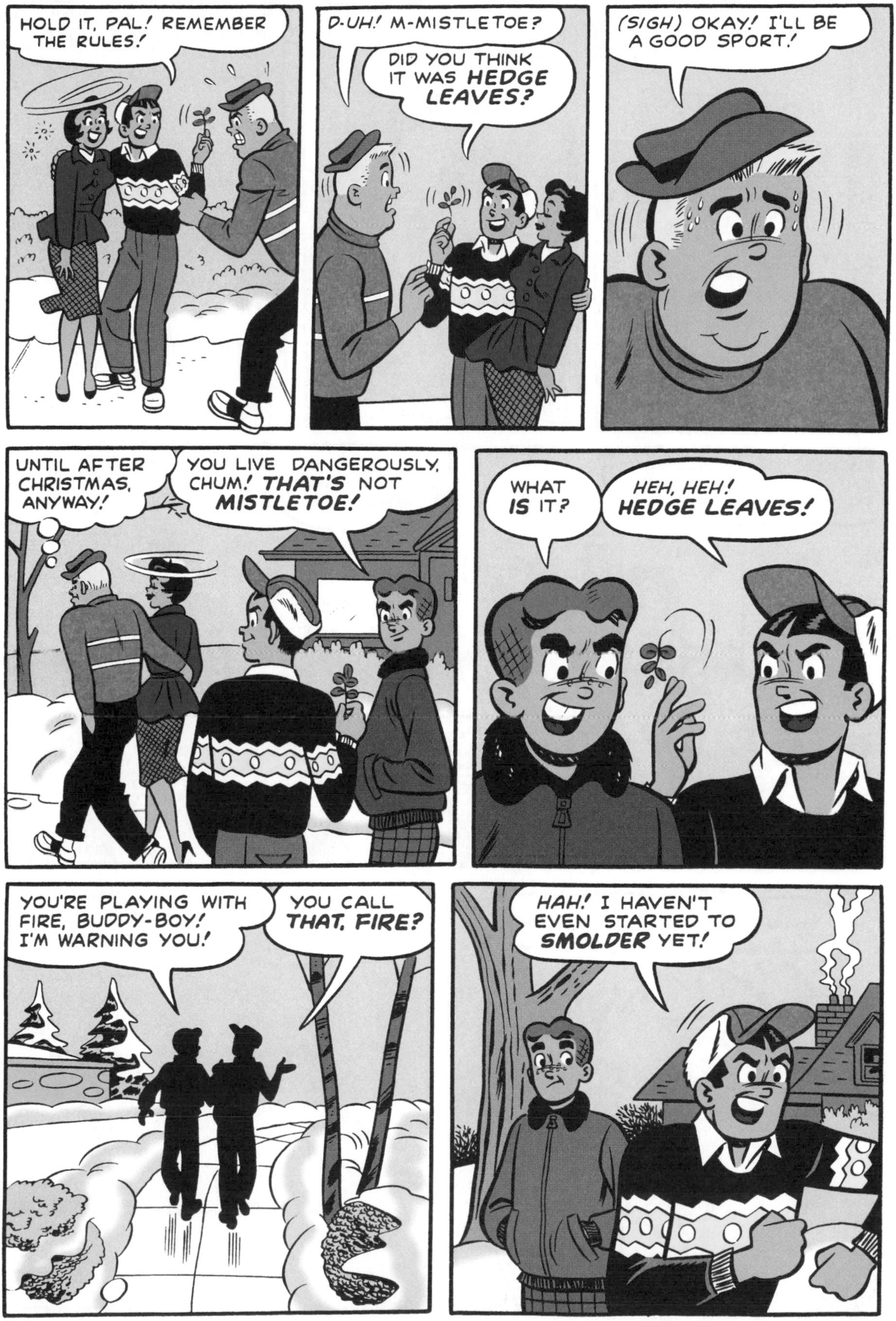
HOLD IT, PAL! REMEMBER THE RULES!
D-UH! M-MISTLETOE?
DID YOU THINK IT WAS HEDGE LEAVES?
(SIGH) OKAY! I'LL BE A GOOD SPORT!
UNTIL AFTER CHRISTMAS, ANYWAY!
YOU LIVE DANGEROUSLY, CHUM! THAT'S NOT MISTLETOE!
WHAT IS IT?
HEH, HEH! HEDGE LEAVES!
YOU'RE PLAYING WITH FIRE, BUDDY-BOY! I'M WARNING YOU!
YOU CALL THAT, FIRE?
HAH! I HAVEN'T EVEN STARTED TO SMOLDER YET!

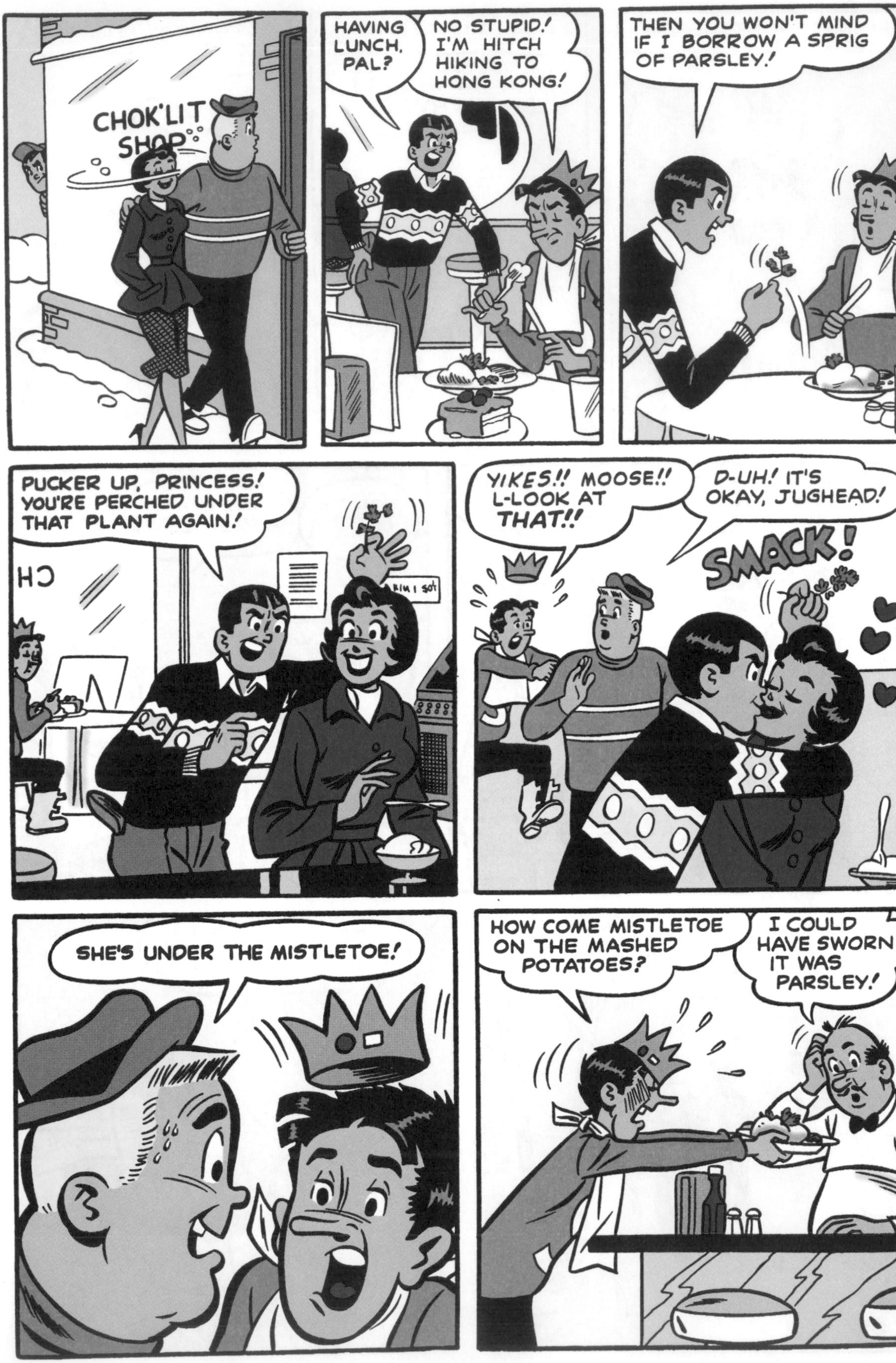
CHOK'LIT SHOP
HAVING LUNCH, PAL?
NO STUPID! I'M HITCH HIKING TO HONG KONG!
THEN YOU WON'T MIND IF I BORROW A SPRIG OF PARSLEY!
PUCKER UP, PRINCESS! YOU'RE PERCHED UNDER THAT PLANT AGAIN!
YIKES!! MOOSE!! L-LOOK AT THAT!!
D-UH! IT'S OKAY, JUGHEAD!
SMACK!
SHE'S UNDER THE MISTLETOE!
HOW COME MISTLETOE ON THE MASHED POTATOES?
I COULD HAVE SWORN IT WAS PARSLEY!

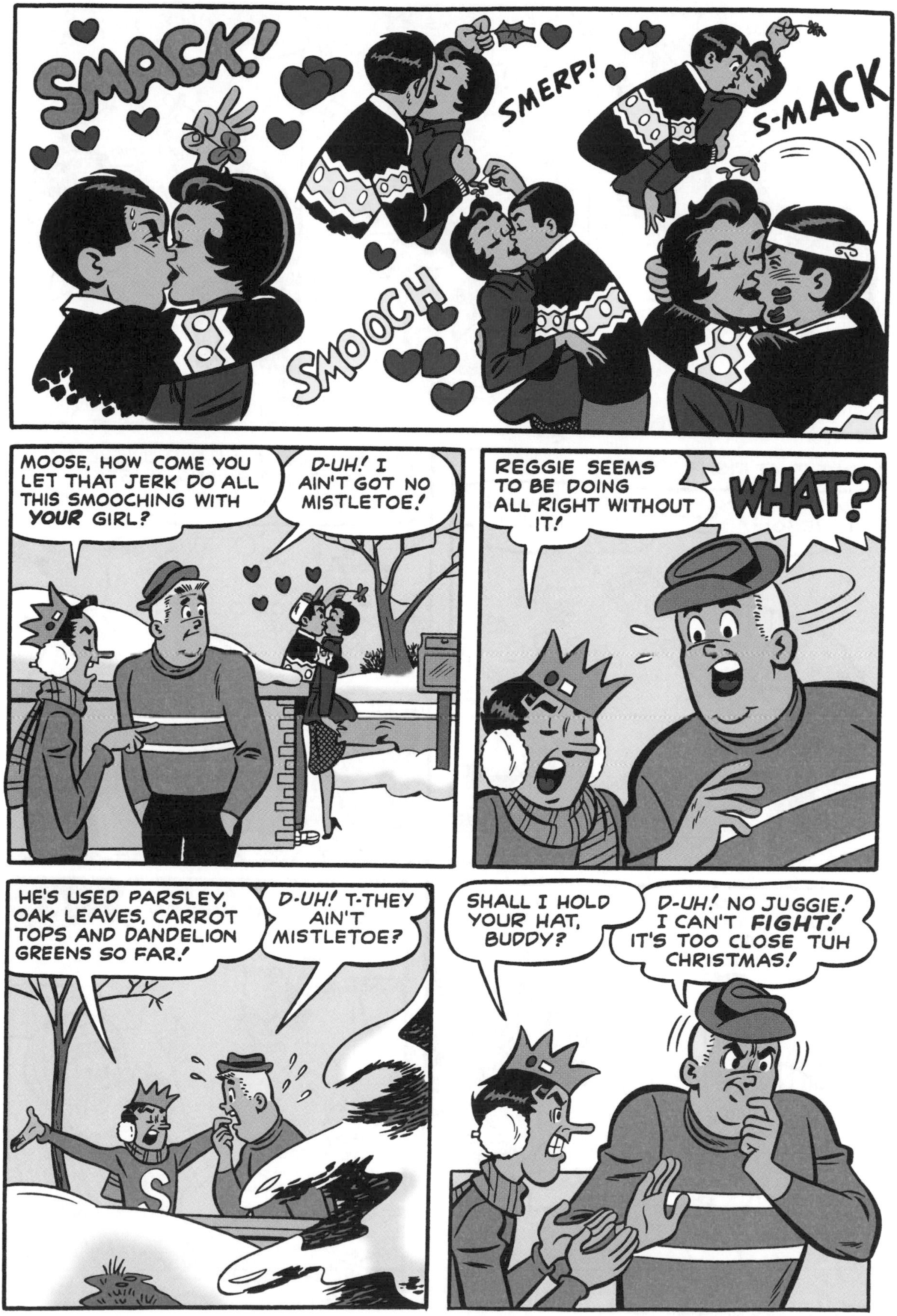
SMACK!
SMERP!
S-MACK
SMOOCH
MOOSE, HOW COME YOU LET THAT JERK DO ALL THIS SMOOCHING WITH YOUR GIRL?
D-UH! I AIN'T GOT NO MISTLETOE!
REGGIE SEEMS TO BE DOING ALL RIGHT WITHOUT IT!
WHAT?
HE'S USED PARSLEY, OAK LEAVES, CARROT TOPS AND DANDELION GREENS SO FAR!
D-UH! T-THEY AIN'T MISTLETOE?
SHALL I HOLD YOUR HAT, BUDDY?
D-UH! NO JUGGIE! I CAN'T FIGHT! IT'S TOO CLOSE TUH CHRISTMAS!

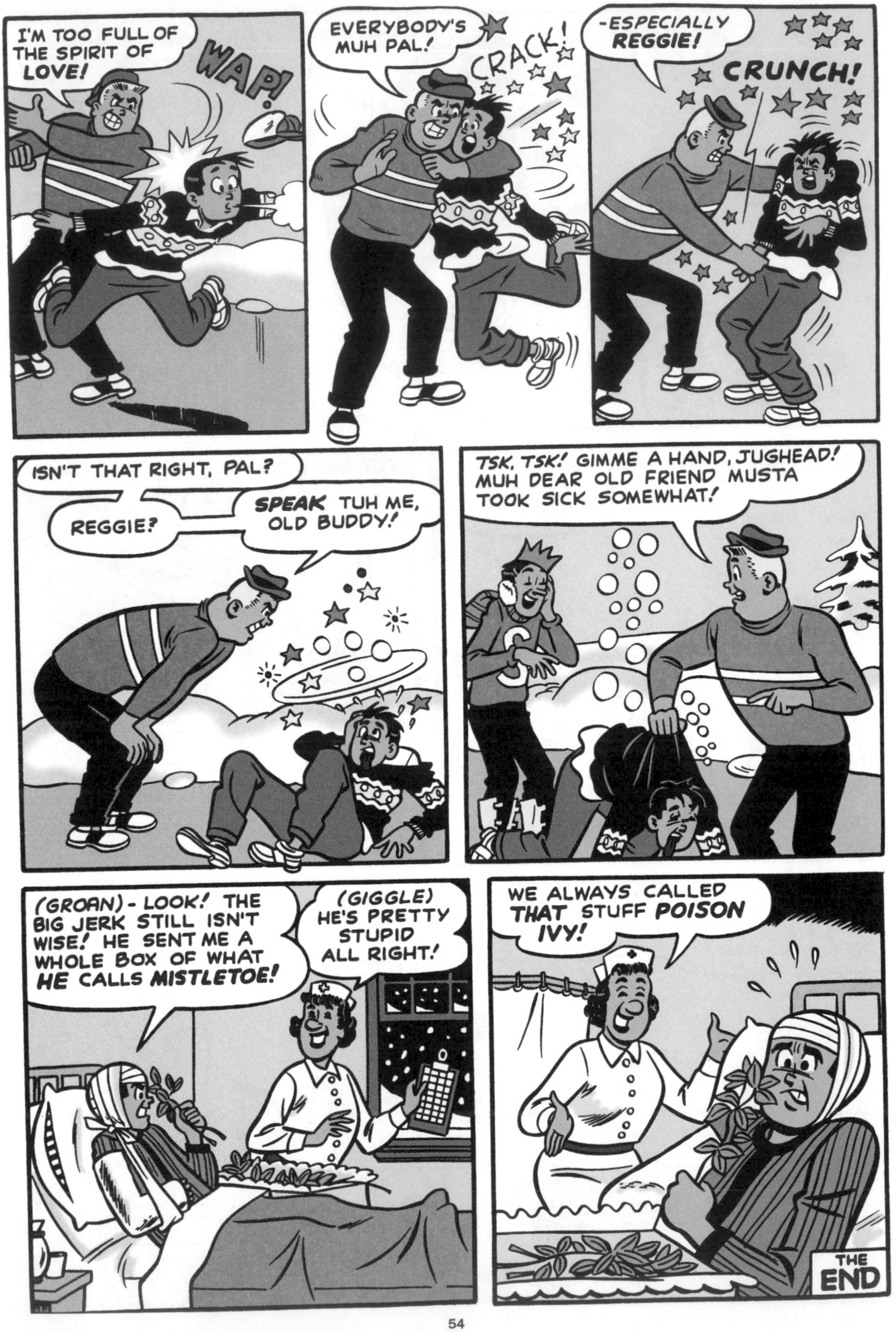
I'M TOO FULL OF THE SPIRIT OF LOVE!
WAP!
EVERYBODY'S MUH PAL!
CRACK!
-ESPECIALLY REGGIE!
CRUNCH!
ISN'T THAT RIGHT, PAL?
REGGIE?
SPEAK TUH ME, OLD BUDDY!
TSK, TSK! GIMME A HAND, JUGHEAD! MUH DEAR OLD FRIEND MUSTA TOOK SICK SOMEWHAT!
(GROAN) - LOOK! THE BIG JERK STILL ISN'T WISE! HE SENT ME A WHOLE BOX OF WHAT HE CALLS MISTLETOE!
(GIGGLE) HE'S PRETTY STUPID ALL RIGHT!
WE ALWAYS CALLED THAT STUFF POISON IVY!
THE END

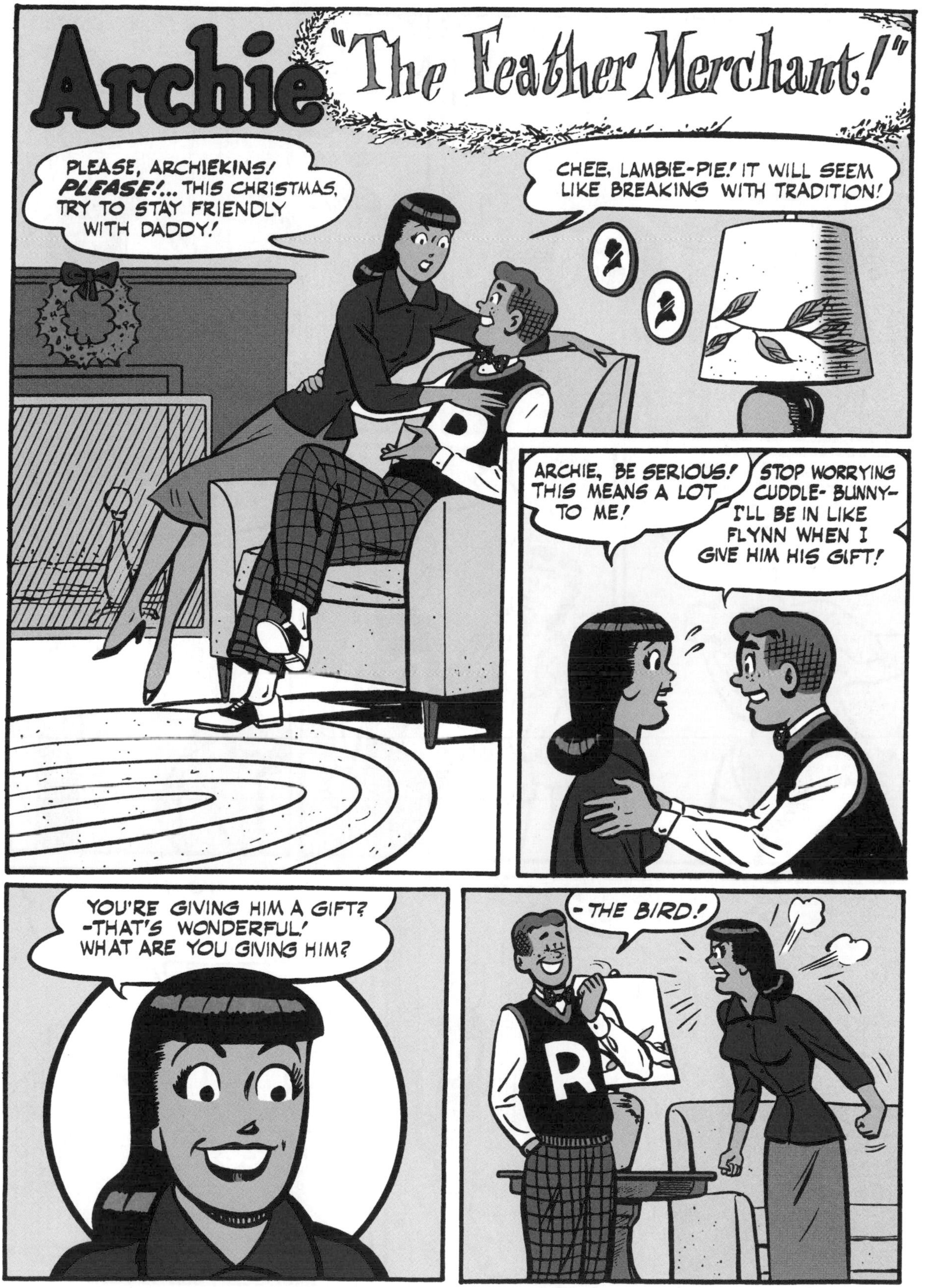
Archie
"The Feather Merchant!"
PLEASE, ARCHIEKINS! PLEASE!... THIS CHRISTMAS, TRY TO STAY FRIENDLY WITH DADDY!
CHEE, LAMBIE-PIE! IT WILL SEEM LIKE BREAKING WITH TRADITION!
ARCHIE, BE SERIOUS! THIS MEANS A LOT TO ME!
STOP WORRYING CUDDLE-BUNNY- I'LL BE IN LIKE FLYNN WHEN I GIVE HIM HIS GIFT!
YOU'RE GIVING HIM A GIFT? -THAT'S WONDERFUL! WHAT ARE YOU GIVING HIM?
-THE BIRD!

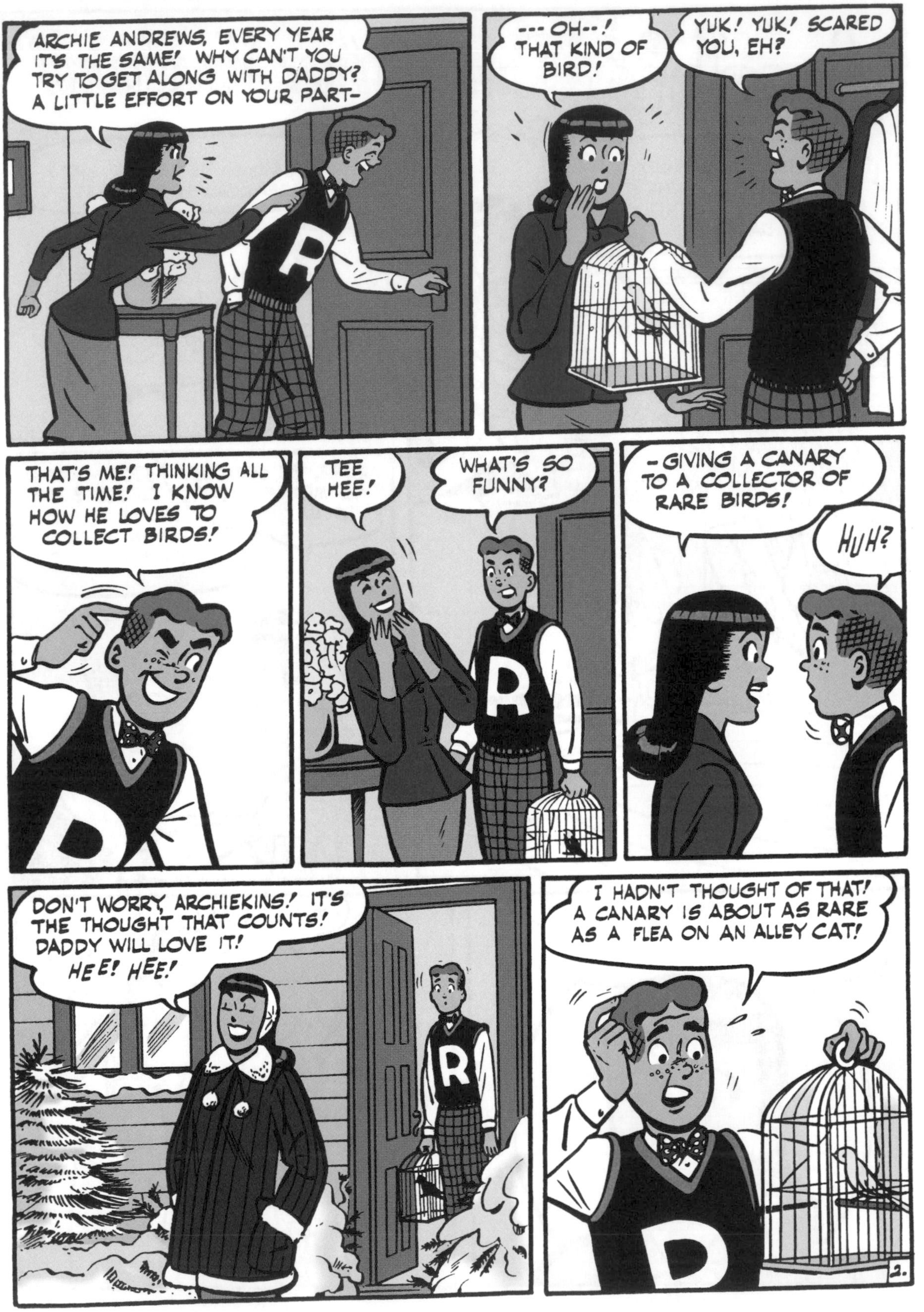
ARCHIE ANDREWS, EVERY YEAR IT'S THE SAME! WHY CAN'T YOU TRY TO GET ALONG WITH DADDY? A LITTLE EFFORT ON YOUR PART-
---OH--! THAT KIND OF BIRD!
YUK! YUK! SCARED YOU, EH?
THAT'S ME! THINKING ALL THE TIME! I KNOW HOW HE LOVES TO COLLECT BIRDS!
TEE HEE!
WHAT'S SO FUNNY?
-GIVING A CANARY TO A COLLECTOR OF RARE BIRDS!
HUH?
DON'T WORRY, ARCHIEKINS! IT'S THE THOUGHT THAT COUNTS! DADDY WILL LOVE IT!
HEE! HEE!
I HADN'T THOUGHT OF THAT! A CANARY IS ABOUT AS RARE AS A FLEA ON AN ALLEY CAT!
2.

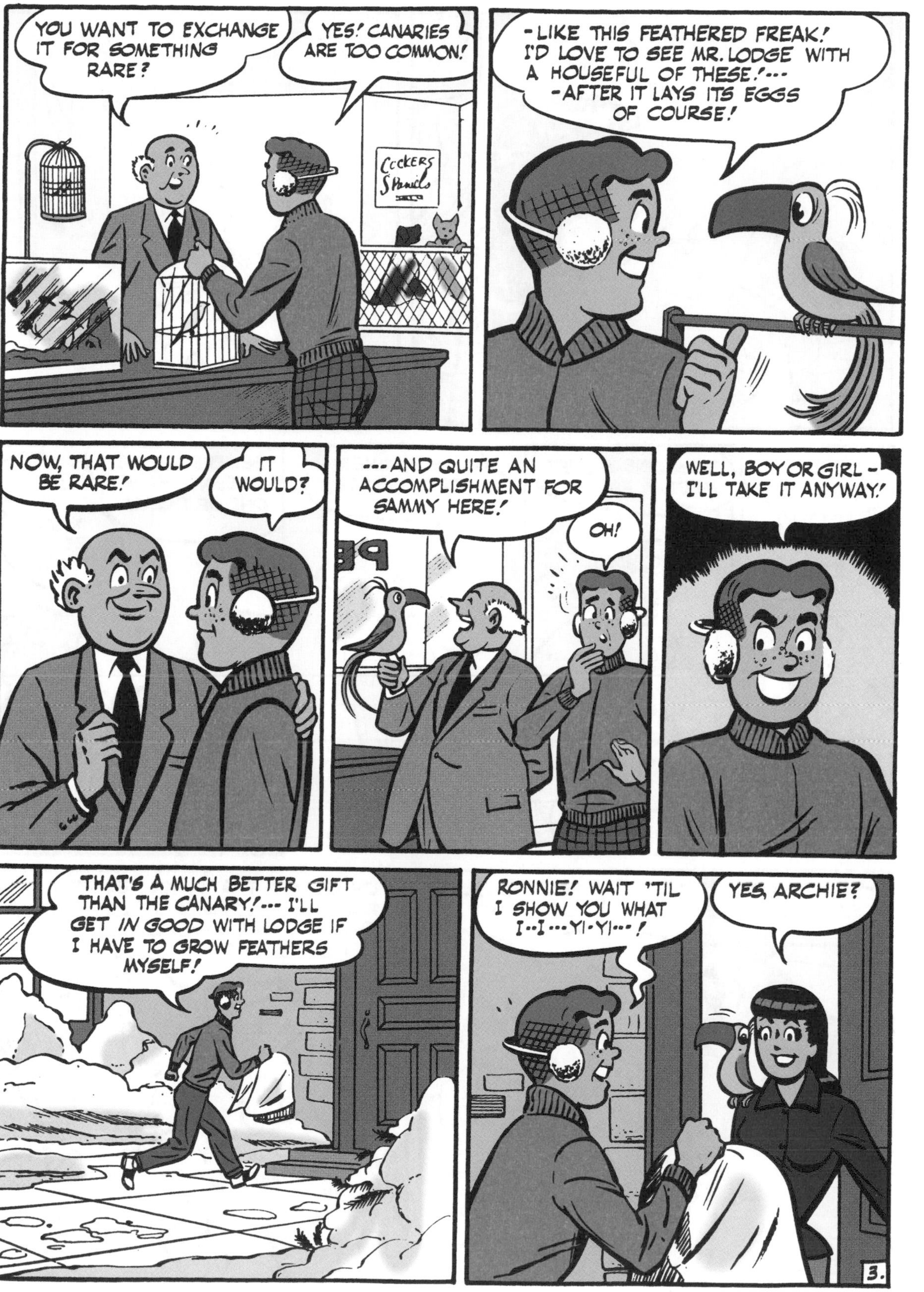
YOU WANT TO EXCHANGE IT FOR SOMETHING RARE?
YES! CANARIES ARE TOO COMMON!
Cockers Spaniels
-LIKE THIS FEATHERED FREAK! I'D LOVE TO SEE MR. LODGE WITH A HOUSEFUL OF THESE!--- -AFTER IT LAYS ITS EGGS OF COURSE!
NOW, THAT WOULD BE RARE!
IT WOULD?
---AND QUITE AN ACCOMPLISHMENT FOR SAMMY HERE!
OH!
WELL, BOY OR GIRL - I'LL TAKE IT ANYWAY!
THAT'S A MUCH BETTER GIFT THAN THE CANARY!--- I'LL GET IN GOOD WITH LODGE IF I HAVE TO GROW FEATHERS MYSELF!
RONNIE! WAIT 'TIL I SHOW YOU WHAT I--I---YI-YI---!
YES, ARCHIE?
3.

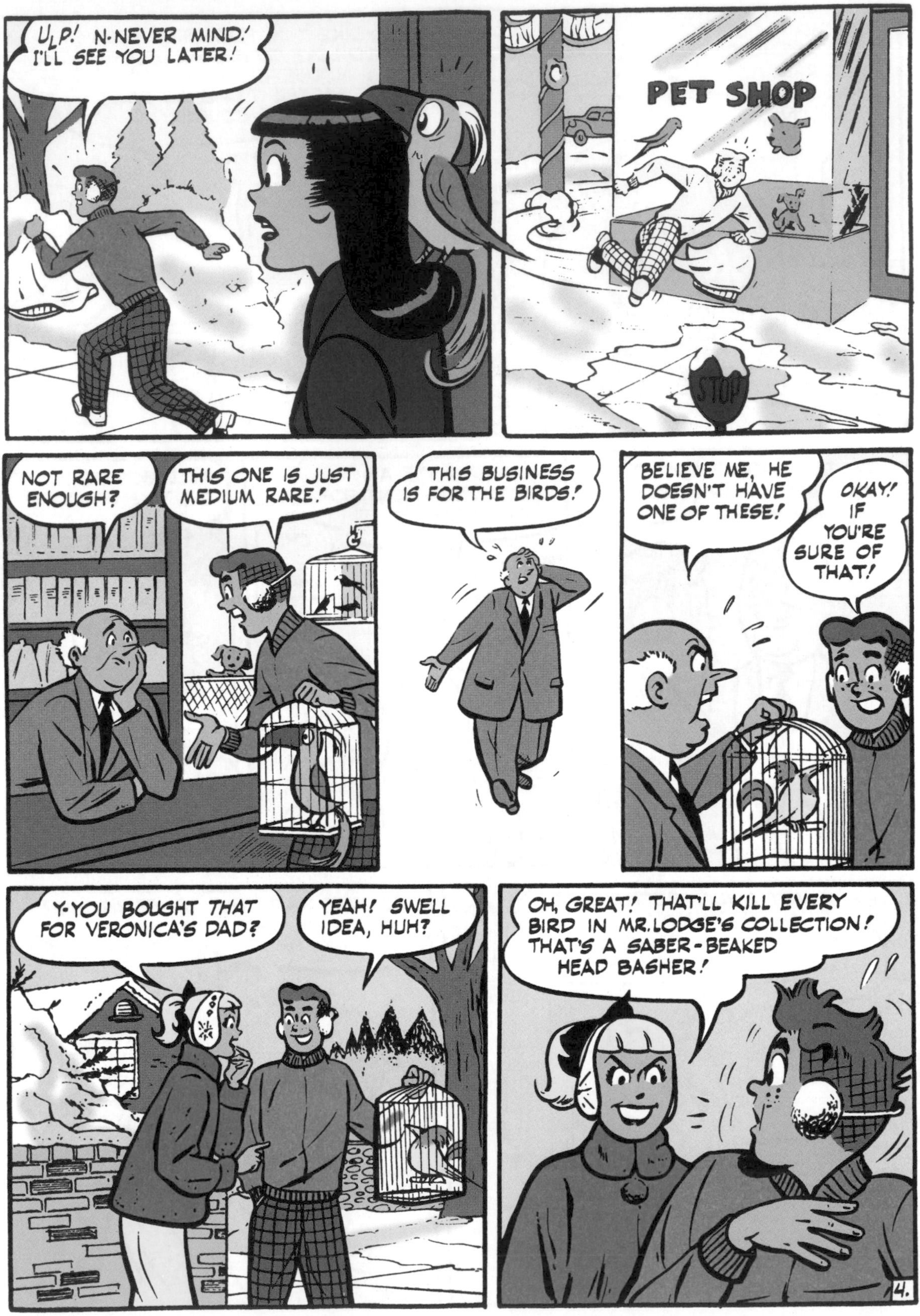
U_LP! N-NEVER MIND! I'LL SEE YOU LATER!
PET SHOP
STOP
NOT RARE ENOUGH?
THIS ONE IS JUST MEDIUM RARE!
THIS BUSINESS IS FOR THE BIRDS!
BELIEVE ME, HE DOESN'T HAVE ONE OF THESE!
OKAY! IF YOU'RE SURE OF THAT!
Y-YOU BOUGHT THAT FOR VERONICA'S DAD?
YEAH! SWELL IDEA, HUH?
OH, GREAT! THAT'LL KILL EVERY BIRD IN MR. LODGE'S COLLECTION! THAT'S A SABER-BEAKED HEAD BASHER!
4.

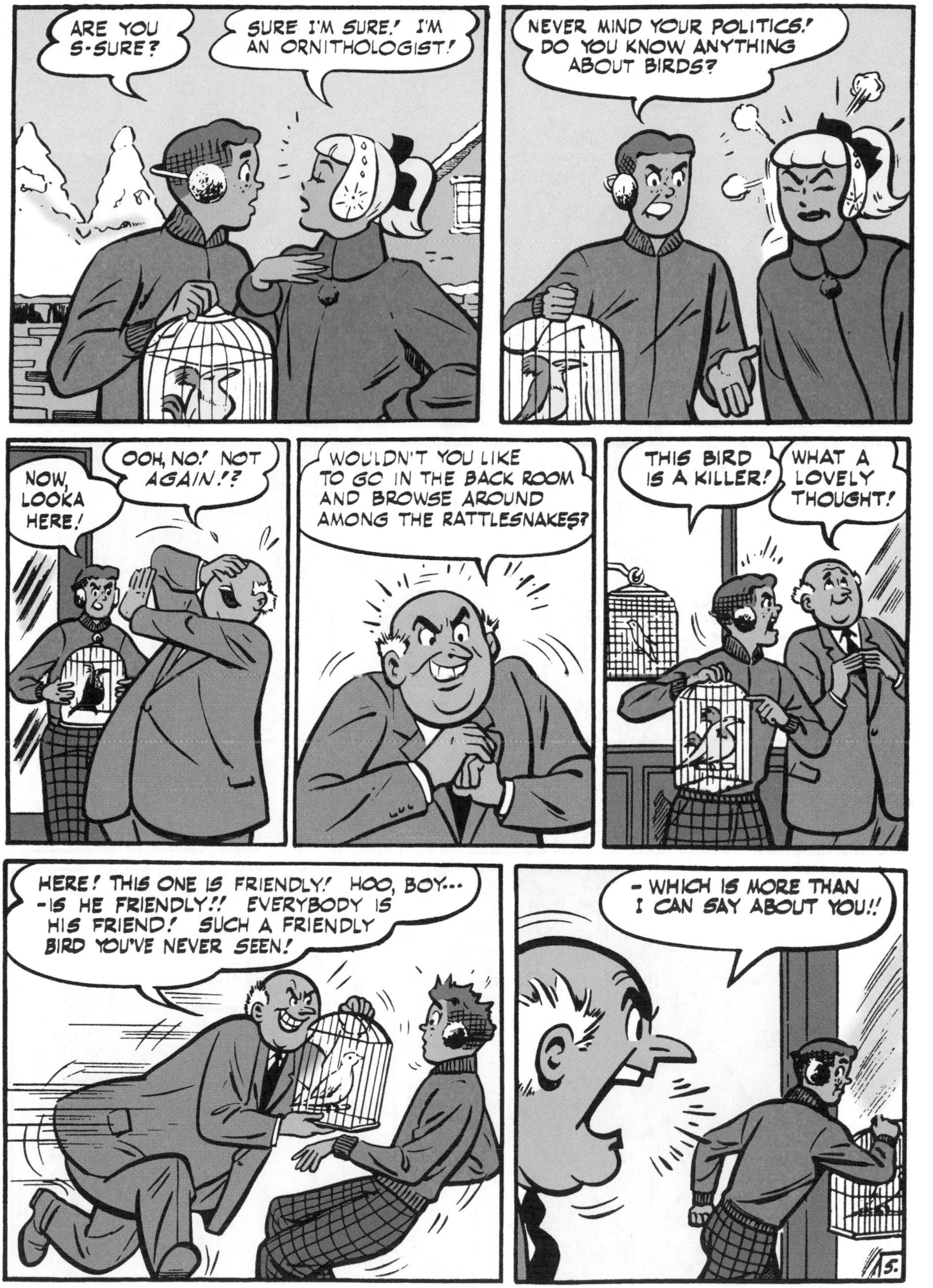
ARE YOU S-SURE?
SURE I'M SURE! I'M AN ORNITHOLOGIST!
NEVER MIND YOUR POLITICS! DO YOU KNOW ANYTHING ABOUT BIRDS?
NOW, LOOKA HERE!
OOH, NO! NOT AGAIN!?
WOULDN'T YOU LIKE TO GO IN THE BACK ROOM AND BROWSE AROUND AMONG THE RATTLESNAKES?
THIS BIRD IS A KILLER!
WHAT A LOVELY THOUGHT!
HERE! THIS ONE IS FRIENDLY! HOO, BOY... -IS HE FRIENDLY!! EVERYBODY IS HIS FRIEND! SUCH A FRIENDLY BIRD YOU'VE NEVER SEEN!
-WHICH IS MORE THAN I CAN SAY ABOUT YOU!!
5.

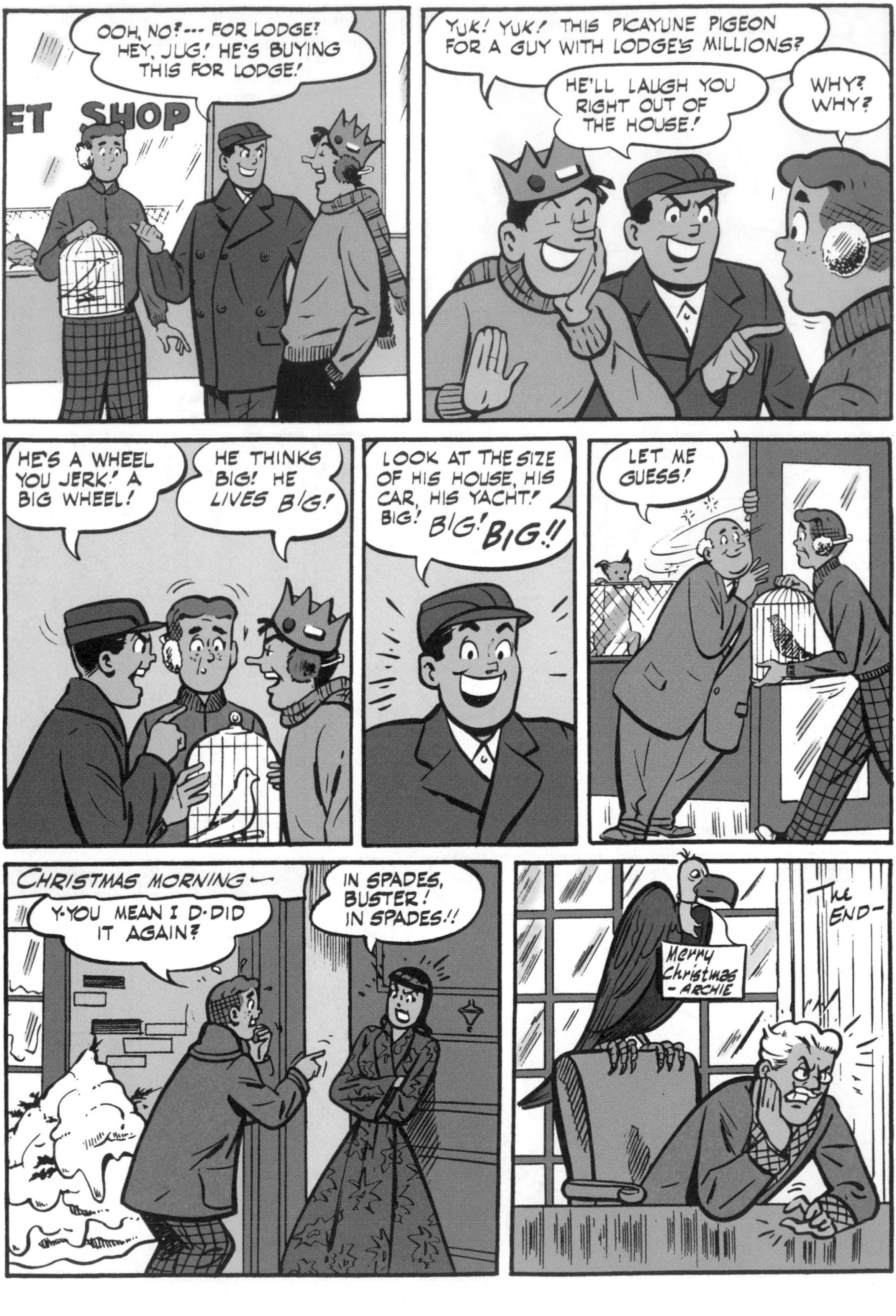
OOH, NO?--- FOR LODGE? HEY, JUG! HE'S BUYING THIS FOR LODGE!
ET SHOP
YUK! YUK! THIS PICAYUNE PIGEON FOR A GUY WITH LODGE'S MILLIONS?
HE'LL LAUGH YOU RIGHT OUT OF THE HOUSE!
WHY? WHY?
HE'S A WHEEL YOU JERK! A BIG WHEEL!
HE THINKS BIG! HE LIVES BIG!
LOOK AT THE SIZE OF HIS HOUSE, HIS CAR, HIS YACHT! BIG! BIG! BIG!!
LET ME GUESS!
CHRISTMAS MORNING —
Y-YOU MEAN I D-DID IT AGAIN?
IN SPADES, BUSTER! IN SPADES!!
Merry Christmas - ARCHIE
The END—

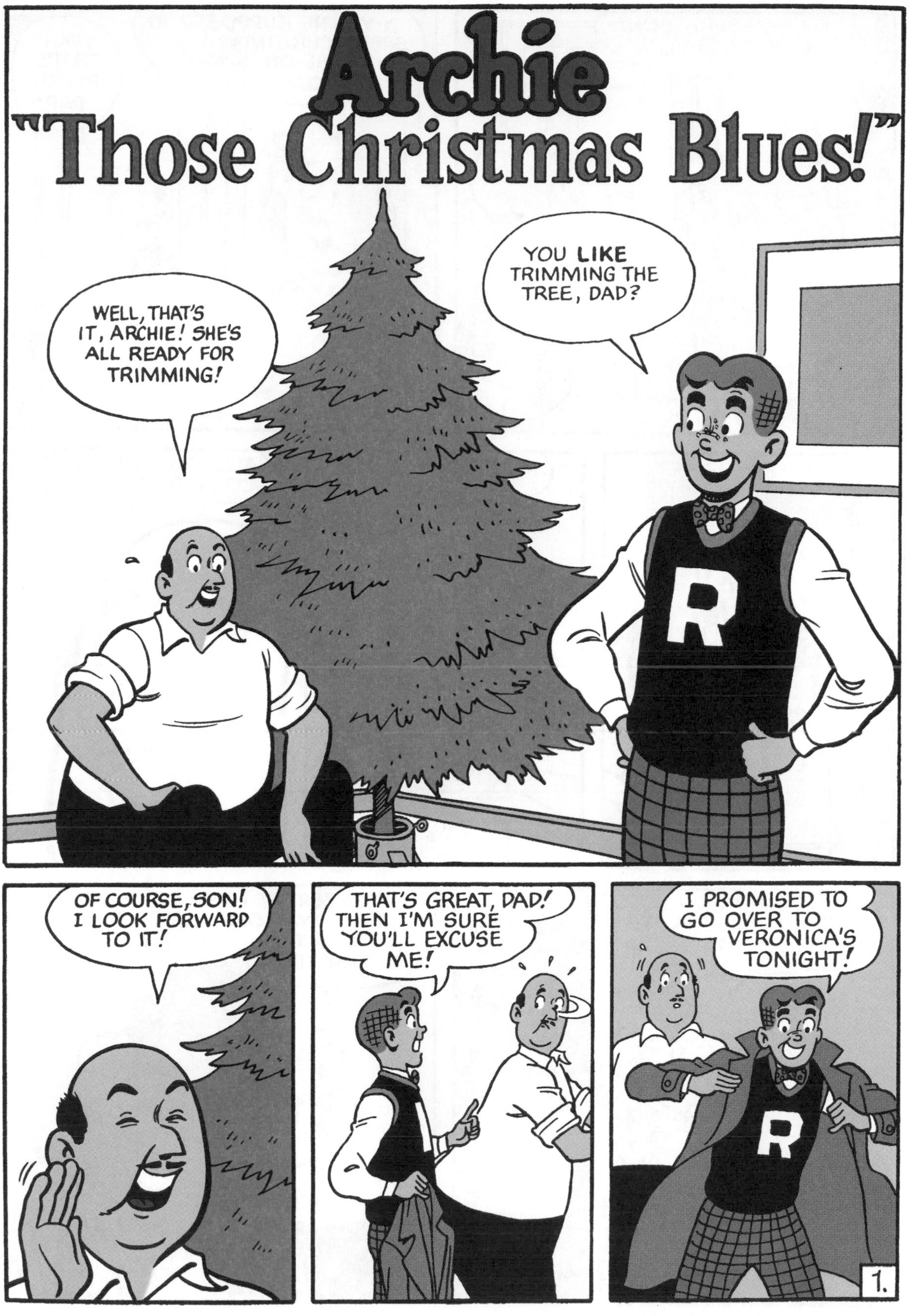
Archie
"Those Christmas Blues!"
WELL, THAT'S IT, ARCHIE! SHE'S ALL READY FOR TRIMMING!
YOU LIKE TRIMMING THE TREE, DAD?
OF COURSE, SON! I LOOK FORWARD TO IT!
THAT'S GREAT, DAD! THEN I'M SURE YOU'LL EXCUSE ME!
I PROMISED TO GO OVER TO VERONICA'S TONIGHT!
1.

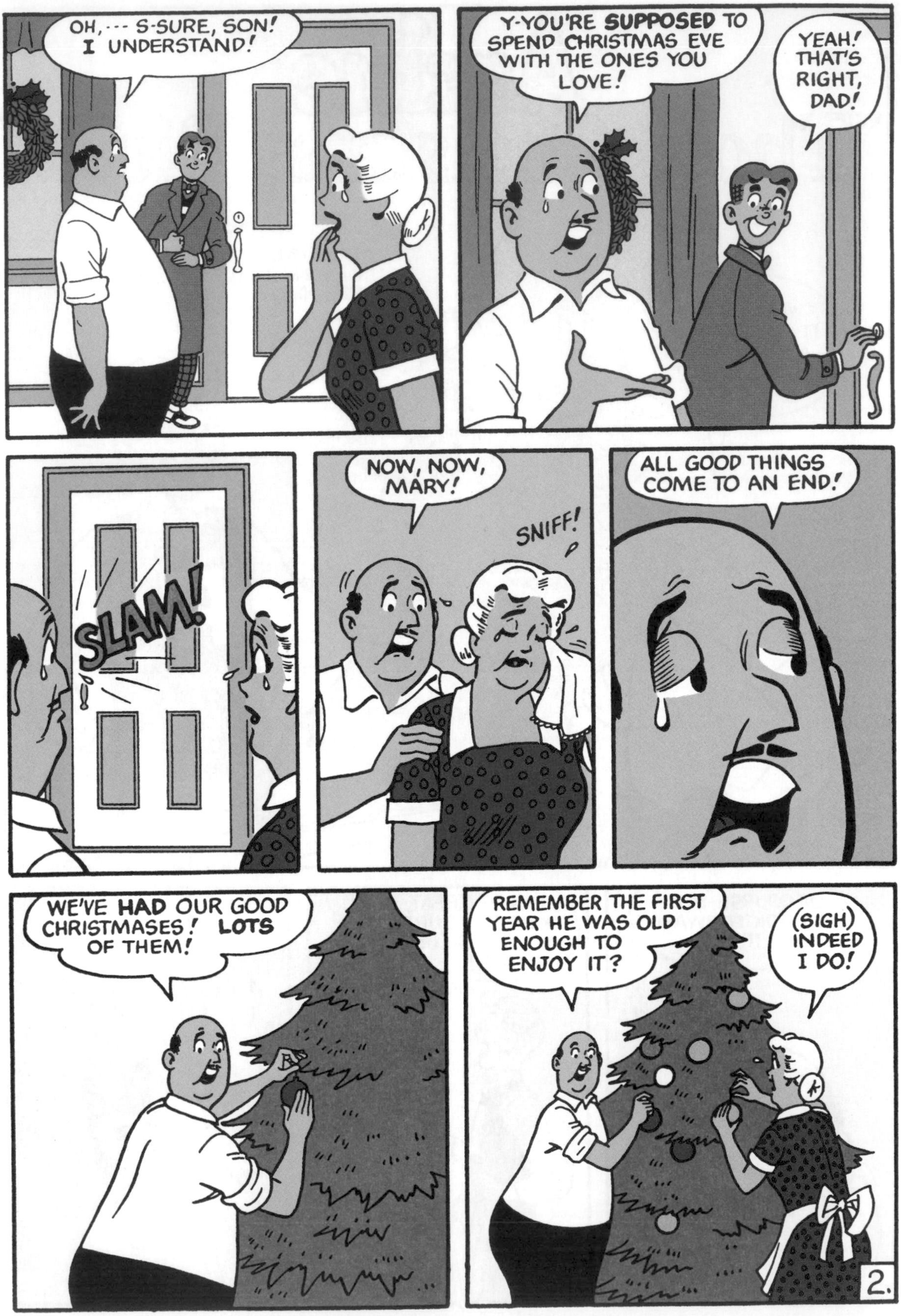

OH, --- S-SURE, SON! I UNDERSTAND!
Y-YOU'RE SUPPOSED TO SPEND CHRISTMAS EVE WITH THE ONES YOU LOVE!
YEAH! THAT'S RIGHT, DAD!
SLAM!
NOW, NOW, MARY!
SNIFF!
ALL GOOD THINGS COME TO AN END!
WE'VE HAD OUR GOOD CHRISTMASES! LOTS OF THEM!
REMEMBER THE FIRST YEAR HE WAS OLD ENOUGH TO ENJOY IT?
(SIGH) INDEED I DO!
2.

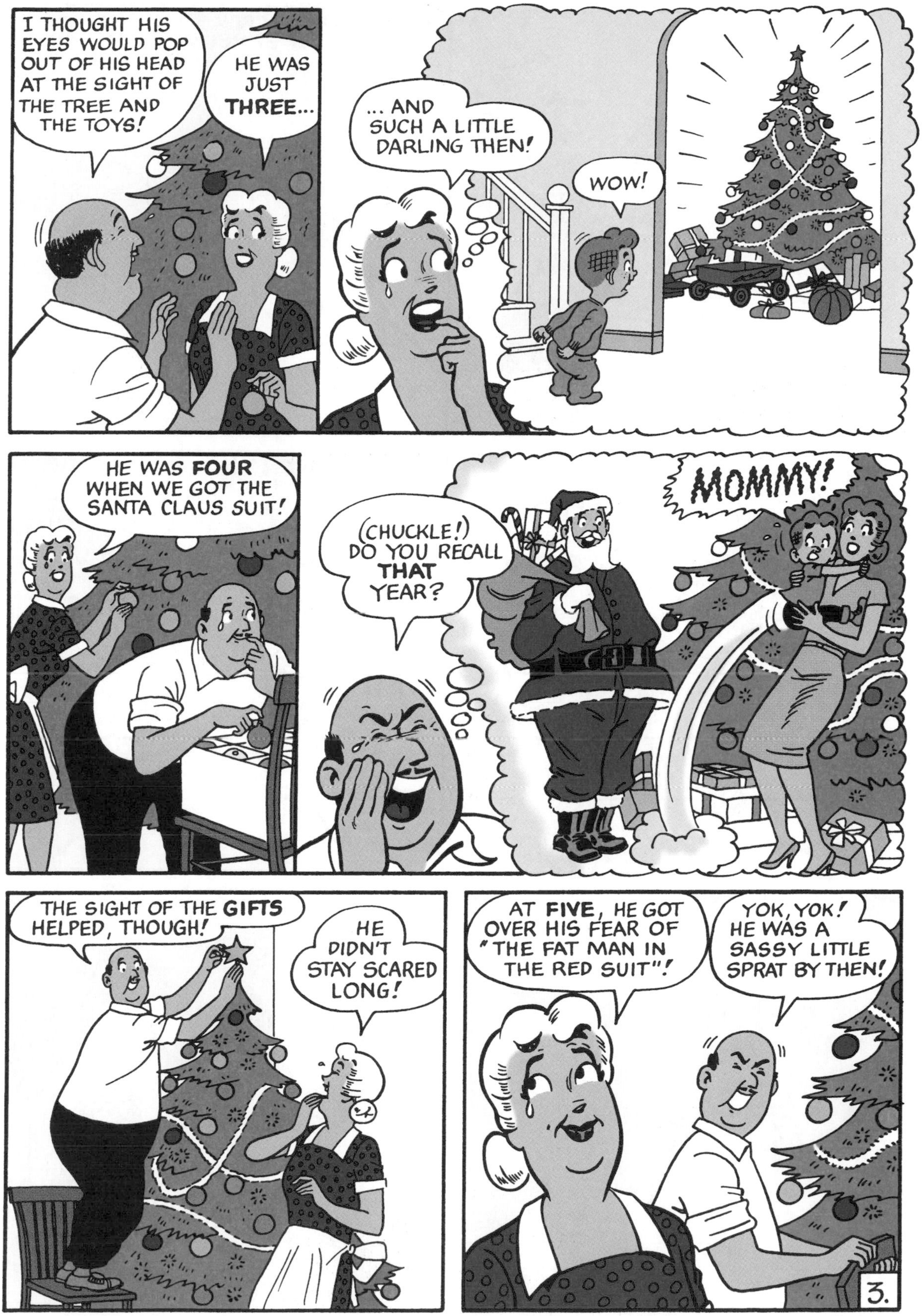
I THOUGHT HIS EYES WOULD POP OUT OF HIS HEAD AT THE SIGHT OF THE TREE AND THE TOYS!
HE WAS JUST THREE...
... AND SUCH A LITTLE DARLING THEN!
WOW!
HE WAS FOUR WHEN WE GOT THE SANTA CLAUS SUIT!
(CHUCKLE!) DO YOU RECALL THAT YEAR?
MOMMY!
THE SIGHT OF THE GIFTS HELPED, THOUGH!
HE DIDN'T STAY SCARED LONG!
AT FIVE, HE GOT OVER HIS FEAR OF "THE FAT MAN IN THE RED SUIT"!
YOK, YOK! HE WAS A SASSY LITTLE SPRAT BY THEN!
3.

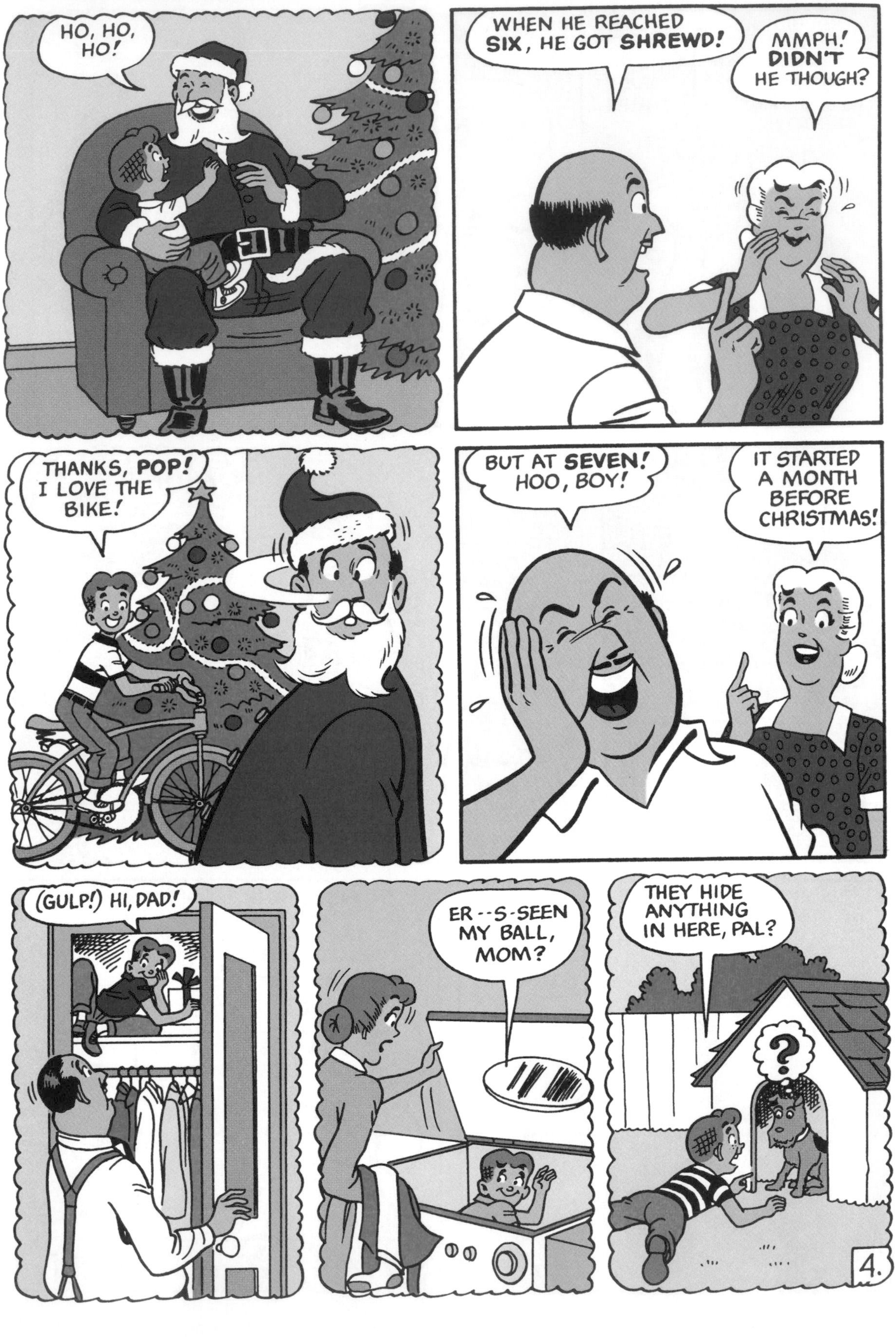
HO, HO, HO!
WHEN HE REACHED **SIX**, HE GOT **SHREWD!**
MMPH! **DIDN'T** HE THOUGH?
THANKS, **POP!** I LOVE THE BIKE!
BUT AT **SEVEN!** HOO, BOY!
IT STARTED A MONTH BEFORE CHRISTMAS!
(GULP!) HI, DAD!
ER--S-SEEN MY BALL, MOM?
THEY HIDE ANYTHING IN HERE, PAL?
?
4.

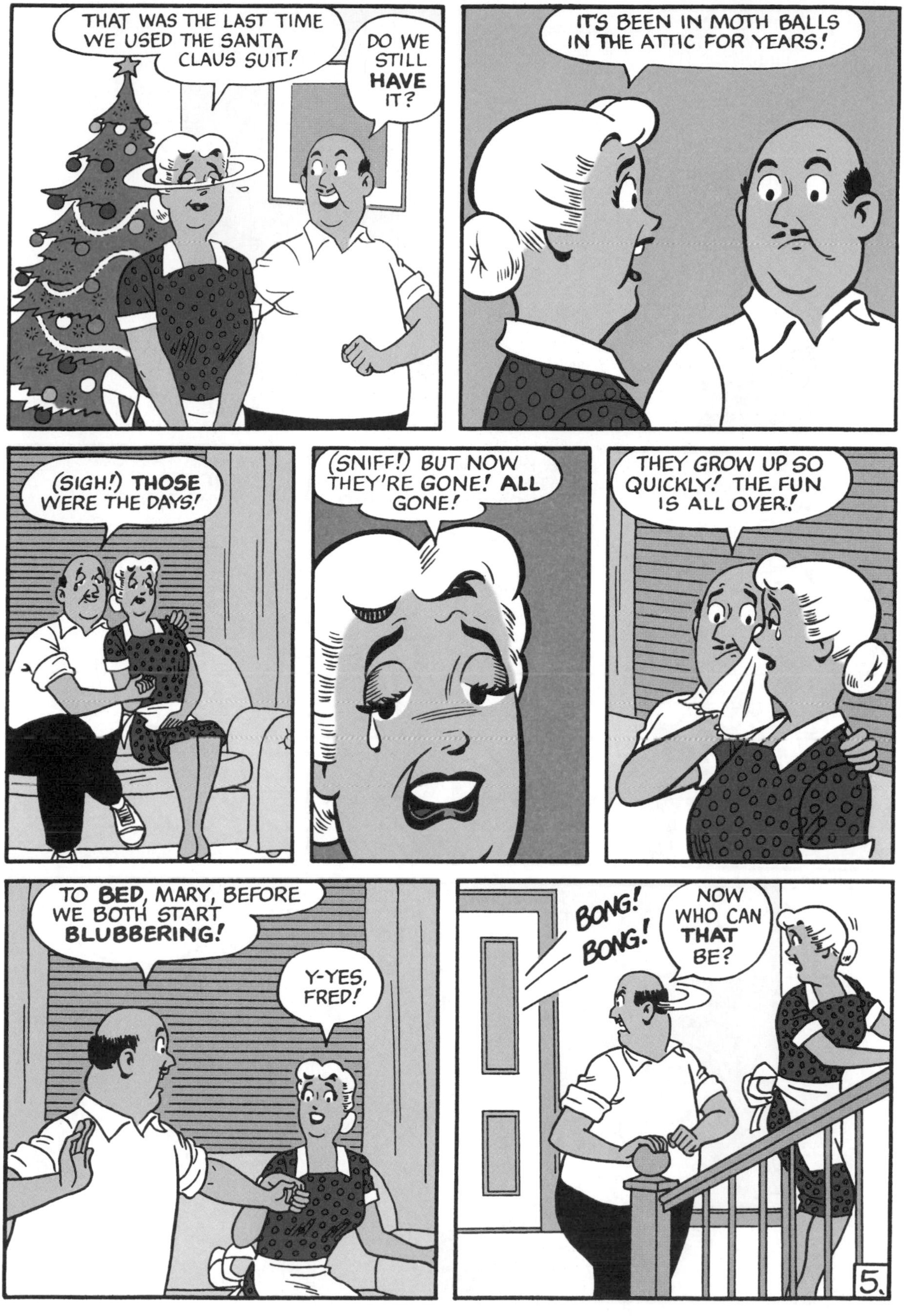
THAT WAS THE LAST TIME WE USED THE SANTA CLAUS SUIT!
DO WE STILL **HAVE** IT?
IT'S BEEN IN MOTH BALLS IN THE ATTIC FOR YEARS!
(SIGH!) **THOSE** WERE THE DAYS!
(SNIFF!) BUT NOW THEY'RE GONE! **ALL** GONE!
THEY GROW UP SO QUICKLY! THE FUN IS ALL OVER!
TO **BED**, MARY, BEFORE WE BOTH START **BLUBBERING!**
Y-YES, FRED!
BONG! BONG!
NOW WHO CAN **THAT** BE?
5.

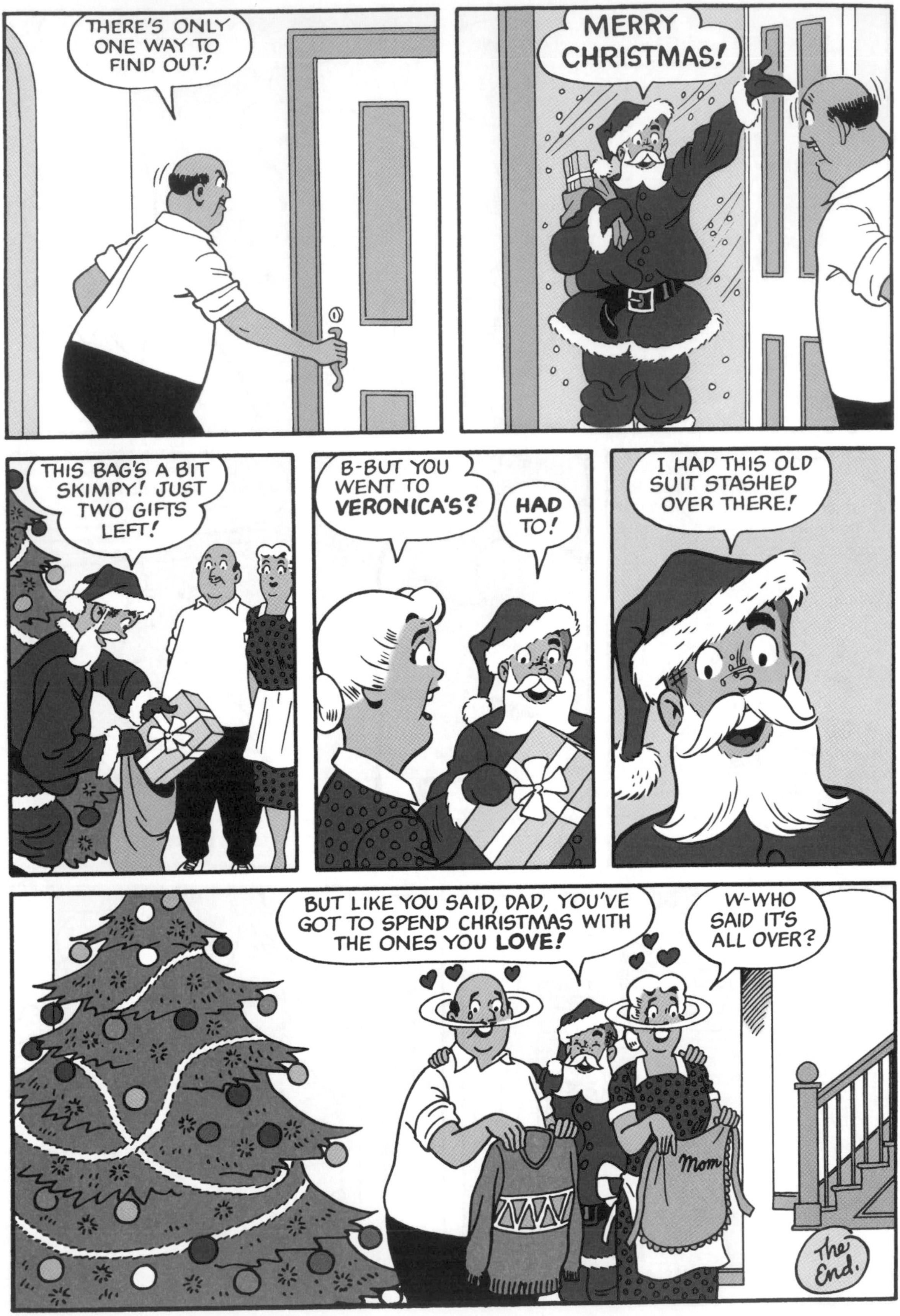
THERE'S ONLY ONE WAY TO FIND OUT!
MERRY CHRISTMAS!
THIS BAG'S A BIT SKIMPY! JUST TWO GIFTS LEFT!
B-BUT YOU WENT TO VERONICA'S?
HAD TO!
I HAD THIS OLD SUIT STASHED OVER THERE!
BUT LIKE YOU SAID, DAD, YOU'VE GOT TO SPEND CHRISTMAS WITH THE ONES YOU LOVE!
W-WHO SAID IT'S ALL OVER?
Mom
The End.

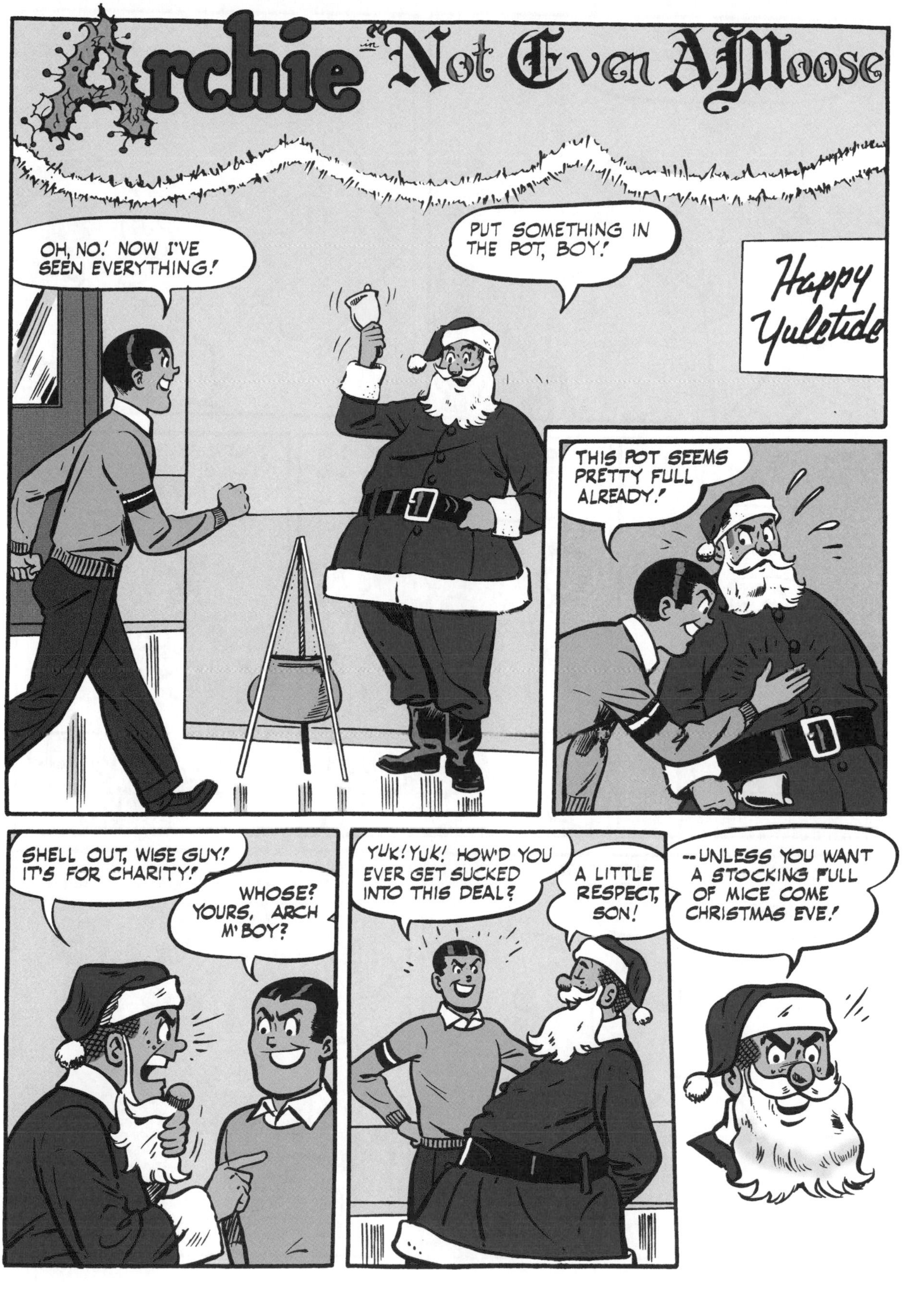
Archie in Not Even A Moose
OH, NO! NOW I'VE SEEN EVERYTHING!
PUT SOMETHING IN THE POT, BOY!
Happy Yuletide
THIS POT SEEMS PRETTY FULL ALREADY!
SHELL OUT, WISE GUY! IT'S FOR CHARITY!
WHOSE? YOURS, ARCH M'BOY?
YUK! YUK! HOW'D YOU EVER GET SUCKED INTO THIS DEAL?
A LITTLE RESPECT, SON!
--UNLESS YOU WANT A STOCKING FULL OF MICE COME CHRISTMAS EVE!

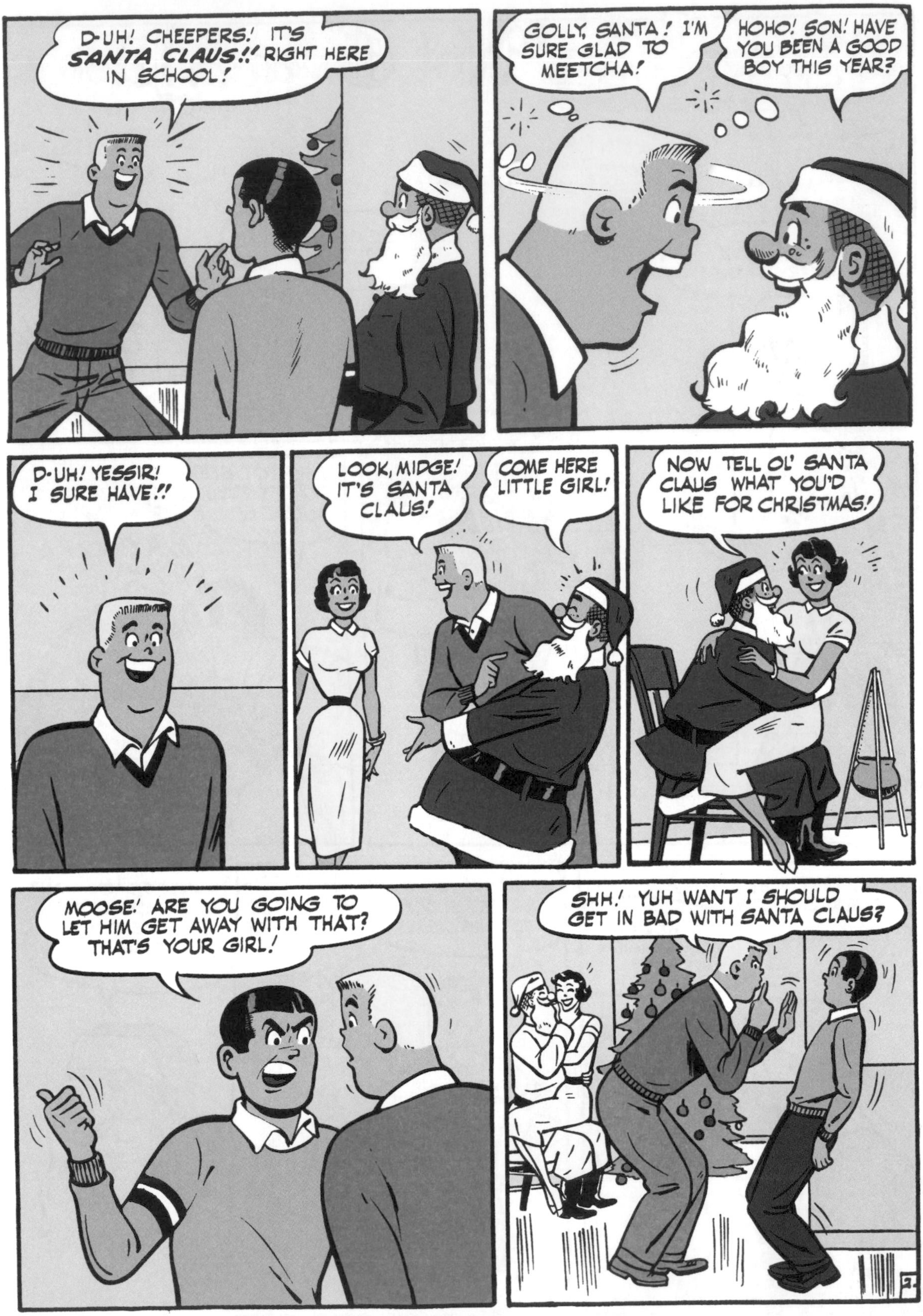
D-UH! CHEEPERS! IT'S SANTA CLAUS!! RIGHT HERE IN SCHOOL!
GOLLY, SANTA! I'M SURE GLAD TO MEETCHA!
HOHO! SON! HAVE YOU BEEN A GOOD BOY THIS YEAR?
D-UH! YESSIR! I SURE HAVE!!
LOOK, MIDGE! IT'S SANTA CLAUS!
COME HERE LITTLE GIRL!
NOW TELL OL' SANTA CLAUS WHAT YOU'D LIKE FOR CHRISTMAS!
MOOSE! ARE YOU GOING TO LET HIM GET AWAY WITH THAT? THAT'S YOUR GIRL!
SHH! YUH WANT I SHOULD GET IN BAD WITH SANTA CLAUS?

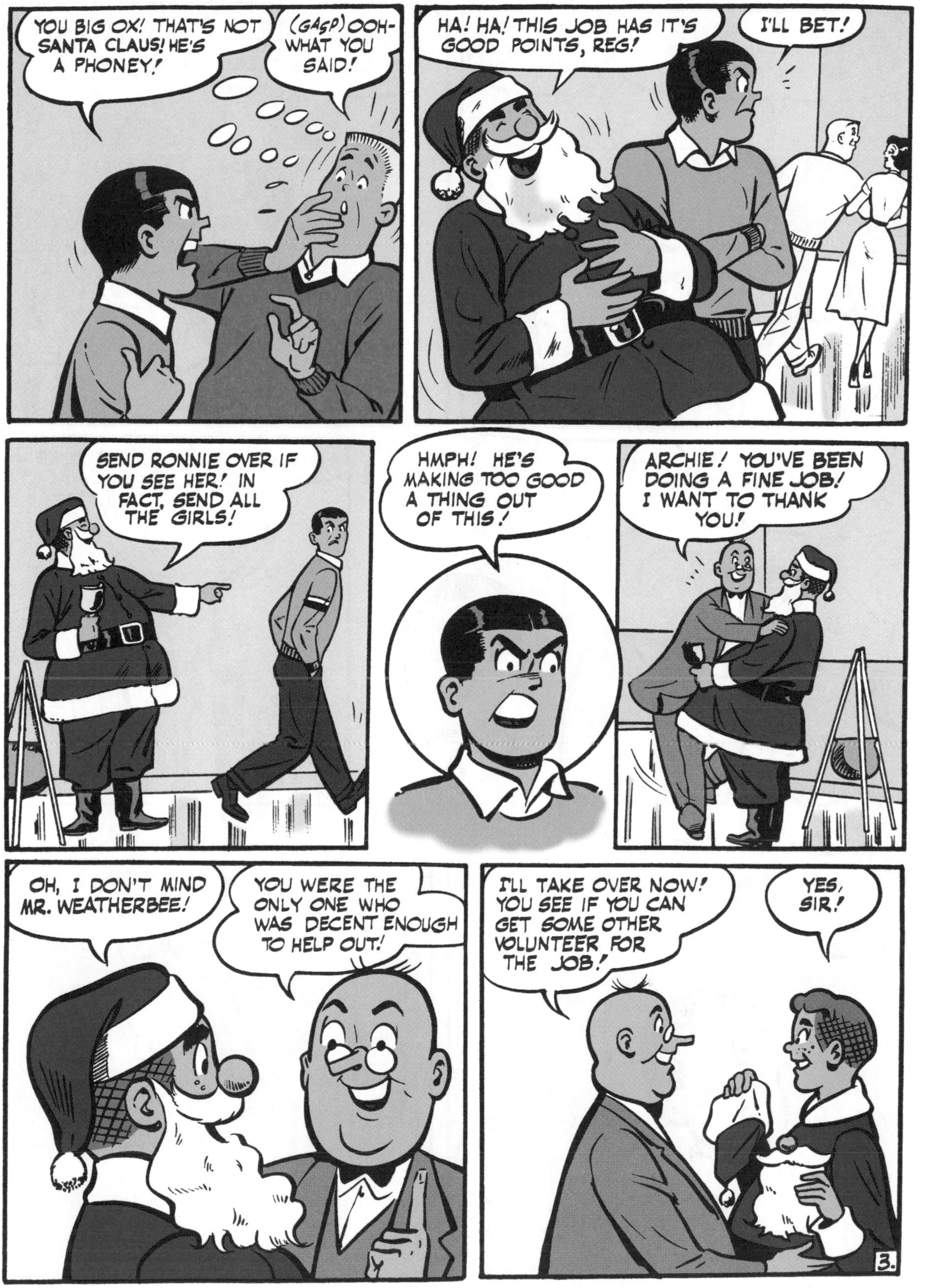
YOU BIG OX! THAT'S NOT SANTA CLAUS! HE'S A PHONEY!
(GASP) OOH- WHAT YOU SAID!
HA! HA! THIS JOB HAS IT'S GOOD POINTS, REG!
I'LL BET!
SEND RONNIE OVER IF YOU SEE HER! IN FACT, SEND ALL THE GIRLS!
HMPH! HE'S MAKING TOO GOOD A THING OUT OF THIS!
ARCHIE! YOU'VE BEEN DOING A FINE JOB! I WANT TO THANK YOU!
OH, I DON'T MIND MR. WEATHERBEE!
YOU WERE THE ONLY ONE WHO WAS DECENT ENOUGH TO HELP OUT!
I'LL TAKE OVER NOW! YOU SEE IF YOU CAN GET SOME OTHER VOLUNTEER FOR THE JOB!
YES, SIR!
3.

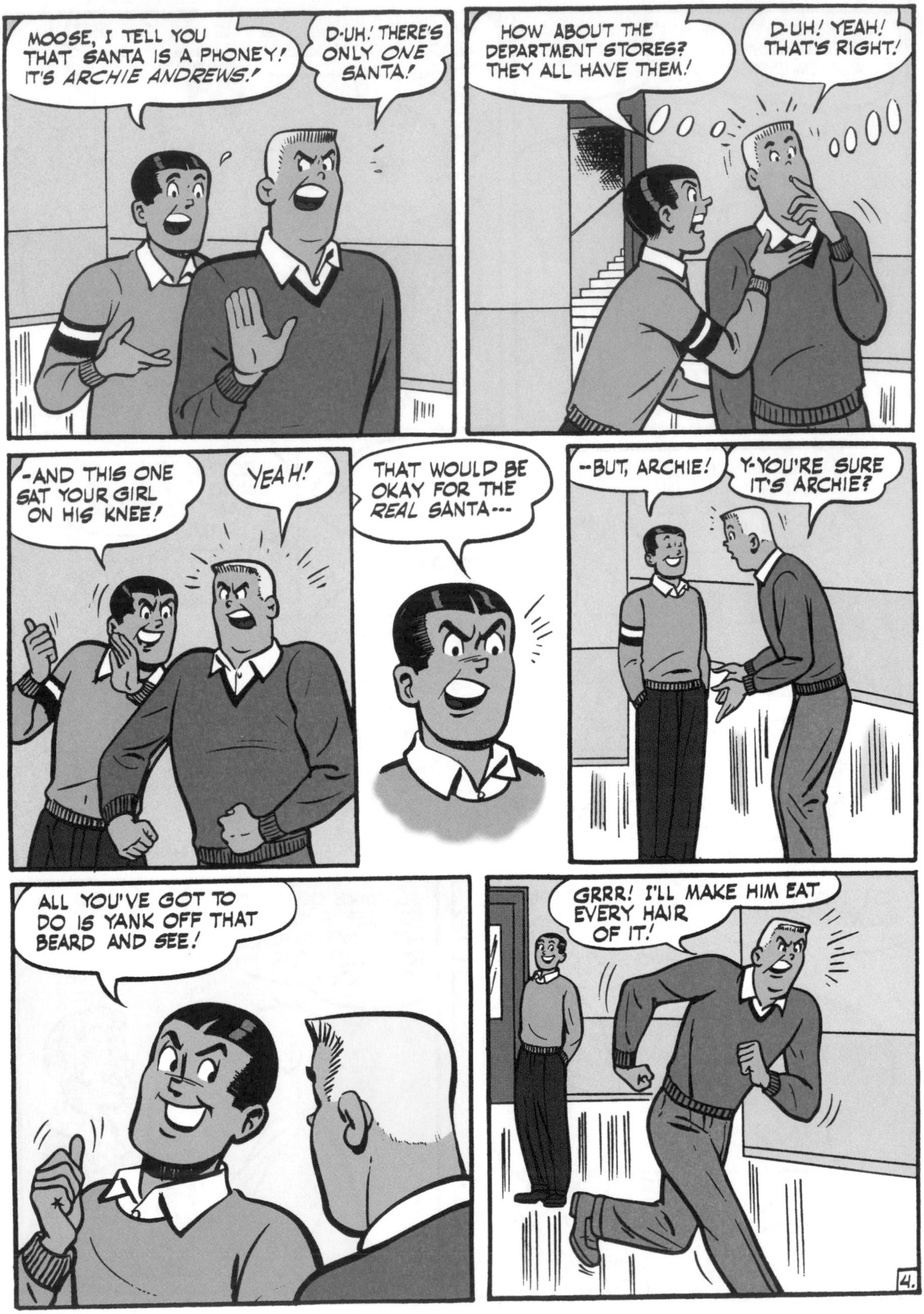
MOOSE, I TELL YOU THAT SANTA IS A PHONEY! IT'S ARCHIE ANDREWS!
D-UH! THERE'S ONLY ONE SANTA!
HOW ABOUT THE DEPARTMENT STORES? THEY ALL HAVE THEM!
D-UH! YEAH! THAT'S RIGHT!
-AND THIS ONE SAT YOUR GIRL ON HIS KNEE!
YEAH!
THAT WOULD BE OKAY FOR THE REAL SANTA---
--BUT, ARCHIE!
Y-YOU'RE SURE IT'S ARCHIE?
ALL YOU'VE GOT TO DO IS YANK OFF THAT BEARD AND SEE!
GRRR! I'LL MAKE HIM EAT EVERY HAIR OF IT!
4.

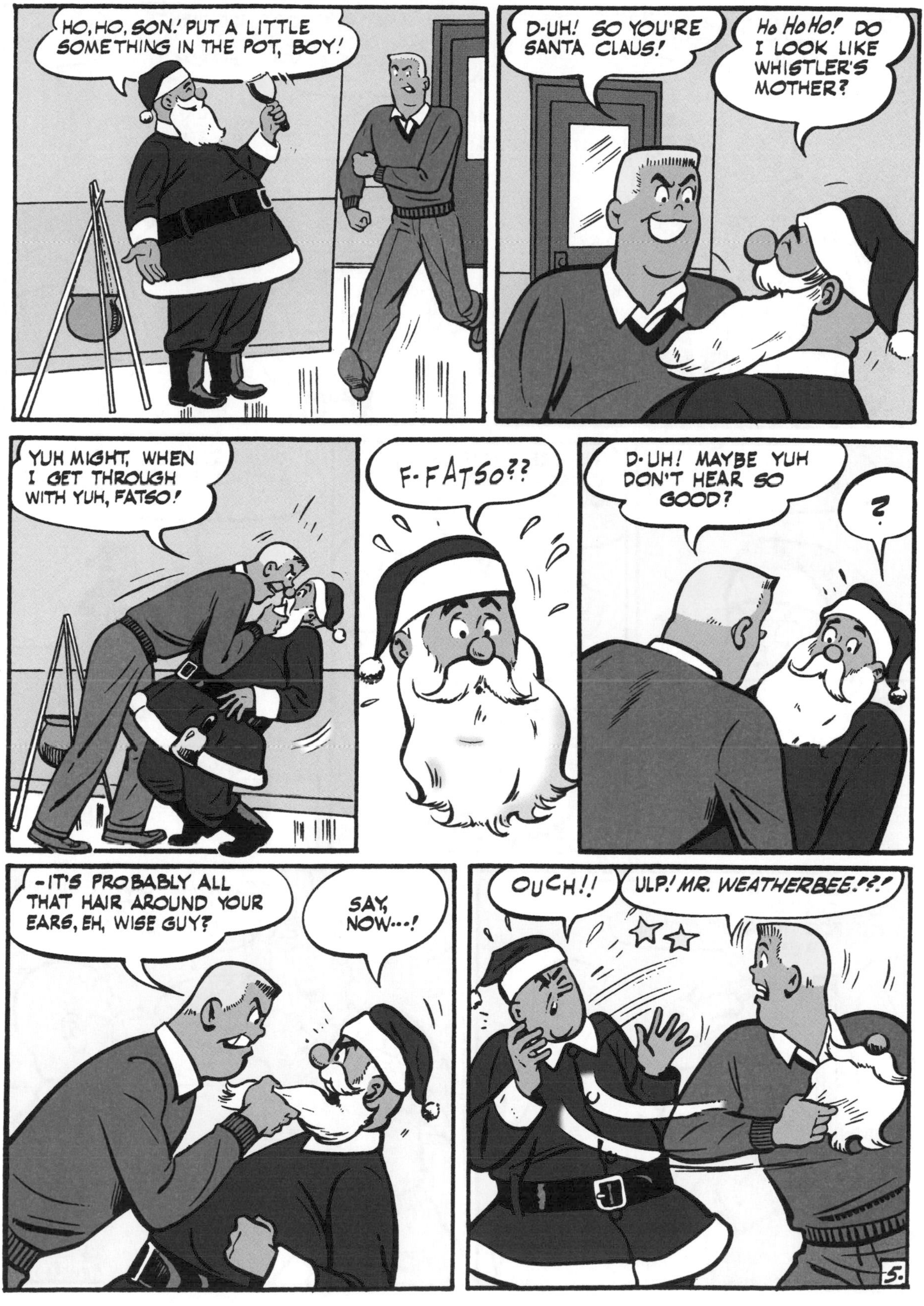
HO, HO, SON! PUT A LITTLE SOMETHING IN THE POT, BOY!
D-UH! SO YOU'RE SANTA CLAUS!
Ho Ho Ho! DO I LOOK LIKE WHISTLER'S MOTHER?
YUH MIGHT, WHEN I GET THROUGH WITH YUH, FATSO!
F-FATSO??
D-UH! MAYBE YUH DON'T HEAR SO GOOD?
?
-IT'S PROBABLY ALL THAT HAIR AROUND YOUR EARS, EH, WISE GUY?
SAY, NOW...!
OUCH!!
ULP! MR. WEATHERBEE!?!
5.

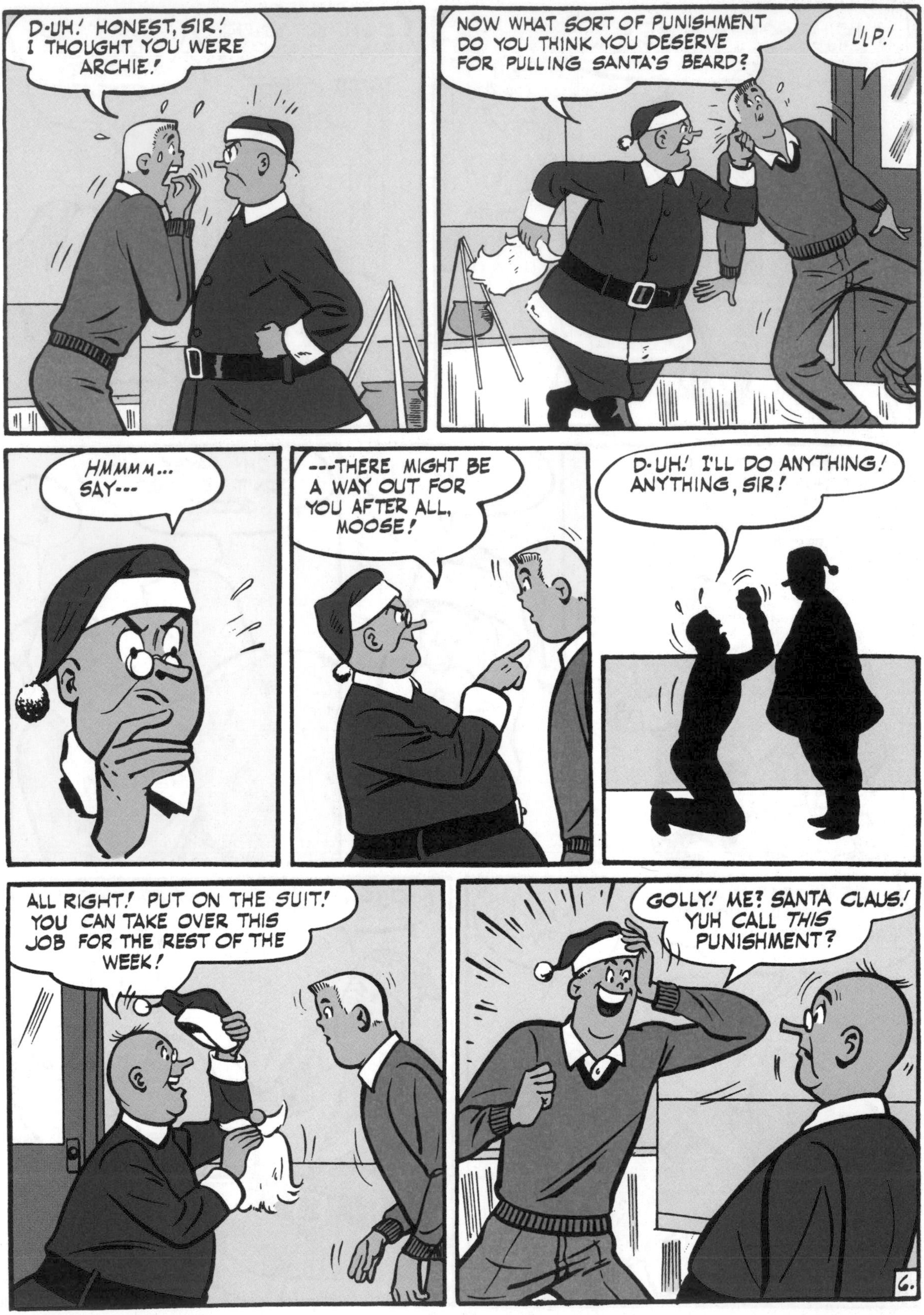
D-UH! HONEST, SIR! I THOUGHT YOU WERE ARCHIE!
NOW WHAT SORT OF PUNISHMENT DO YOU THINK YOU DESERVE FOR PULLING SANTA'S BEARD?
ULP!
HMMMM... SAY---
---THERE MIGHT BE A WAY OUT FOR YOU AFTER ALL, MOOSE!
D-UH! I'LL DO ANYTHING! ANYTHING, SIR!
ALL RIGHT! PUT ON THE SUIT! YOU CAN TAKE OVER THIS JOB FOR THE REST OF THE WEEK!
GOLLY! ME? SANTA CLAUS! YUH CALL *THIS* PUNISHMENT?
6.

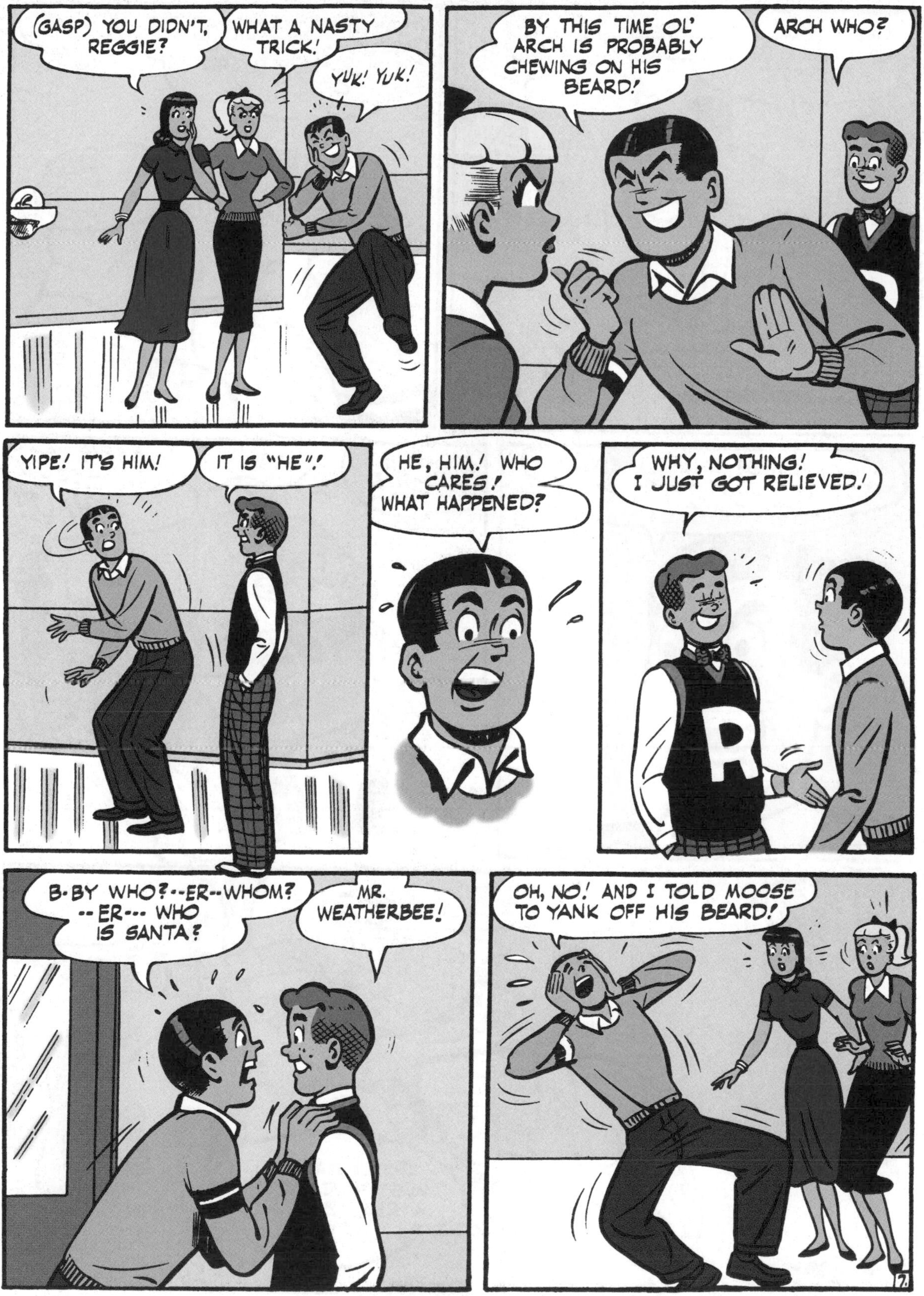
(GASP) YOU DIDN'T, REGGIE?
WHAT A NASTY TRICK!
YUK! YUK!
BY THIS TIME OL' ARCH IS PROBABLY CHEWING ON HIS BEARD!
ARCH WHO?
YIPE! IT'S HIM!
IT IS "HE"!
HE, HIM! WHO CARES! WHAT HAPPENED?
WHY, NOTHING! I JUST GOT RELIEVED!
B-BY WHO?--ER--WHOM? --ER--- WHO IS SANTA?
MR. WEATHERBEE!
OH, NO! AND I TOLD MOOSE TO YANK OFF HIS BEARD!
7.

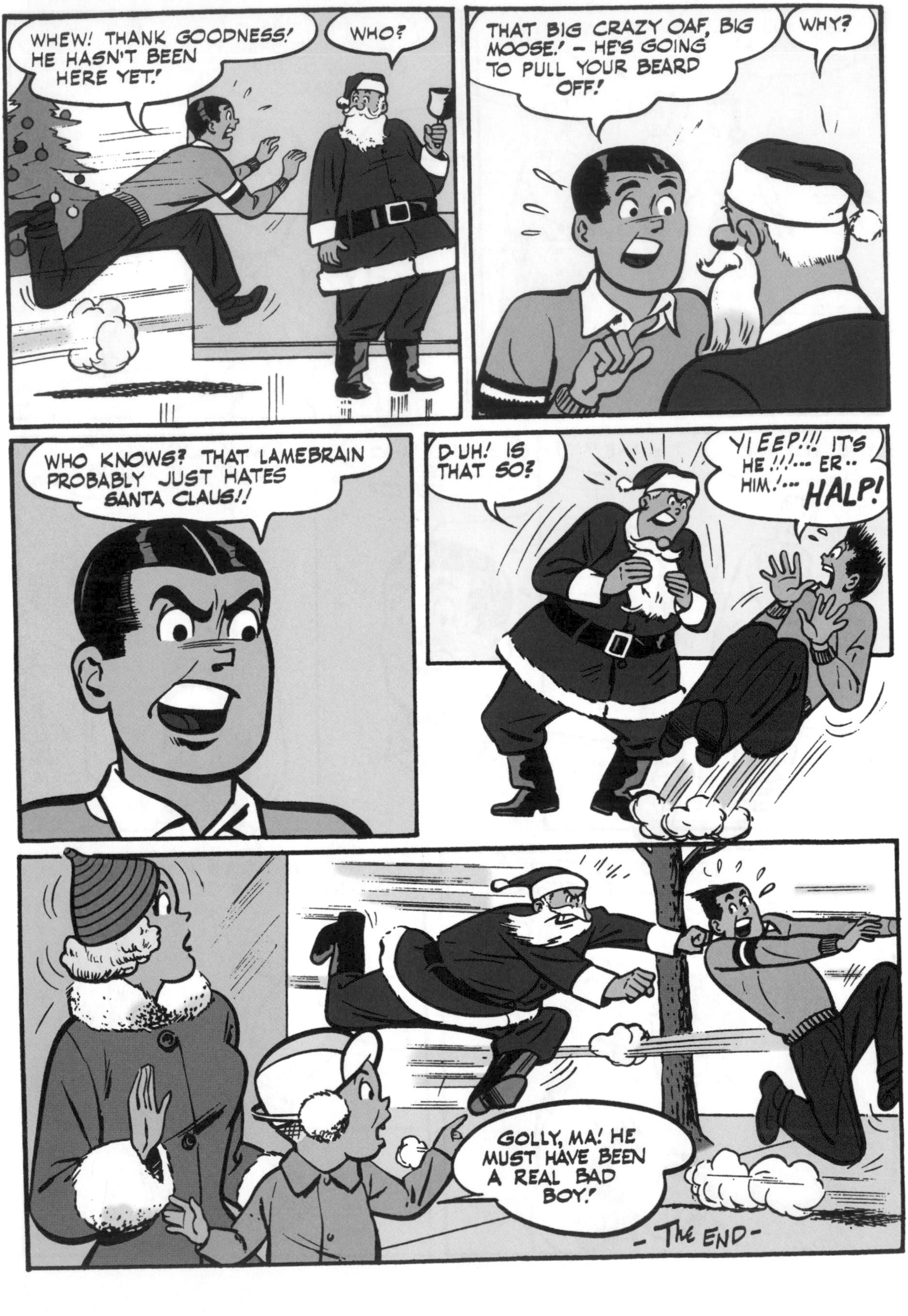
WHEW! THANK GOODNESS! HE HASN'T BEEN HERE YET!
WHO?
THAT BIG CRAZY OAF, BIG MOOSE! – HE'S GOING TO PULL YOUR BEARD OFF!
WHY?
WHO KNOWS? THAT LAMEBRAIN PROBABLY JUST HATES SANTA CLAUS!!
D-UH! IS THAT SO?
YI EEP!!! IT'S HE!!!... ER.. HIM!... HALP!
GOLLY, MA! HE MUST HAVE BEEN A REAL BAD BOY!
- THE END -

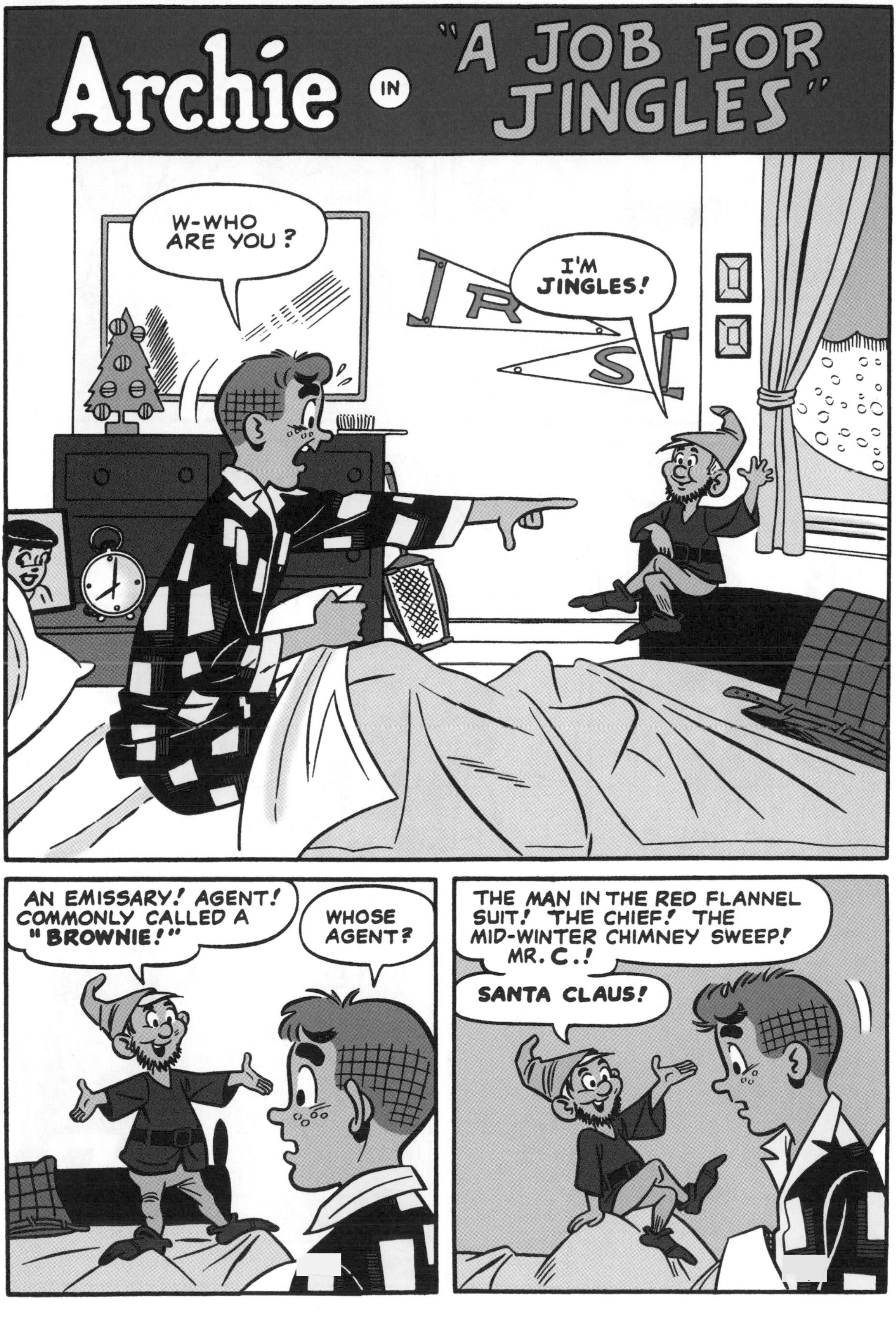
Archie in "A JOB FOR JINGLES"
W-WHO ARE YOU ?
I'M JINGLES!
AN EMISSARY! AGENT! COMMONLY CALLED A "BROWNIE!"
WHOSE AGENT?
THE MAN IN THE RED FLANNEL SUIT! THE CHIEF! THE MID-WINTER CHIMNEY SWEEP! MR. C.!
SANTA CLAUS!

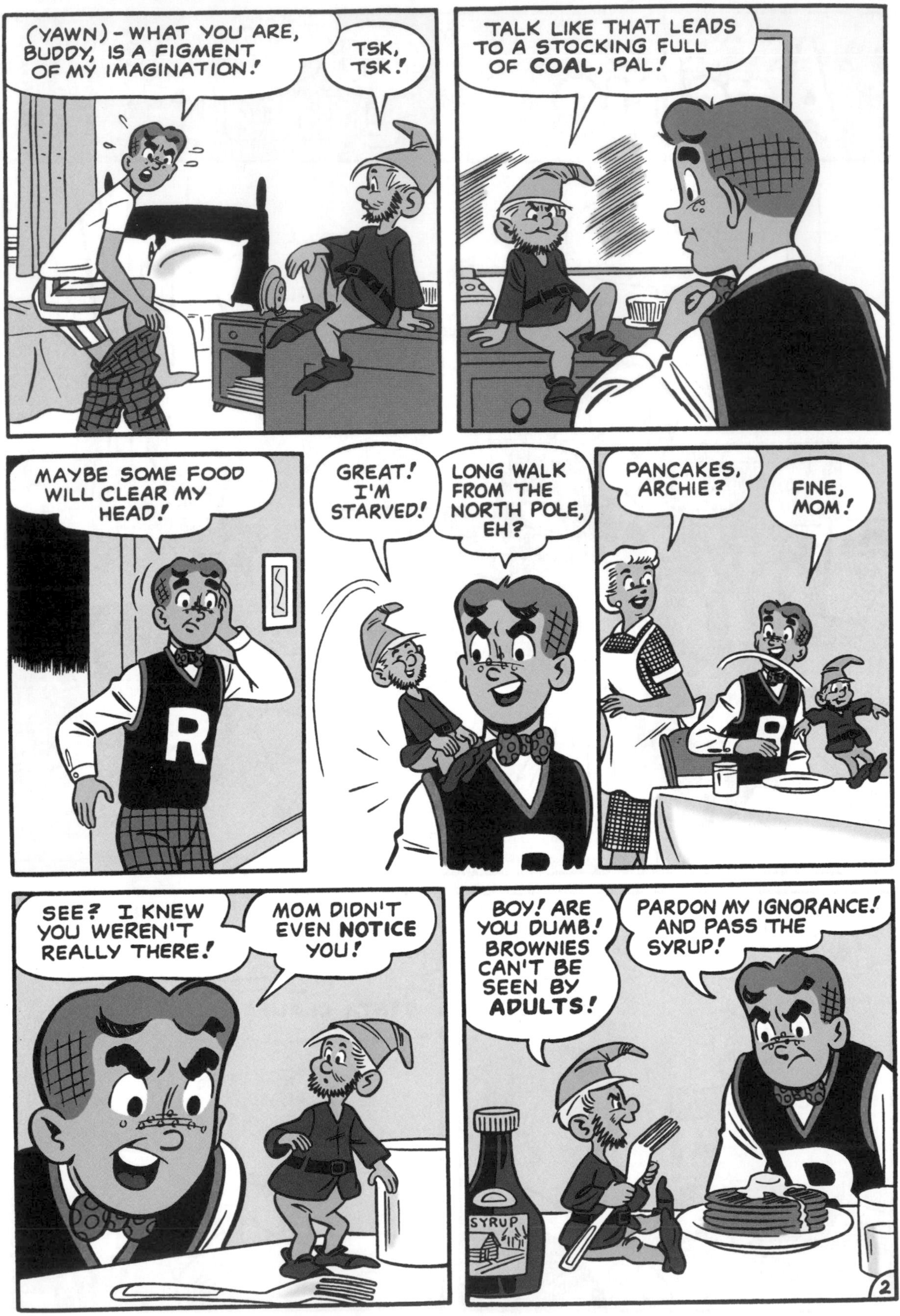
(YAWN) - WHAT YOU ARE, BUDDY, IS A FIGMENT OF MY IMAGINATION!
TSK, TSK!
TALK LIKE THAT LEADS TO A STOCKING FULL OF COAL, PAL!
MAYBE SOME FOOD WILL CLEAR MY HEAD!
GREAT! I'M STARVED!
LONG WALK FROM THE NORTH POLE, EH?
PANCAKES, ARCHIE?
FINE, MOM!
SEE? I KNEW YOU WEREN'T REALLY THERE!
MOM DIDN'T EVEN NOTICE YOU!
BOY! ARE YOU DUMB! BROWNIES CAN'T BE SEEN BY ADULTS!
PARDON MY IGNORANCE! AND PASS THE SYRUP!
SYRUP
2

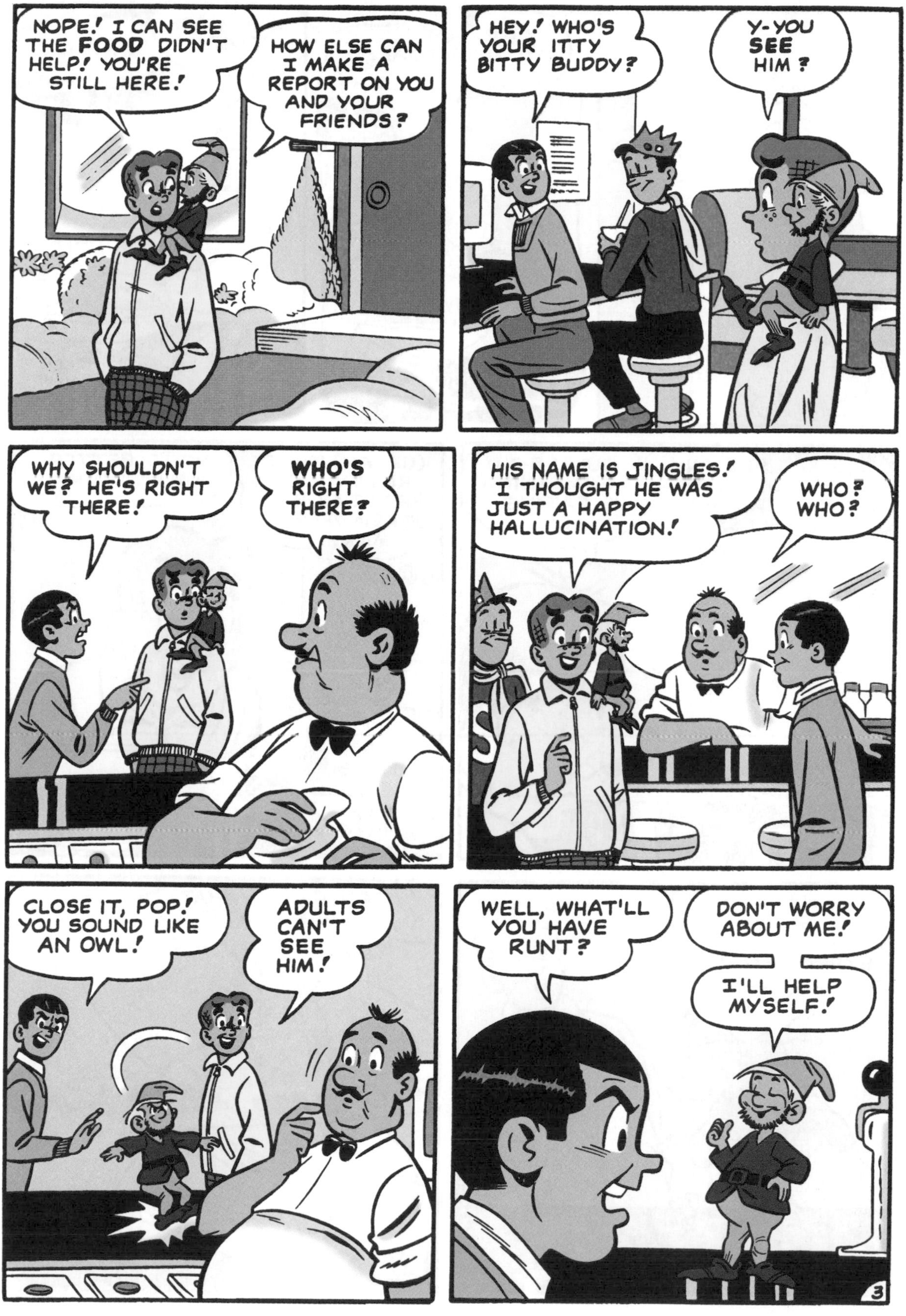
NOPE! I CAN SEE THE FOOD DIDN'T HELP! YOU'RE STILL HERE!
HOW ELSE CAN I MAKE A REPORT ON YOU AND YOUR FRIENDS?
HEY! WHO'S YOUR ITTY BITTY BUDDY?
Y-YOU SEE HIM?
WHY SHOULDN'T WE? HE'S RIGHT THERE!
WHO'S RIGHT THERE?
HIS NAME IS JINGLES! I THOUGHT HE WAS JUST A HAPPY HALLUCINATION!
WHO? WHO?
CLOSE IT, POP! YOU SOUND LIKE AN OWL!
ADULTS CAN'T SEE HIM!
WELL, WHAT'LL YOU HAVE RUNT?
DON'T WORRY ABOUT ME!
I'LL HELP MYSELF!
3

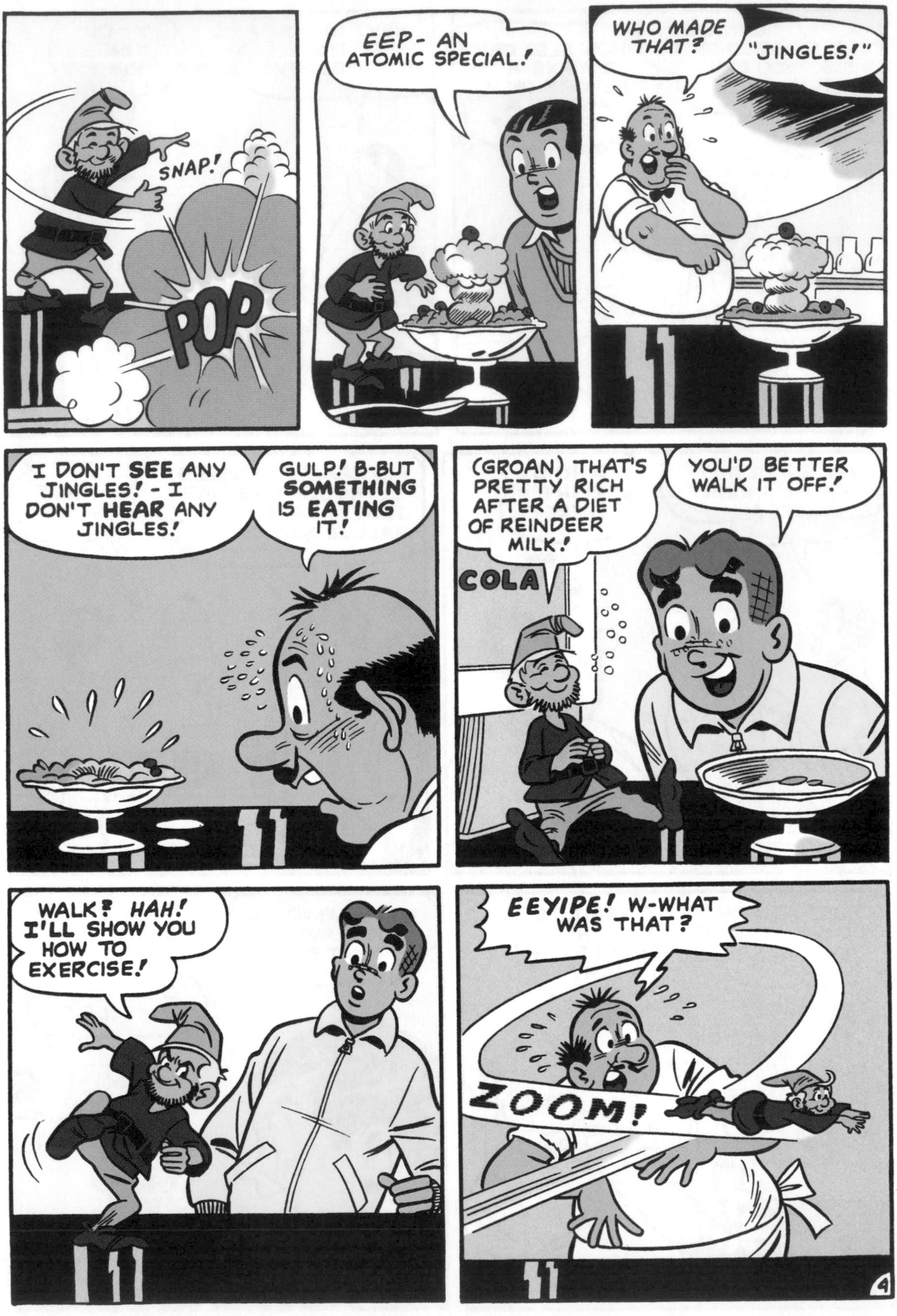
SNAP!
POP
EEP- AN ATOMIC SPECIAL!
WHO MADE THAT?
"JINGLES!"
I DON'T **SEE** ANY JINGLES! - I DON'T **HEAR** ANY JINGLES!
GULP! B-BUT **SOMETHING** IS **EATING** IT!
(GROAN) THAT'S PRETTY RICH AFTER A DIET OF REINDEER MILK!
COLA
YOU'D BETTER WALK IT OFF!
WALK? HAH! I'LL SHOW YOU HOW TO EXERCISE!
EEYIPE! W-WHAT WAS THAT?
ZOOM!
4

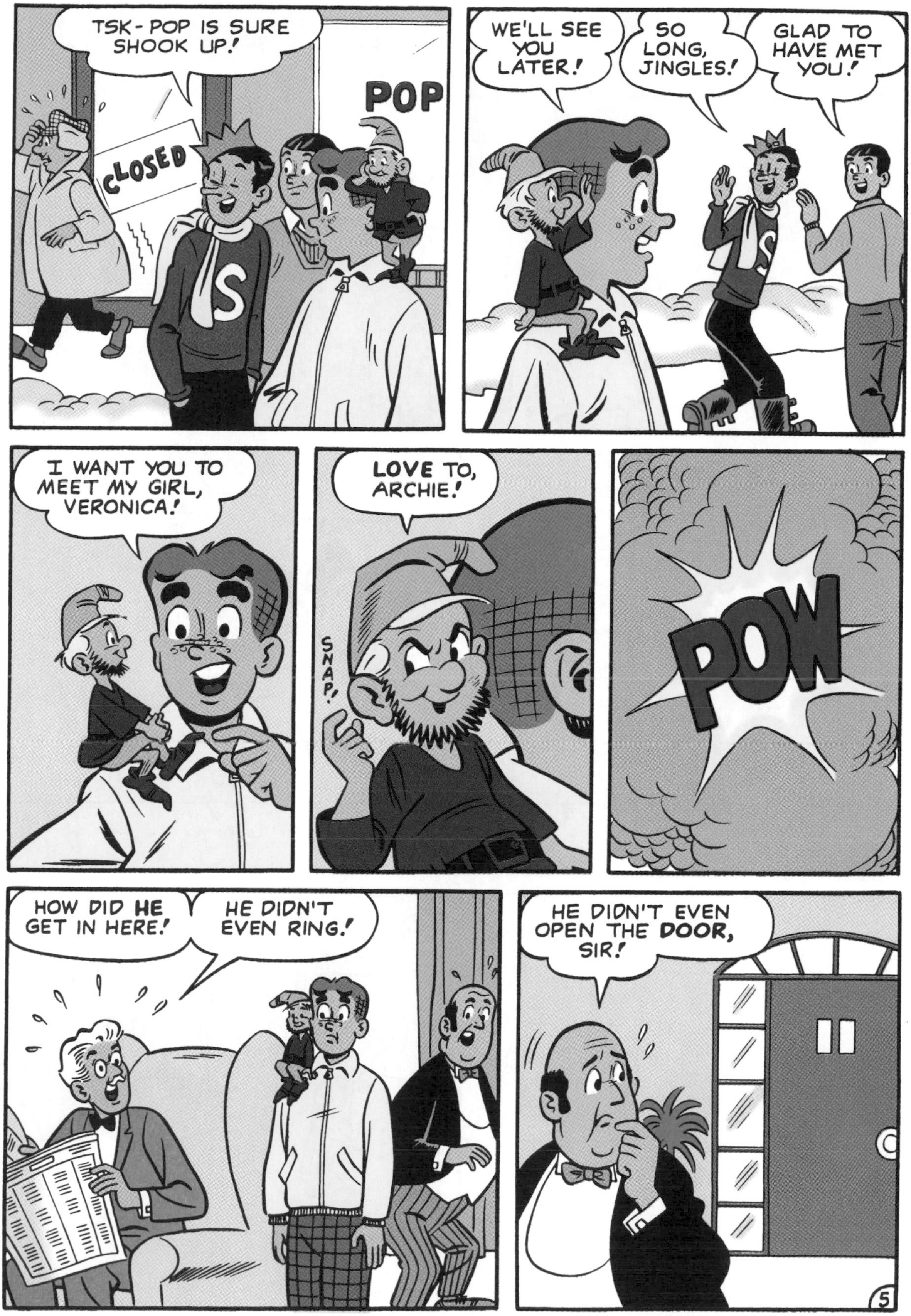
TSK-POP IS SURE SHOOK UP!
POP
CLOSED
WE'LL SEE YOU LATER!
SO LONG, JINGLES!
GLAD TO HAVE MET YOU!
I WANT YOU TO MEET MY GIRL, VERONICA!
LOVE TO, ARCHIE!
SNAP!
POW
HOW DID HE GET IN HERE!
HE DIDN'T EVEN RING!
HE DIDN'T EVEN OPEN THE DOOR, SIR!
5

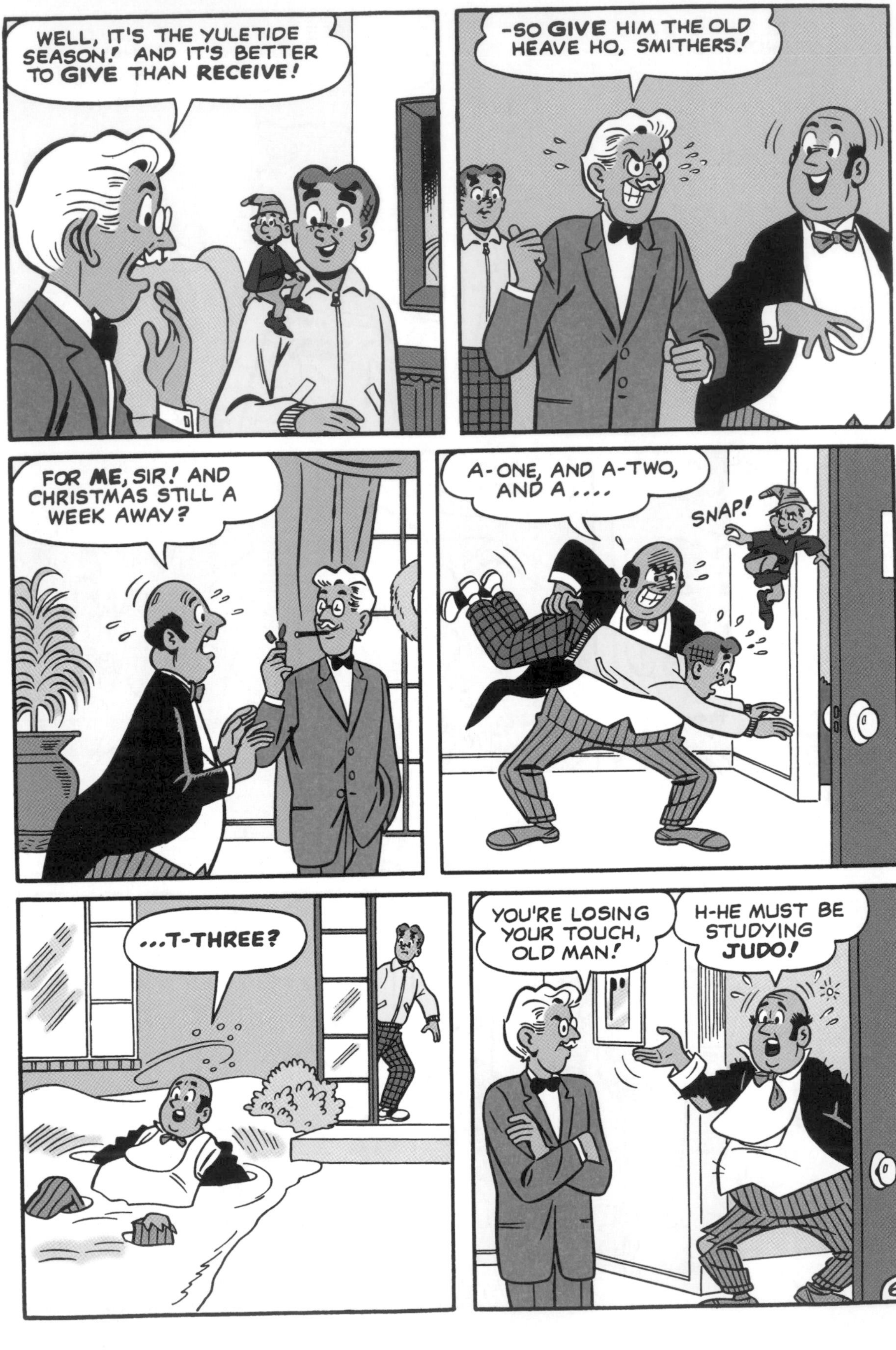

WELL, IT'S THE YULETIDE SEASON! AND IT'S BETTER TO GIVE THAN RECEIVE!
-SO GIVE HIM THE OLD HEAVE HO, SMITHERS!
FOR ME, SIR! AND CHRISTMAS STILL A WEEK AWAY?
A-ONE, AND A-TWO, AND A....
SNAP!
...T-THREE?
YOU'RE LOSING YOUR TOUCH, OLD MAN!
H-HE MUST BE STUDYING JUDO!
6

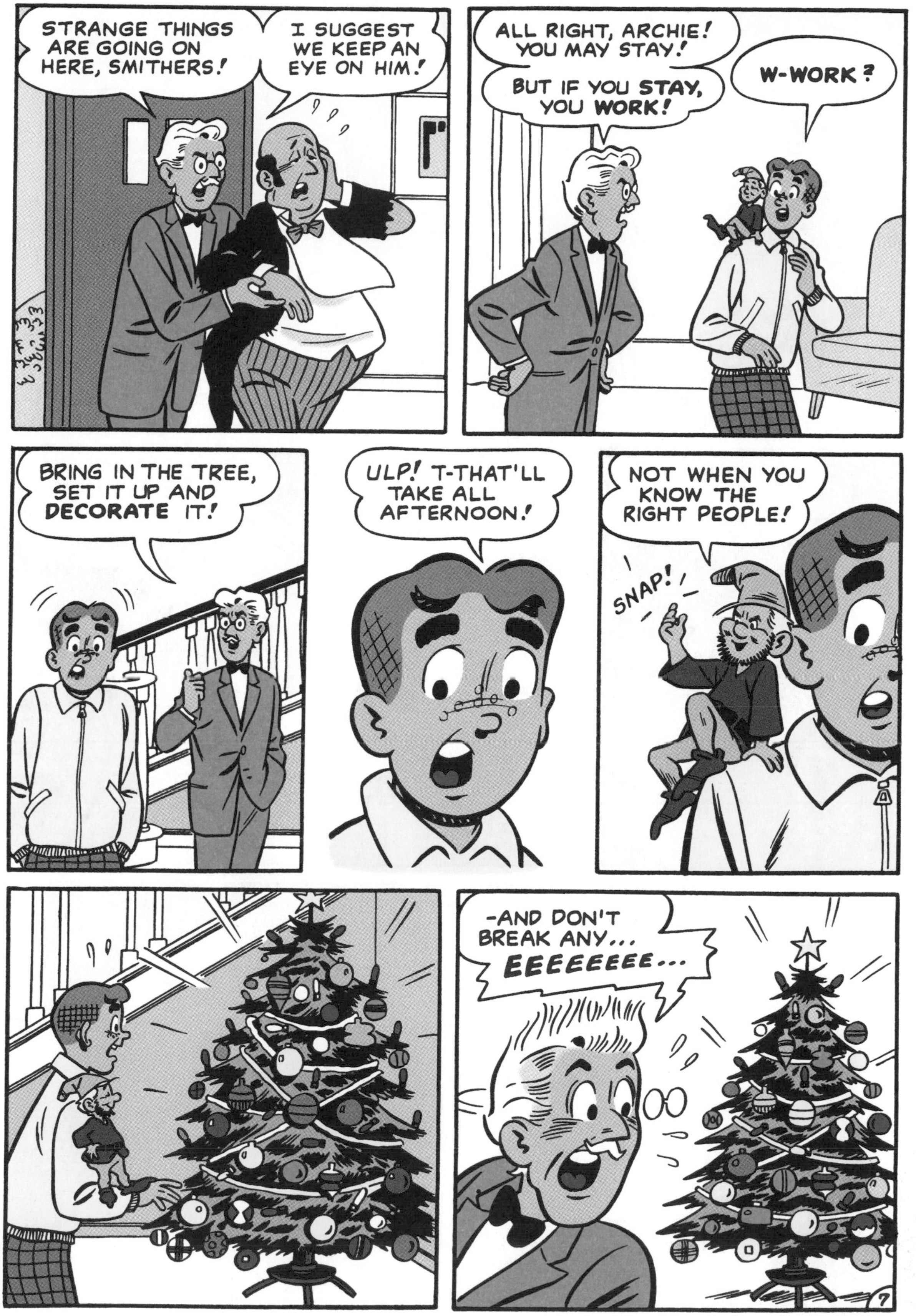
STRANGE THINGS ARE GOING ON HERE, SMITHERS!
I SUGGEST WE KEEP AN EYE ON HIM!
ALL RIGHT, ARCHIE! YOU MAY STAY!
BUT IF YOU STAY, YOU WORK!
W-WORK?
BRING IN THE TREE, SET IT UP AND DECORATE IT!
ULP! T-THAT'LL TAKE ALL AFTERNOON!
NOT WHEN YOU KNOW THE RIGHT PEOPLE!
SNAP!
-AND DON'T BREAK ANY... EEEEEEEE...
7

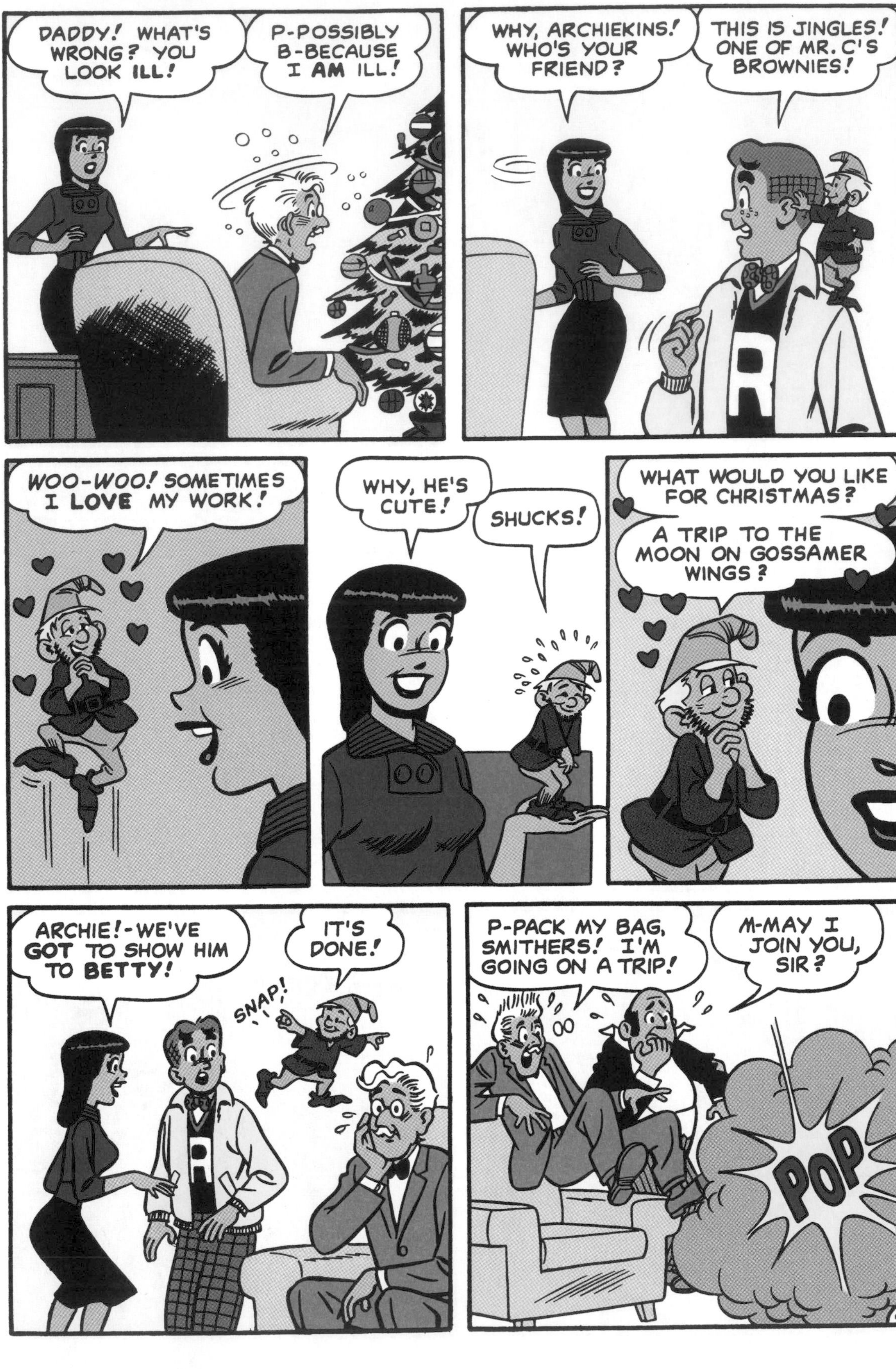
DADDY! WHAT'S WRONG? YOU LOOK ILL!
P-POSSIBLY B-BECAUSE I AM ILL!
WHY, ARCHIEKINS! WHO'S YOUR FRIEND?
THIS IS JINGLES! ONE OF MR. C'S BROWNIES!
WOO-WOO! SOMETIMES I LOVE MY WORK!
WHY, HE'S CUTE!
SHUCKS!
WHAT WOULD YOU LIKE FOR CHRISTMAS?
A TRIP TO THE MOON ON GOSSAMER WINGS?
ARCHIE!-WE'VE GOT TO SHOW HIM TO BETTY!
IT'S DONE!
SNAP!
P-PACK MY BAG, SMITHERS! I'M GOING ON A TRIP!
M-MAY I JOIN YOU, SIR?
POP
8

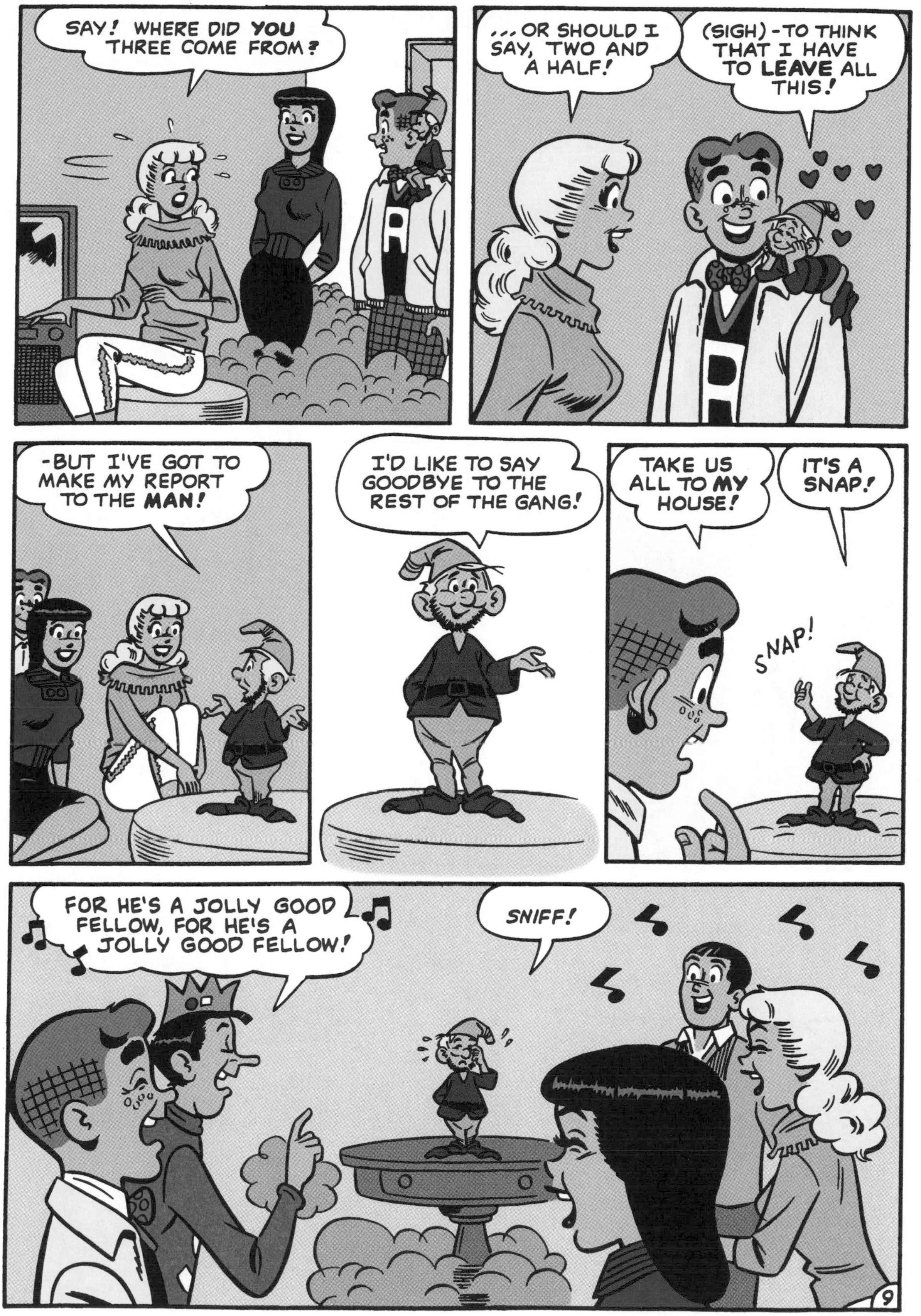
SAY! WHERE DID **YOU** THREE COME FROM?
...OR SHOULD I SAY, TWO AND A HALF!
(SIGH)-TO THINK THAT I HAVE TO **LEAVE** ALL THIS!
-BUT I'VE GOT TO MAKE MY REPORT TO THE **MAN**!
I'D LIKE TO SAY GOODBYE TO THE REST OF THE GANG!
TAKE US ALL TO **MY** HOUSE!
IT'S A SNAP!
SNAP!
FOR HE'S A JOLLY GOOD FELLOW, FOR HE'S A JOLLY GOOD FELLOW!
SNIFF!
9

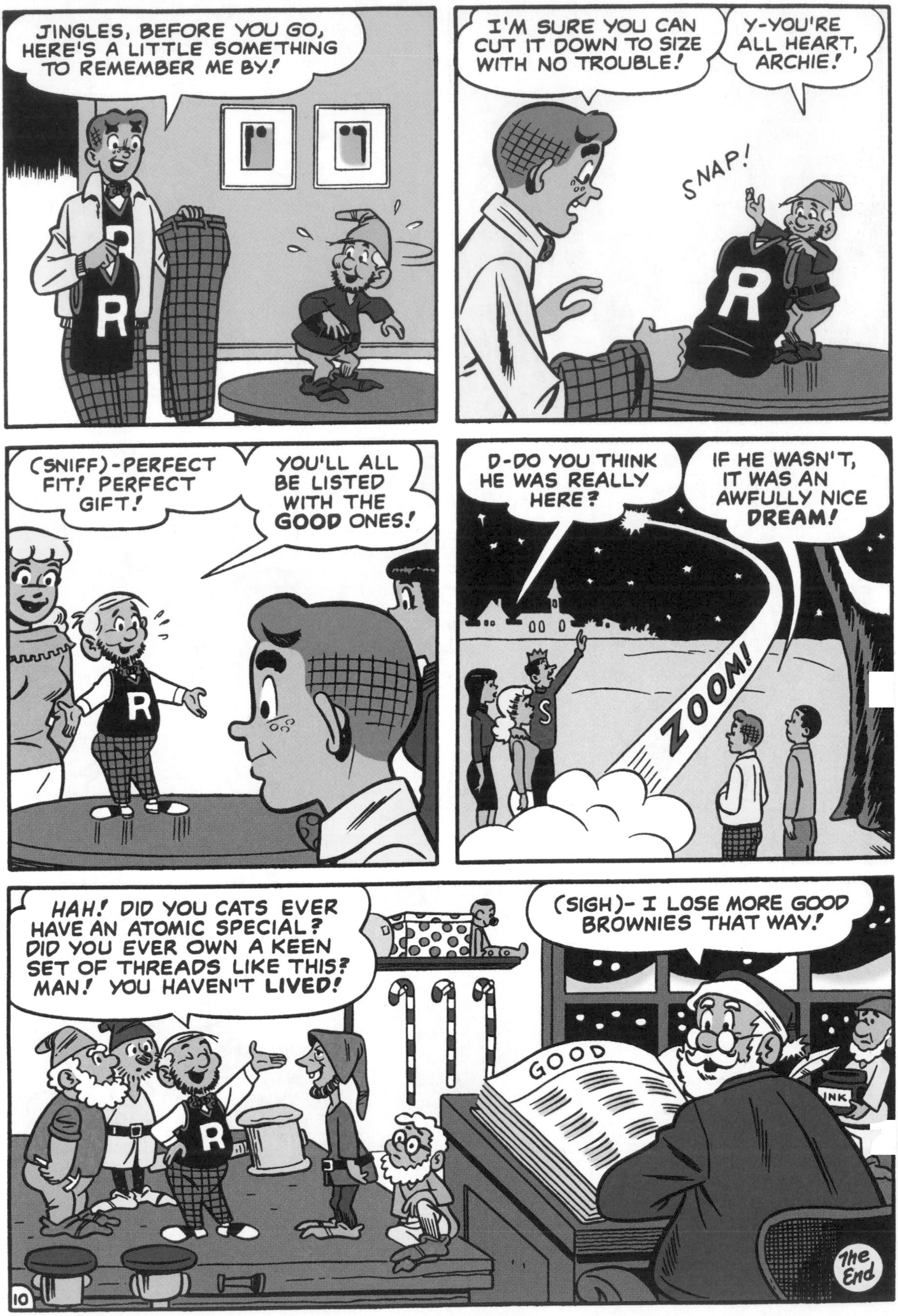
JINGLES, BEFORE YOU GO, HERE'S A LITTLE SOMETHING TO REMEMBER ME BY!
I'M SURE YOU CAN CUT IT DOWN TO SIZE WITH NO TROUBLE!
Y-YOU'RE ALL HEART, ARCHIE!
SNAP!
R
(SNIFF)-PERFECT FIT! PERFECT GIFT!
YOU'LL ALL BE LISTED WITH THE GOOD ONES!
D-DO YOU THINK HE WAS REALLY HERE?
IF HE WASN'T, IT WAS AN AWFULLY NICE DREAM!
ZOOM!
HAH! DID YOU CATS EVER HAVE AN ATOMIC SPECIAL? DID YOU EVER OWN A KEEN SET OF THREADS LIKE THIS? MAN! YOU HAVEN'T LIVED!
(SIGH)- I LOSE MORE GOOD BROWNIES THAT WAY!
GOOD
INK
10
The End

Archie in 'ESCAPE'

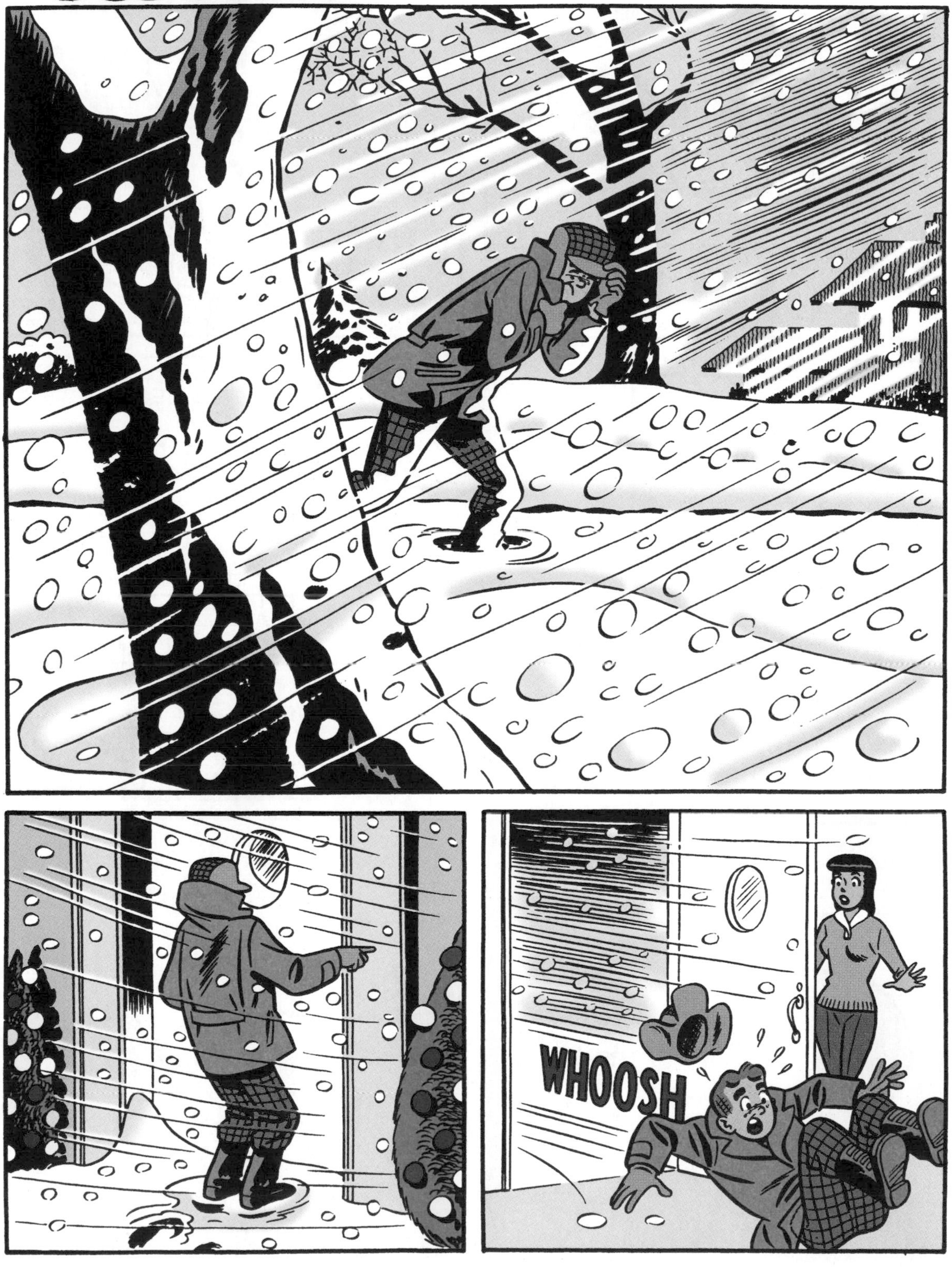
WHOOSH

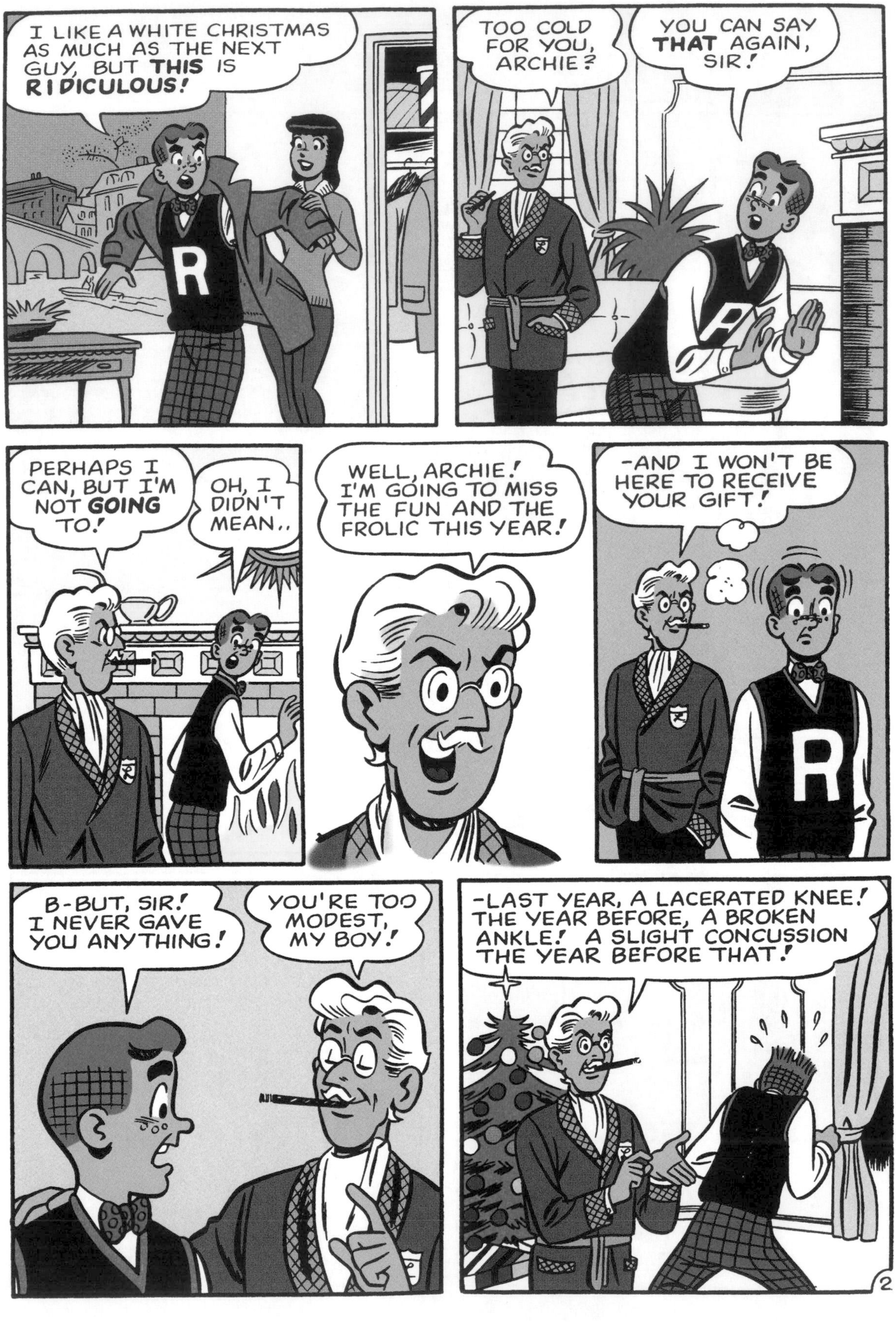
I LIKE A WHITE CHRISTMAS AS MUCH AS THE NEXT GUY, BUT **THIS** IS **RIDICULOUS!**
TOO COLD FOR YOU, ARCHIE?
YOU CAN SAY **THAT** AGAIN, SIR!
PERHAPS I CAN, BUT I'M NOT **GOING** TO!
OH, I DIDN'T MEAN..
WELL, ARCHIE! I'M GOING TO MISS THE FUN AND THE FROLIC THIS YEAR!
-AND I WON'T BE HERE TO RECEIVE YOUR GIFT!
B-BUT, SIR! I NEVER GAVE YOU ANYTHING!
YOU'RE TOO MODEST, MY BOY!
-LAST YEAR, A LACERATED KNEE! THE YEAR BEFORE, A BROKEN ANKLE! A SLIGHT CONCUSSION THE YEAR BEFORE THAT!
2

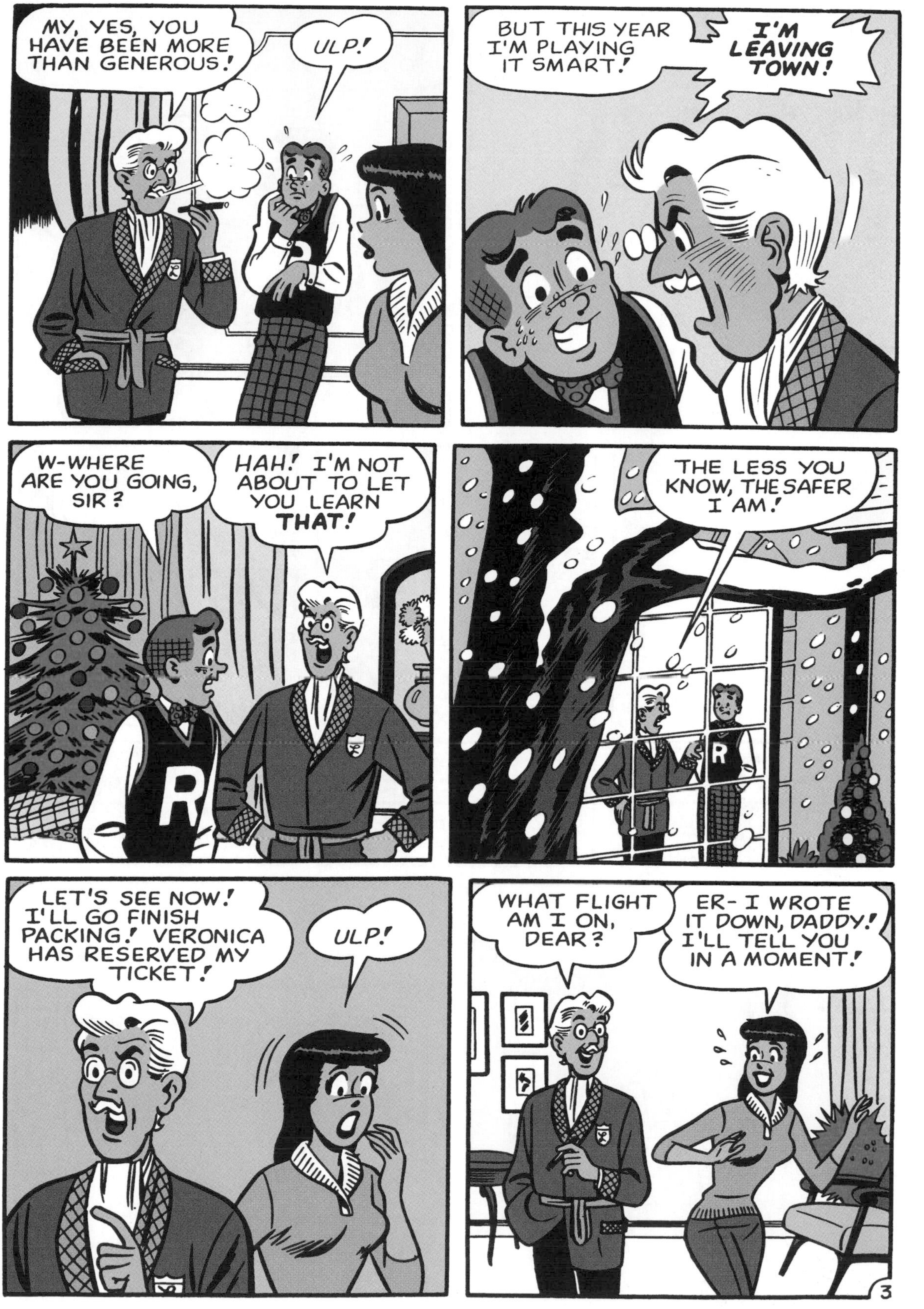
MY, YES, YOU HAVE BEEN MORE THAN GENEROUS!
ULP!
BUT THIS YEAR I'M PLAYING IT SMART!
I'M LEAVING TOWN!
W-WHERE ARE YOU GOING, SIR?
HAH! I'M NOT ABOUT TO LET YOU LEARN THAT!
THE LESS YOU KNOW, THE SAFER I AM!
LET'S SEE NOW! I'LL GO FINISH PACKING! VERONICA HAS RESERVED MY TICKET!
ULP!
WHAT FLIGHT AM I ON, DEAR?
ER- I WROTE IT DOWN, DADDY! I'LL TELL YOU IN A MOMENT!
3

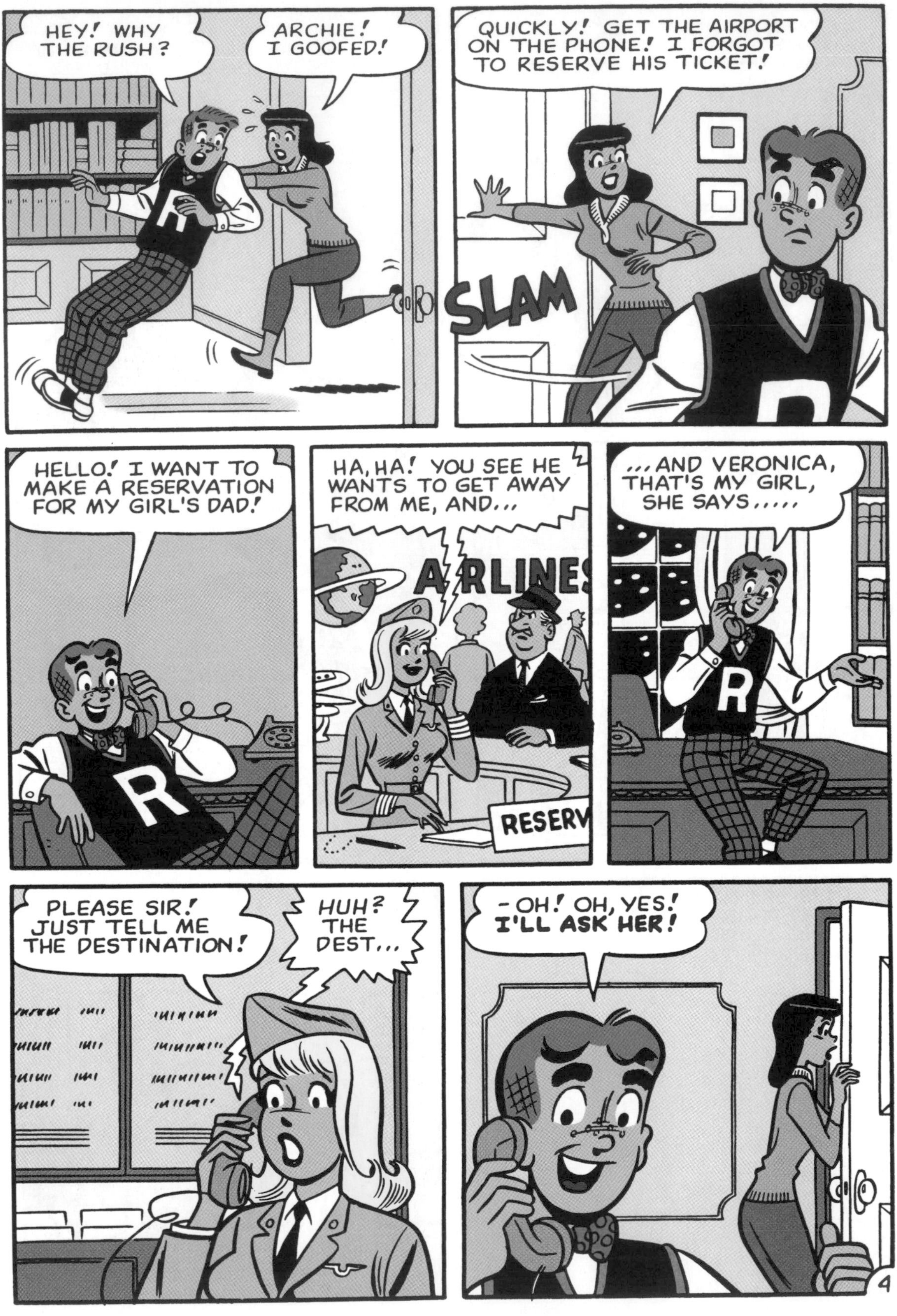
HEY! WHY THE RUSH?
ARCHIE! I GOOFED!
QUICKLY! GET THE AIRPORT ON THE PHONE! I FORGOT TO RESERVE HIS TICKET!
SLAM
HELLO! I WANT TO MAKE A RESERVATION FOR MY GIRL'S DAD!
HA, HA! YOU SEE HE WANTS TO GET AWAY FROM ME, AND...
AIRLINES
RESERV
...AND VERONICA, THAT'S MY GIRL, SHE SAYS.....
PLEASE SIR! JUST TELL ME THE DESTINATION!
HUH? THE DEST...
-OH! OH, YES! I'LL ASK HER!
4

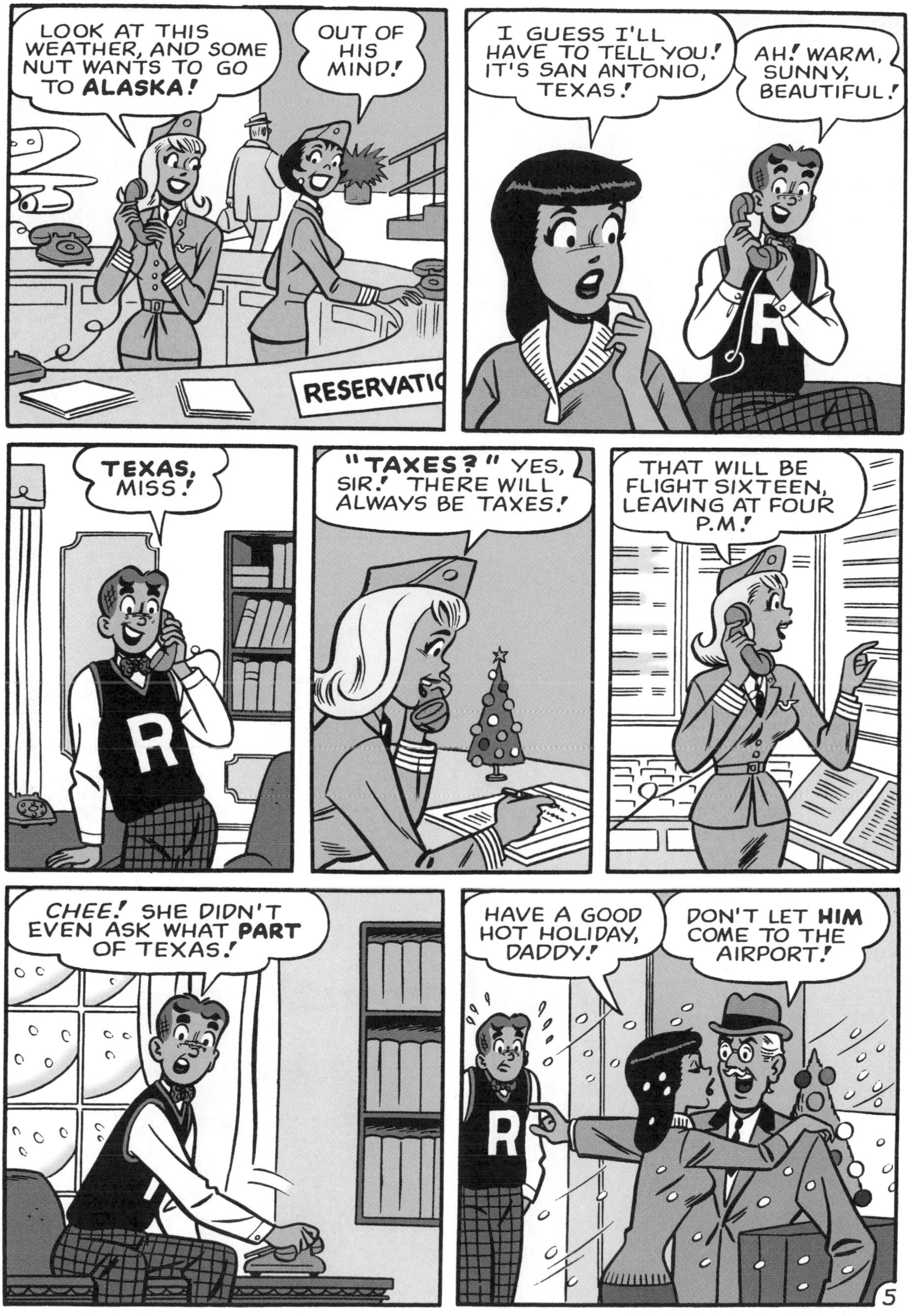
LOOK AT THIS WEATHER, AND SOME NUT WANTS TO GO TO ALASKA!
OUT OF HIS MIND!
RESERVATIO
I GUESS I'LL HAVE TO TELL YOU! IT'S SAN ANTONIO, TEXAS!
AH! WARM, SUNNY, BEAUTIFUL!
TEXAS, MISS!
"TAXES?" YES, SIR! THERE WILL ALWAYS BE TAXES!
THAT WILL BE FLIGHT SIXTEEN, LEAVING AT FOUR P.M!
CHEE! SHE DIDN'T EVEN ASK WHAT PART OF TEXAS!
HAVE A GOOD HOT HOLIDAY, DADDY!
DON'T LET HIM COME TO THE AIRPORT!
5

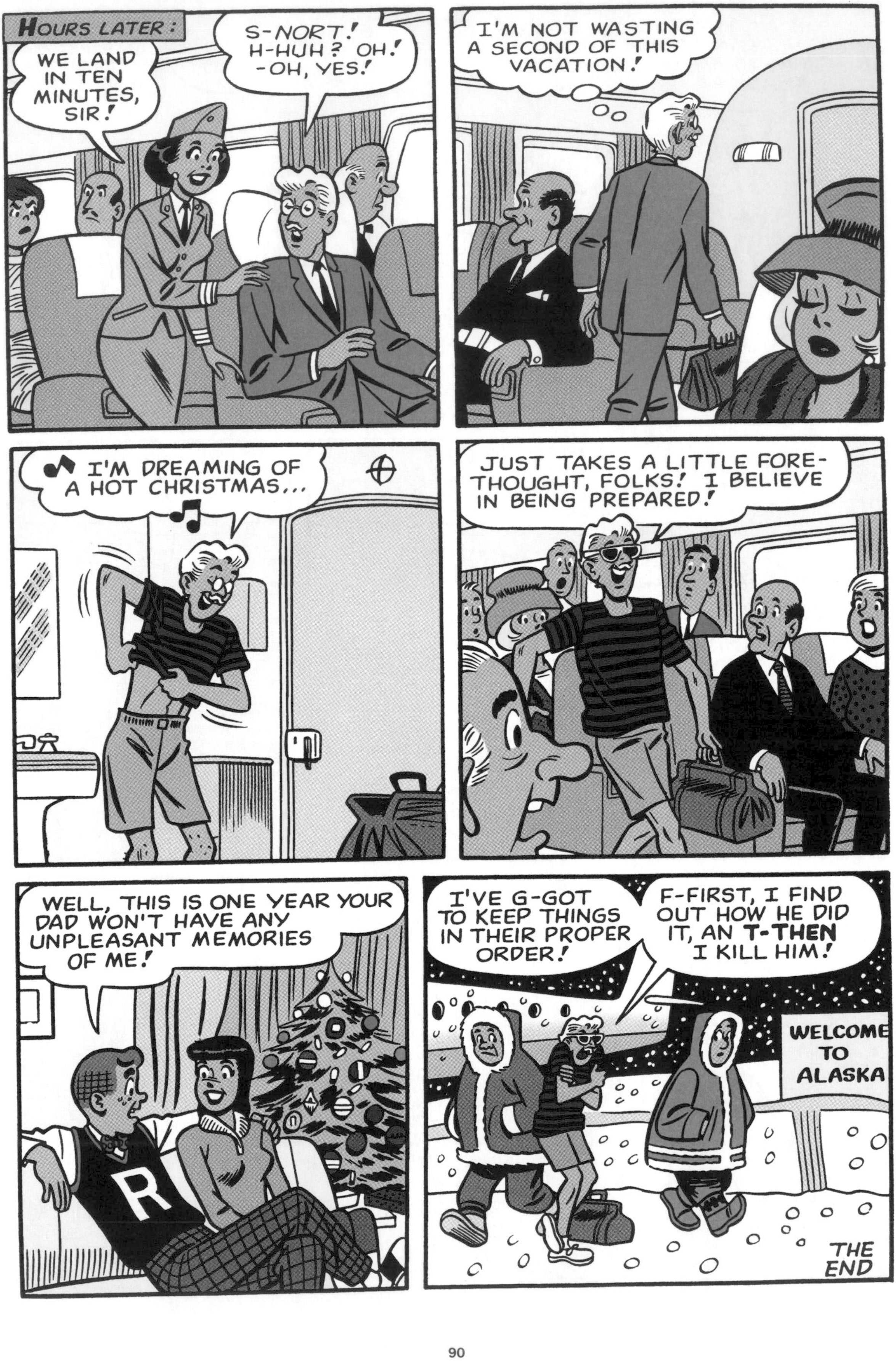
HOURS LATER:
WE LAND IN TEN MINUTES, SIR!
S-NORT! H-HUH? OH! -OH, YES!
I'M NOT WASTING A SECOND OF THIS VACATION!
I'M DREAMING OF A HOT CHRISTMAS...
JUST TAKES A LITTLE FORE-THOUGHT, FOLKS! I BELIEVE IN BEING PREPARED!
WELL, THIS IS ONE YEAR YOUR DAD WON'T HAVE ANY UNPLEASANT MEMORIES OF ME!
I'VE G-GOT TO KEEP THINGS IN THEIR PROPER ORDER!
F-FIRST, I FIND OUT HOW HE DID IT, AN **T-THEN** I KILL HIM!
WELCOME TO ALASKA
THE END

Archie in 'The Return of JINGLES'

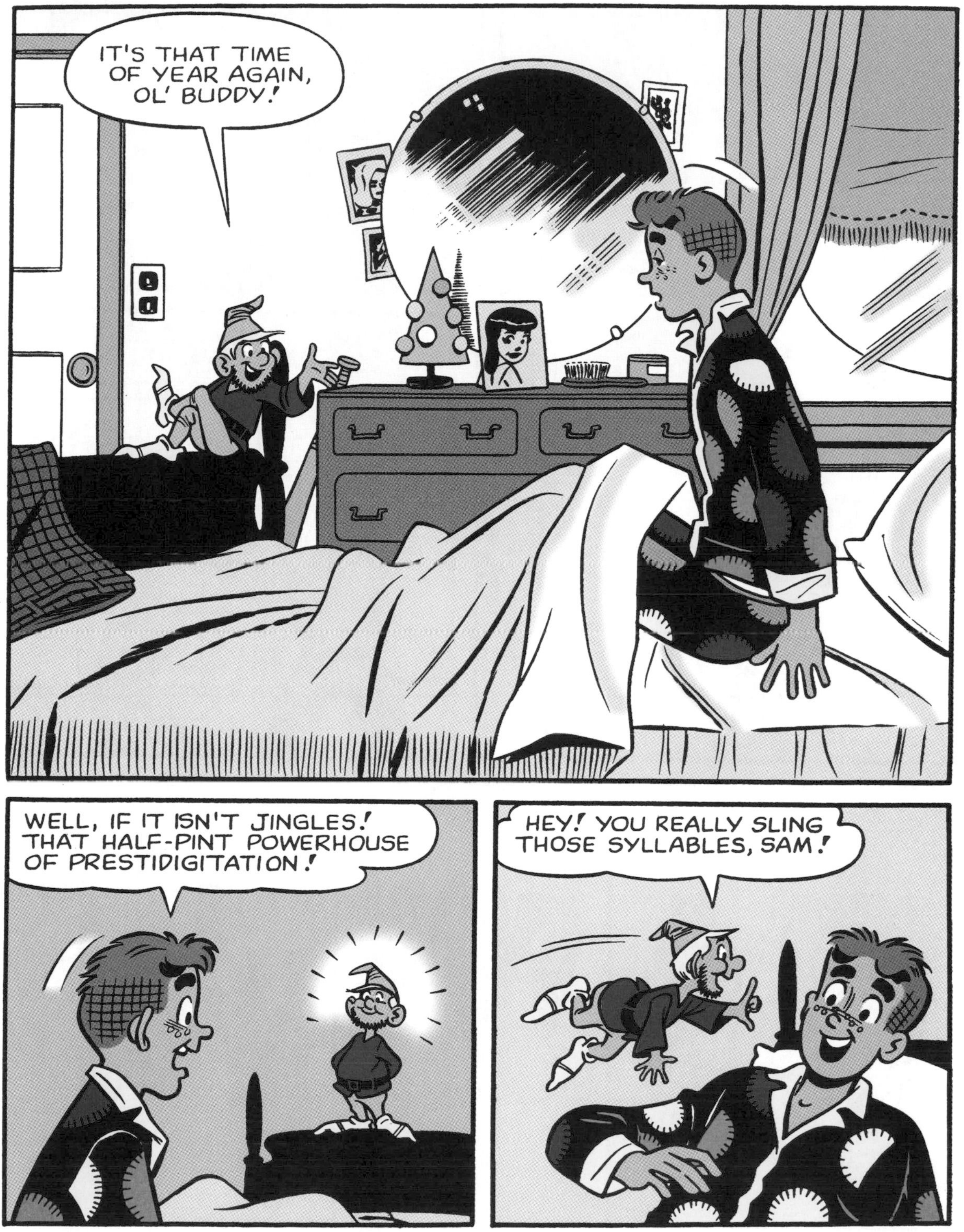
IT'S THAT TIME OF YEAR AGAIN, OL' BUDDY!
WELL, IF IT ISN'T JINGLES! THAT HALF-PINT POWERHOUSE OF PRESTIDIGITATION!
HEY! YOU REALLY SLING THOSE SYLLABLES, SAM!

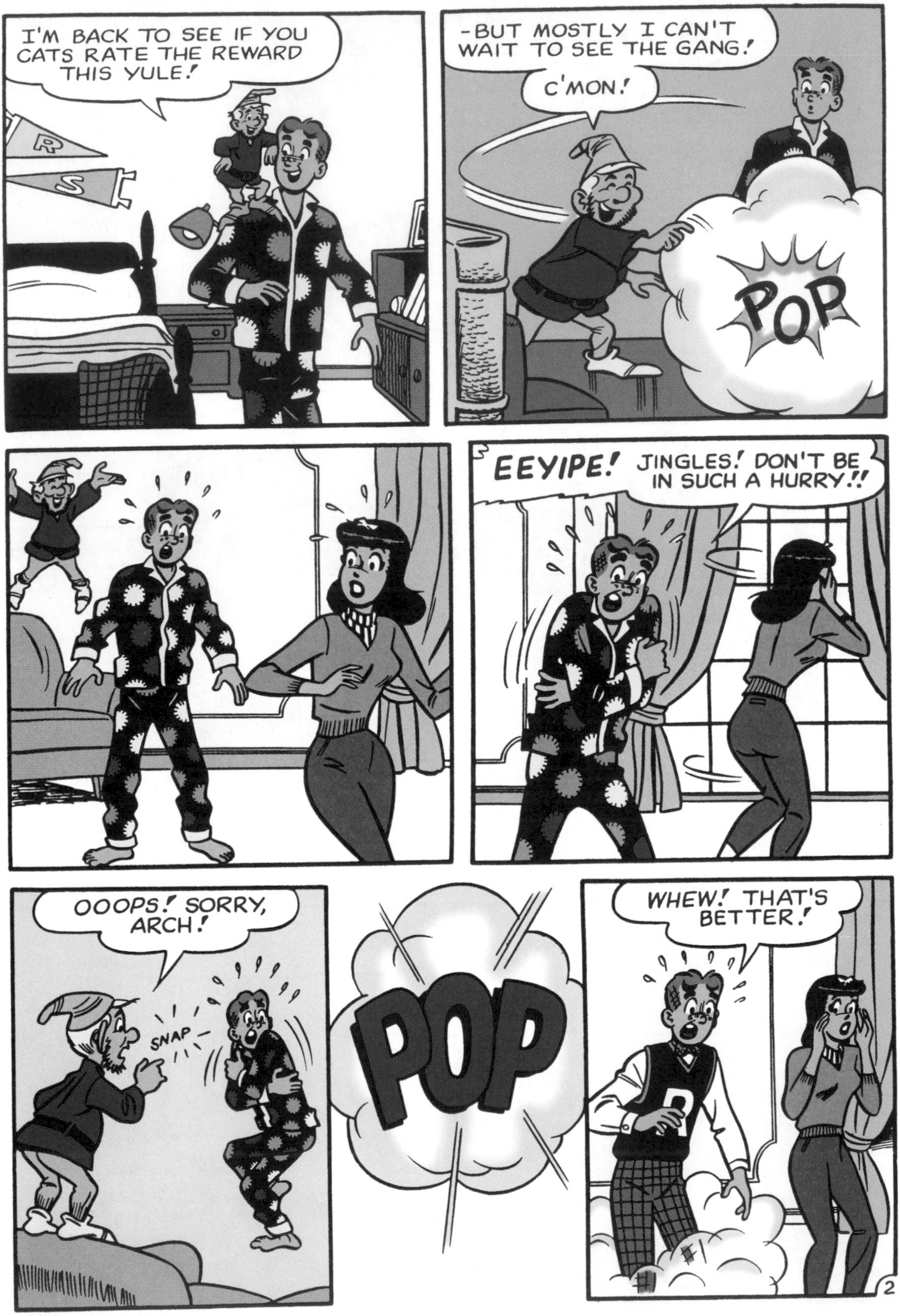
I'M BACK TO SEE IF YOU CATS RATE THE REWARD THIS YULE!
-BUT MOSTLY I CAN'T WAIT TO SEE THE GANG!
C'MON!
POP
EEYIPE!
JINGLES! DON'T BE IN SUCH A HURRY!!
OOOPS! SORRY, ARCH!
SNAP
POP
WHEW! THAT'S BETTER!
2

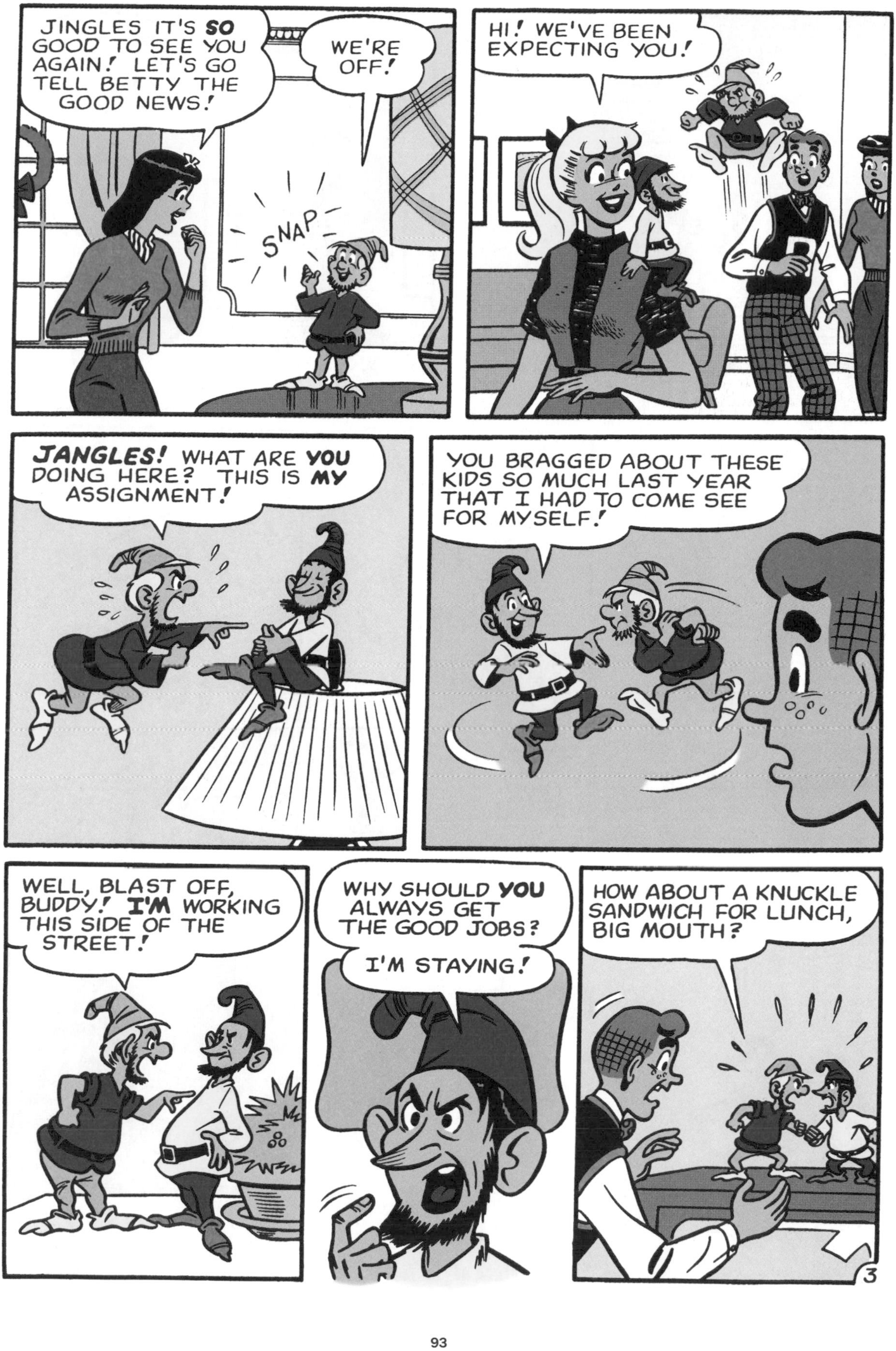
JINGLES IT'S **SO** GOOD TO SEE YOU AGAIN! LET'S GO TELL BETTY THE GOOD NEWS!
WE'RE OFF!
SNAP
HI! WE'VE BEEN EXPECTING YOU!
JANGLES! WHAT ARE **YOU** DOING HERE? THIS IS **MY** ASSIGNMENT!
YOU BRAGGED ABOUT THESE KIDS SO MUCH LAST YEAR THAT I HAD TO COME SEE FOR MYSELF!
WELL, BLAST OFF, BUDDY! **I'M** WORKING THIS SIDE OF THE STREET!
WHY SHOULD **YOU** ALWAYS GET THE GOOD JOBS?
I'M STAYING!
HOW ABOUT A KNUCKLE SANDWICH FOR LUNCH, BIG MOUTH?
3

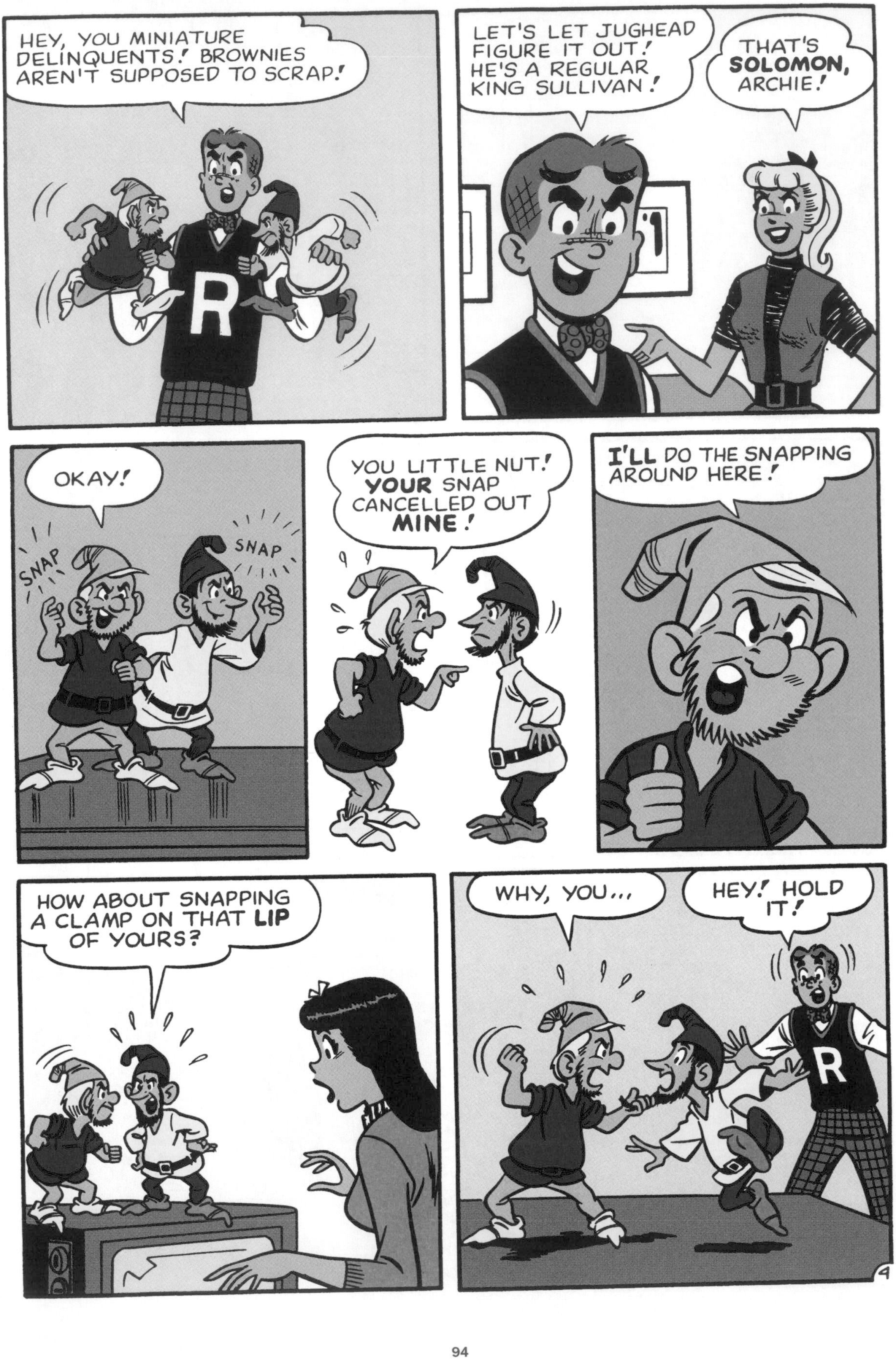
HEY, YOU MINIATURE DELINQUENTS! BROWNIES AREN'T SUPPOSED TO SCRAP!
LET'S LET JUGHEAD FIGURE IT OUT! HE'S A REGULAR KING SULLIVAN!
THAT'S SOLOMON, ARCHIE!
OKAY!
SNAP
SNAP
YOU LITTLE NUT! YOUR SNAP CANCELLED OUT MINE!
I'LL DO THE SNAPPING AROUND HERE!
HOW ABOUT SNAPPING A CLAMP ON THAT LIP OF YOURS?
WHY, YOU...
HEY! HOLD IT!
4

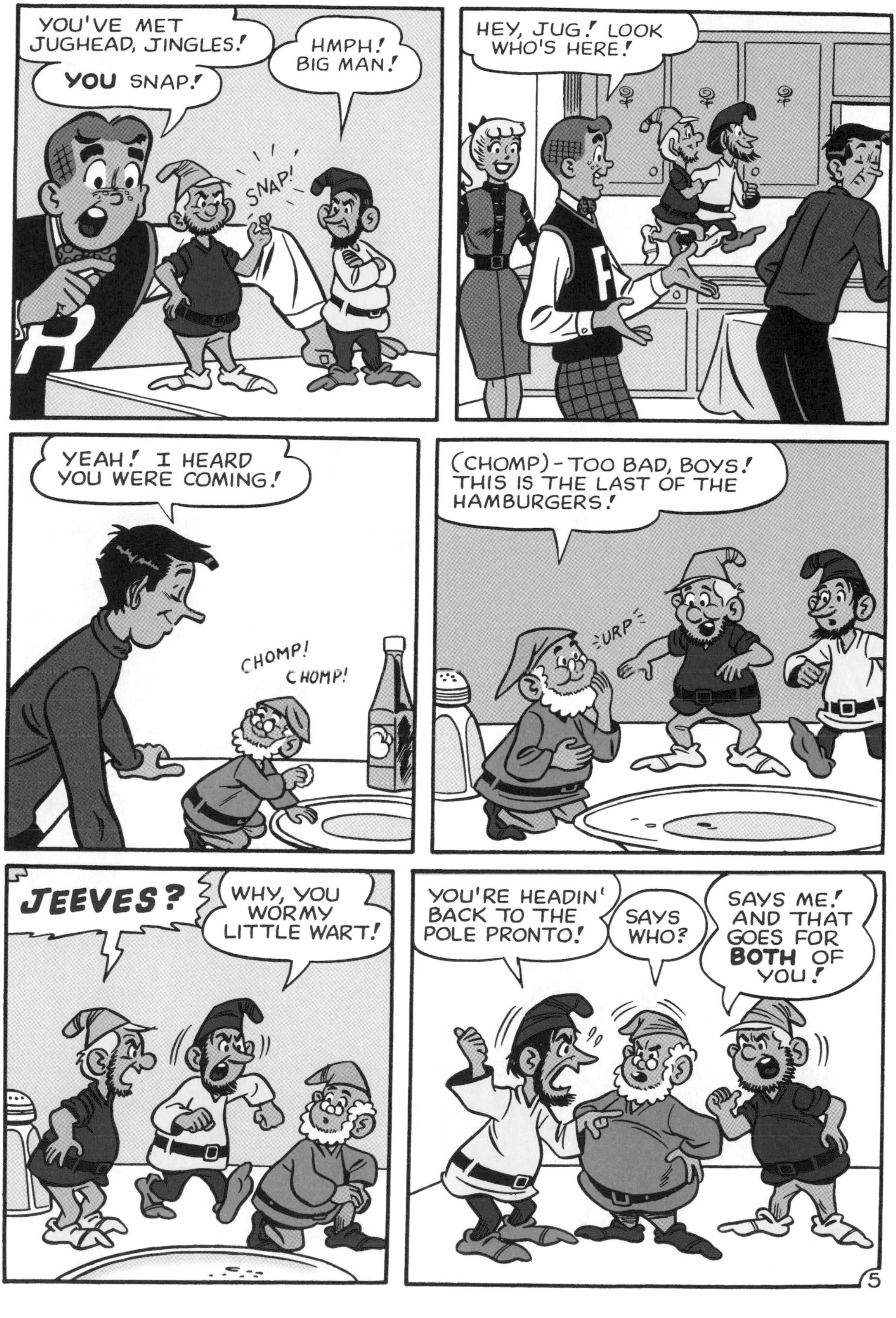
YOU'VE MET JUGHEAD, JINGLES!
YOU SNAP!
HMPH! BIG MAN!
SNAP!
HEY, JUG! LOOK WHO'S HERE!
YEAH! I HEARD YOU WERE COMING!
CHOMP!
CHOMP!
(CHOMP) - TOO BAD, BOYS! THIS IS THE LAST OF THE HAMBURGERS!
URP
JEEVES?
WHY, YOU WORMY LITTLE WART!
YOU'RE HEADIN' BACK TO THE POLE PRONTO!
SAYS WHO?
SAYS ME! AND THAT GOES FOR BOTH OF YOU!
5

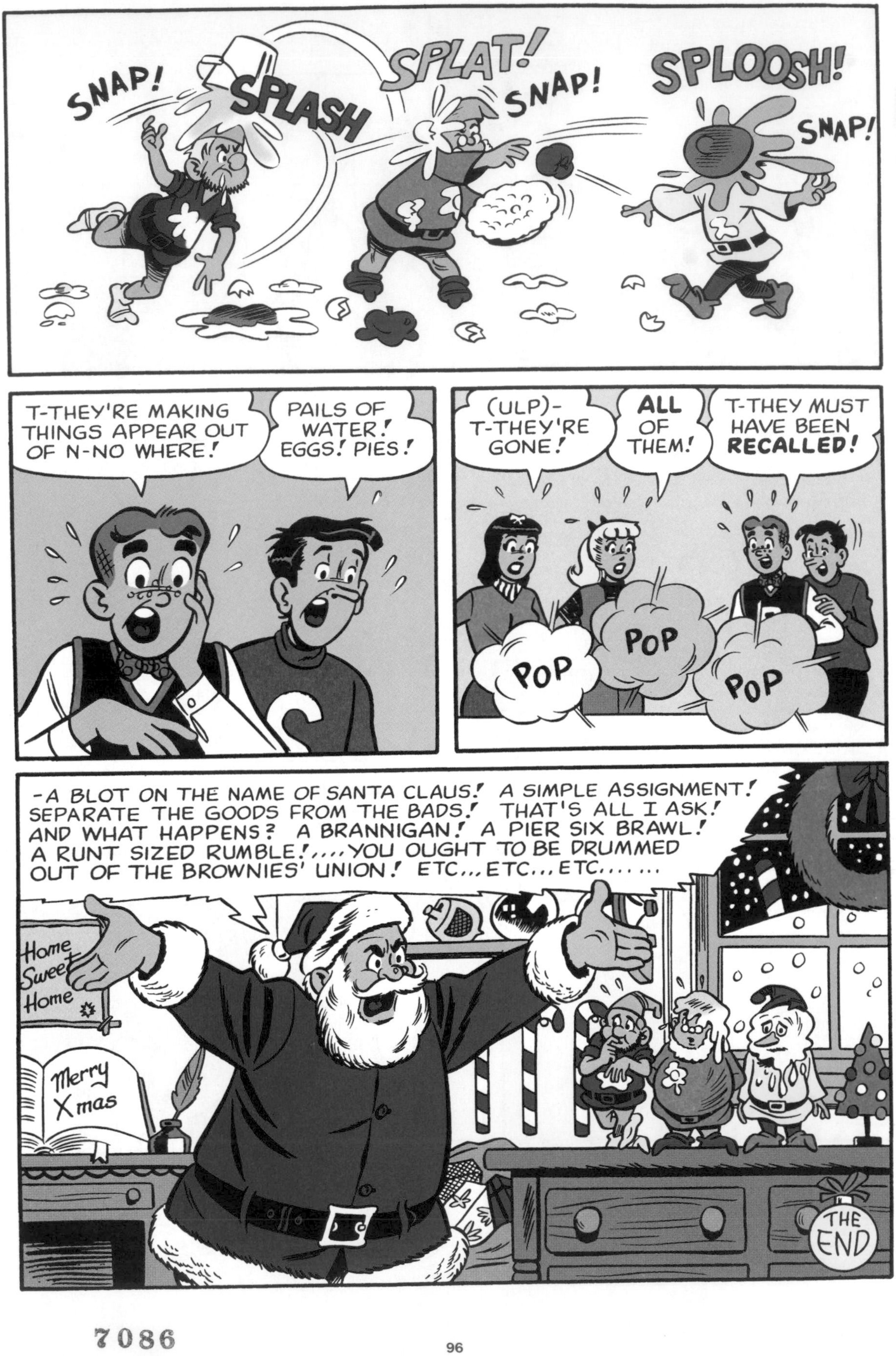
SNAP!
SPLASH
SPLAT!
SNAP!
SPLOOSH!
SNAP!
T-THEY'RE MAKING THINGS APPEAR OUT OF N-NO WHERE!
PAILS OF WATER! EGGS! PIES!
(ULP)- T-THEY'RE GONE!
ALL OF THEM!
T-THEY MUST HAVE BEEN RECALLED!
POP
POP
POP
-A BLOT ON THE NAME OF SANTA CLAUS! A SIMPLE ASSIGNMENT! SEPARATE THE GOODS FROM THE BADS! THAT'S ALL I ASK! AND WHAT HAPPENS? A BRANNIGAN! A PIER SIX BRAWL! A RUNT SIZED RUMBLE!.... YOU OUGHT TO BE DRUMMED OUT OF THE BROWNIES' UNION! ETC... ETC... ETC......
Home Sweet Home
Merry Xmas
THE END

7086